Large Print

COB   Coble, Colleen.

             The lightkeeper's
             daughter.

$33.95

Large Print

   COB   Coble, Colleen.

                The lightkeeper's
                daughter.

   $33.95

DATE	BORROWER'S NAME	

THE LIGHTKEEPER'S DAUGHTER

Center Point Large Print

Also by Colleen Coble
and available from Center Point Large Print:

Cry in the Night
Anathema

**This Large Print Book carries the
Seal of Approval of N.A.V.H.**

THE LIGHTKEEPER'S DAUGHTER

A Mercy Falls Novel

Colleen Coble

CENTER POINT PUBLISHING
THORNDIKE, MAINE

This Center Point Large Print edition
is published in the year 2010 by arrangement with
Thomas Nelson Publishers.

The text of this Large Print edition is unabridged.
In other aspects, this book may vary
from the original edition.
Printed in the United States of America
on permanent paper.
Set in 16-point Times New Roman type.

ISBN: 978-1-60285-704-9

Library of Congress Cataloging-in-Publication Data

Coble, Colleen.
  The lightkeeper's daughter / Colleen Coble.
    p. cm.
  ISBN 978-1-60285-704-9 (library binding : alk. paper)
  1. Nannies--Fiction. 2. California--History--1850-1950--Fiction. 3. Domestic fiction.
  4. Large type books. I. Title.
  PS3553.O2285L54 2010b
  813'.54--dc22
  2009045407

For Ami,
I'm so glad you encouraged me
to write this book!
Thanks for always being my champion.

PROLOGUE

1884

THE SHIP'S DECK rolled under his feet, and he widened his stance to protect his balance and the toddler in his arms. Where was she? He'd been from one end of the steamer to the other. Laura was nowhere to be found. He shifted the sleeping child and eyed the black clouds hovering low on the horizon. A lighthouse winked in the darkening seascape. The wind whipped the waves into a frenzy and tore at the masts. The boat fell into a trough, and the stern rose as the bow tipped. He grabbed at the railing for support. A rumble came to his ears. Thunder? Deckhands rushed by him, and he caught the faint stench of smoke.

"Fire!" a man shouted. "There's been an explosion!"

He turned to see smoke pouring from the hold. People milled on the deck, and crewmen rushed to lower the lifeboat. He grabbed the arm of a passing crewman and shouted over the howling wind. "The pretty woman with the red hair in a pompadour. Have you seen her?"

"She's gone. Left first thing this morning before we left the dock. This ship is going down, mate. Get on the lifeboat now!" The man jerked his arm away.

7

He watched the crewman rush to help panicking passengers into the lifeboat. Gone. How could she leave without a word? Laura would never leave her child. Other people streamed by him on their way to safety, but he stood rooted to the deck until the little girl in his arms whimpered.

"Mama," she said. "Papa."

He studied her eyes, so like her mother's. "We must get you to shore," he said. His purpose found, he strode to the lifeboat. Wide-eyed passengers crammed every seat. Some had other people on their laps. There was no room. Not for him.

He held up the little girl. "Please, someone save her!"

"Hurry, mister!" a crewman yelled. "Throw her into the boat."

A woman held out her arms. "I'll take her."

Julia clutched him and wailed. "It's okay, darling," he soothed. He kissed her smooth cheek, then lowered her into the woman's arms. The woman had barely settled the child when the steamer lurched and shuddered. It began to break apart as the lifeboat hit the roiling waves. He watched the men in the boat strain at the oars, but the waves swamped it, and it was making little headway.

He couldn't stay here or he'd go down with the steamer. Shucking his morning coat and shoes, he climbed to the rail and dived overboard. Cold salt water filled his mouth and nose. He struggled to the surface and gulped in air before another wave caught him. The fury of the current took him under again, and he lost track of how many times he managed to snatch a breath before being thrust toward the ocean floor once more. A dozen? A hundred?

Finally his knees scraped rock, and a wave vomited him from the sea to the shore. Nearly unconscious, he lay gasping on blessed ground. He swam in and out of darkness until his brain regained enough function to remember Julia. His stomach heaved seawater onto the sand, and the retching brought him around. He managed to get on his hands and knees and stayed there a few moments until his head cleared and he could stumble to his feet. He gawked at the devastation scattered across the beach.

The sea had torn the lifeboat to splinters. Bodies and debris lay strewn up and down the coast. Shudders racked his body, and he lurched along the rocks. "Julia!" he called. The wind tossed his words back at him. She had to be alive. He ran up and down the littered shore but found no trace of the little girl he loved nearly as much as he loved her mother.

ONE

1907

ADDIE SULLIVAN'S STIFF fingers refused to obey her as she struggled to unbutton her voluminous nightgown. The lighthouse bucked with the wind, and she swallowed hard. Her room was freezing, because they'd run out of coal last week and had no money to buy more. Her German shepherd, Gideon, whined and licked her hand. She had to get dressed, but she stood paralyzed.

A storm like this never failed to bring the familiar nightmares to mind. She could taste the salt water on her tongue and feel the helplessness of being at the mercy of the waves. Her parents insisted she'd never been in a shipwreck, but throughout her life she'd awakened screaming in the night, imagining she was drowning. In her nightmare, she struggled against a faceless man who tossed her into the water from a burning ship.

Thunder rumbled outside like a beast rising from the raging waves, and the sound drew her unwilling attention again. "The LORD on high is mightier than the noise of many waters, yea, than the mighty waves of the sea," she whispered. Her agitation eased, and she reached for her dress.

The front door slammed, and her mother's voice called out. "Addie, I need your help! Get your kit."

The urgency in her words broke Addie's paralysis. She grabbed her dressing gown. The medical kit was in the bottom of her chifforobe cabinet. "Come, Gideon," she said.

Carrying the metal box of bandages, acetylsalicylic acid powder, and carbolic acid, she rushed down the steps with her dog on her heels. She found her mother in the parlor. The patient lay on the rug by the fireplace. Her mother, lighthouse keeper Josephine Sullivan, stepped back when Addie entered the room. The woman's overalls and jacket were drenched from the rain and surf.

"You took long enough, girlie," she said. "I suppose you were hiding in your room."

Addie eyed her mother's set mouth, then knelt by the man. "What's happened? Where is he injured?"

"His arm is swollen. I think it's sprained. He has several cuts. I found him at the foot of the stairs to the lighthouse. I think he fell. He passed out as soon as I got him in here." Her mother stepped over to turn on the gaslights. Their hiss could barely be heard above the storm.

"I'll get you some tea after I tend to our patient," she said to her mother.

The wind had whipped her mother's hair free of its pins. Her gray locks lay plastered against her head. The wind rattled the shutters and lashed rain against the windows. "And food. You should have brought me something."

Addie clamped her mouth shut. The last time she'd tried to take food to her mother as a storm rolled in, her efforts were met with a tantrum. She turned her attention back to her patient. He was in his fifties and had little color in his face. Judging by his clean-shaven jaw, she guessed him to be wealthy and following the fashion of the day. His expensive suit, though shredded, bore out her speculation.

"Help me get his coat off," Addie said.

Her mother reached for the scissors from her sewing basket. "Cut it off. The clothing is useless anyway."

"But what will he wear?"

"Something of your father's."

Addie choked back her objections and took the scissors. The man's tie was missing, and blood showed through the white shirt under the jacket. She cut the shirt to gain access to his swollen arm. "I think it's only sprained."

Her mother dropped into a chair and pushed her wet hair out of her face. "As I said."

"It's God's blessing that he's unconscious. He might need the doctor."

"The isthmus is covered. I'd have to wait until low tide to reach the mainland."

"I'll secure his arm in a sling. He'll be fine in a few days," Addie said. He flinched and moaned, and she knew he'd awaken soon. She pulled out a bandage and secured his arm, then sprayed the cuts with carbolic acid and bandaged the worst of them. "Was there a shipwreck?" she asked.

Her mother shook her head. "Not that I know of. Just this man lying by the steps."

Addie silently prayed for him while she immobilized the arm in a sling of muslin. He moaned again. His eyelids fluttered, then opened. He blinked a few times, then struggled to sit up.

"No, don't move," she said.

He squinted into her face. "Where am I?"

"At Battery Point Lighthouse. Outside Crescent City," Addie said. "California," she added in case he was a bit addled. She touched his clammy forehead.

"The steep hillside," he muttered. "I fell."

"The steps are treacherous in this kind of weather. But you're going to be fine in a few days. I think your arm is sprained, but that's the worst of it."

His eyes lingered on her face, then moved to the locket nestled against her chest. He frowned, then struggled to sit up as he reached for it. "Where did you get that?"

Addie flinched and clutched the locket. "It was my grandmother's." She looked away from the intensity in his face.

"Laura." He clutched his arm. "My arm hurts."

Laura? She touched his head to check for fever. "Let's get you to the chair."

She helped him stand and stagger to the armchair

13

protected with crocheted doilies. He nearly collapsed onto the cushion, but his attention remained fixed on her locket.

She was ready to escape his piercing stare. "I'll make us some tea."

In the kitchen she stirred the embers of the fire in the wood range, then poured out hot water from the reservoir into the cracked teapot. The storm was beginning to blow itself out, and she no longer saw the flashes of lightning that had so terrified her. She ladled vegetable soup into chipped bowls from the pot she'd kept warm for her mother. The sound of her mother's raised voice came to her ears and nearly caused her to spill the hot tea.

"You have no proof!" her mother shouted.

"What on earth?" Addie placed cups and the teapot on a tray, then rushed to the parlor. The man and her mother were tight-lipped and tense when she entered.

"Is everything all right?"

When neither the man nor her mother answered her, Addie set the tray on the fireplace hearth and poured tea into the mismatched cups. What could they possibly be arguing about?

She stirred honey into her mother's tea, then handed it over. "Honey?" Addie asked their guest.

He shook his head. "Black, please." He took the cup in his left hand, which shook. The tea sloshed. He didn't take his eyes off Addie. "I didn't believe it until I saw you."

"What?"

He set his tea down and glared at her mother before turning his attention back to Addie. His lips tightened. "The way you stand, the shape of your eyes. Just like your mother's."

Addie's eyes flitted to her mother. "Is your vision blurry?" she asked the man. Addie had often coveted the lovely brunette hair she'd seen in photos of her mother as a young woman. It was so straight and silky, and quite unlike her own mop of auburn locks that reached her waist. She actually looked more like her grandmother, the woman in the picture held by her locket. "What is your name?"

"Walter Driscoll. From Mercy Falls."

"Near Ferndale," she said. "There's a lighthouse there."

"That's right."

"What are you doing in Crescent City?"

"Looking for you," he said. His voice was still weak, and he was pale.

He must be delirious. She noticed the swelling in his elbow had increased. "Is your arm paining you?"

He nodded. "It's getting quite bad."

She reached for her medical supplies and pulled out the acetylsalicylic acid. She stirred some into his tea and added honey to cover the bitterness. "Drink that. It will help." She waited until he gulped it down. "Let me help you to the guest room," she said. "Sleep is the best thing." He wobbled when she helped him up the steps to the spare room across the hall from hers.

Her mother followed close behind with Gideon. "I'll help him prepare for bed," she said. "It's not appropriate for a young woman."

Addie studied her mother's face. The woman's mouth was set, and Addie could have sworn she saw panic in her eyes. "Of course, Mama. Call if you need anything."

Closing the door behind her, she went to her bedroom and shut herself in with Gideon. The dog leaped onto her bed and curled up at the foot. She petted his ears. The foghorn tolled out across the water. The fury of the waves had subsided, leaving behind only the lulling sound of the surf against the shore. She left the dog and stepped to the window. She opened it and drew in a fresh breath of salt-laden air. The light from the lighthouse tower pierced the fog hovering near the shore. She saw no other ships in the dark night, but the fog might be hiding them.

The voices across the hall rose. Her mother quite disliked nosiness, but Addie went to the door anyway. Gideon jumped down from the bed and followed her. Addie wanted to know the reason for the animosity between Mr. Driscoll and her mother. She caught only a few floating words. "Paid handsomely," she heard her mother say. And "truth must be told" came from Mr. Driscoll.

What did her mother mean? They had no wealth to speak of. Many times since Papa died of consumption, they'd had little more for food than fish they could catch or soup made from leeks from their garden. The small amount of money Addie brought in from the dressmaking helped her mother, but there was never enough. Someday she wanted to walk into a shop and buy a ready-made dress. New shoes were a luxury she hadn't had in five years.

"She's not your child," she heard Mr. Driscoll say.

Addie put her hand to her throat. Did her mother have another child? Gideon whined at her side. "It's okay, boy." She had to know the truth even if it made her mother furious. She opened the door and stepped into the hall.

"If you don't tell her, I will," Mr. Driscoll said. "She has the right to know about her heritage."

Heritage? Who were they talking about? The door opened, and she was face-to-face with her mother.

Her mother's shoulders were back, and her mouth was stiff. "Spying on me?"

"No, Mama, of course not. I heard arguing. Is something wrong?"

"It's none of your business, girlie."

Mr. Driscoll's shoulders loomed behind her mother. "It most certainly *is* her business. You must tell her."

Her mother scowled over her shoulder at the man, then turned back to Addie. "Oh, very well," she said. "Come downstairs."

"Of course." Addie still wore her dressing gown, so she followed her mother down the stairs. Gideon stayed close to Addie, and Mr. Driscoll brought up the rear.

"Sit down." Her mother indicated the armless Lady's chair.

Addie's eyes were gritty and burning with fatigue. She obeyed her mother's directive. She glanced at Mr. Driscoll. He wore her father's shirt and pants, the blue ones with the patches on the knees.

Addie turned her attention back to her grim-faced mother. "What is it, Mama? What's wrong?"

"Wait here." Her mother went down the hall and into the office. She returned with a metal lockbox in her hands. "Your father never wanted you to know. I told him this day would come, but he wouldn't hear of it."

Addie's muscles bunched, and her hands began to shake. "Know?"

Her mother thrust a key into the lock and opened the box. "Perhaps it is best if you simply read through these items." She laid the box on Addie's lap.

The papers inside were old and yellowed. Mr. Driscoll stood watching them with a hooded gaze. "Mama, you're frightening me," Addie said.

"What are these papers?" She didn't dare touch them.

Mr. Driscoll's Adam's apple bobbed. "They deal with your heritage, Addie. This woman is not your real mother."

Two

ADDIE CURLED HER hands in her lap. Where was her fan? She was suffocating. "You're my stepmother? Why did you never tell me?"

"You are the most irritating child," her mother said. "Just read the things in the box."

Addie glanced at the yellowed papers. "Can't you just tell me what this is all about?"

Her mother chewed on her lip. "The nightmares of drowning you've suffered all your life? You experienced a shipwreck when you were about two. Roy found you on the shore and brought you home. He insisted we tell no one how we'd found you."

Addie examined her mother's words. Surely she didn't mean Papa hadn't been her real father. "You're jesting." She pressed her trembling lips together and studied her mother's face. The defiance in her eyes convinced Addie she spoke the truth.

Roy Sullivan had not been her father? He'd saved his pennies to buy her every Elizabeth Barrett Browning book that lined the shelf in her room.

19

He'd bought her the treadle sewing machine. Even the stacks of fabric in her sewing room were purchased by him to give her the start she needed. She'd seen him make many sacrifices for her over the years on his modest lightkeeper's salary.

Pain pulsed behind her eyes. And in her heart. She needed air. She started to rise to go outside, then sank back to her chair when her muscles refused to obey. "What do you have to do with this?" she asked Driscoll.

"I believe I'm your uncle," he said. Cradling his sling with his good hand, he settled on the sofa.

Her hand crept to the locket at her neck. "My uncle?" She rubbed the engraved gold. "I don't understand."

Gideon thrust his head against her leg. She entwined her fingers in his fur and found a measure of comfort. "Is Addie even my name?" she managed to ask past a throat too tight to swallow a sip of water.

Her mother looked away as if she couldn't hold Addie's gaze. "Not if my suspicions are right," Mr. Driscoll said.

"Then who am I?" Addie pressed her quivering lips together.

He smoothed the sling. "I believe you're Julia Eaton, daughter of Henry and Laura Eaton. There are newspaper clippings in the file that lead me to that conclusion." He nodded at the metal box. "Laura was my sister."

Addie focused on the woman standing by the fireplace. Josephine Sullivan. Not her mother. No wonder Addie had always sensed a wall between the two of them. It explained so much. She'd often wondered why her auburn hair and green eyes didn't match either of her parents' features. Her mother had cruelly teased her about being left by fairies until her father put a stop to it.

"Why didn't you tell me?" Addie asked.

"Roy refused to allow the truth to come out. You were his little darling."

"You never loved me," Addie whispered. "Even before Papa died."

"Your disobedience killed him," Josephine said. "If I'd told you once, I told you a thousand times not to go swimming out past the breakers."

Addie dropped her gaze. "And it's something I'll have to live with the rest of my life."

"What's this?" Mr. Driscoll asked. "She killed her father?"

Josephine hunched her shoulders. "He took this post hoping the sea air would cure his consumption, but it never happened. The stress of saving Addie from her own foolish behavior sent Roy into a decline he never recovered from."

Addie bolted to her feet. "I need air."

Josephine caught Addie's arm and forced her back into the chair. "It's time the truth came out."

Addie rubbed her throbbing arm. "If you hate me, why did you keep me?"

"I don't hate you," Josephine said. "But you were a constant reminder of my failure to have our own child."

"Then why keep me?" Addie asked again.

Her mother shrugged. "Money. Someone pays for your upkeep. We receive a monthly check from San Francisco. The attorney who sends the funds would never tell us who his client was, so don't even ask."

"You were *paid* to keep me from my real family?" She struggled to take it in. "So the sewing machine was paid for by someone else? The books, the fabric, my clothes?"

"Roy was much too generous with you. I wanted him to save it for our old age. We earned every penny. He saved some, but not enough. Instead he bought you fripperies you didn't need."

"But we've been paupers since Papa died. Did the money stop?"

"With Roy gone, I was able to save it, as we should have been doing all along."

"That money belongs to Addie," Mr. Driscoll put in. "You'll hand over the bankbook or I'll file charges for kidnapping."

Josephine tipped her chin up. "I raised that girl. It belongs to me."

"I don't want it," Addie said, tightening her grip on Gideon. How foolish she'd been to stay here and try to earn her mother's love. "You should have told me."

"There was no need for you to know," Josephine said.

Addie turned her attention to Mr. Driscoll. "Why are you so sure I'm this Julia Eaton?"

He pointed with his good hand to the locket. "I gave my sister the locket you're wearing. She died right offshore here. The woman in the picture is her mother, your grandmother Vera. You look much like both of them."

"How did you find me?"

"A friend passed through here a couple of months ago. She came out to the lighthouse to take pictures with her new Brownie camera and happened to snap a photo of you fishing. When she showed it to me, something in your posture and the way you smiled reminded me of Laura. I knew she'd died nearby, so I decided to come. I never expected . . ." He swallowed hard.

"The Holy Scriptures say we may entertain angels unawares," Addie said. "I think that is the case this night."

His laugh was uneasy. "I'm hardly an angel, Miss Adeline."

Her father had always told her that truth never stayed hidden forever. God laughed at mankind's plans. What would her father say if he were alive today to face the revelation of the lies he'd told her? Everything she thought she knew about her life was in ashes.

She rubbed her forehead. "I don't understand

anything. Why would someone pay you to care for me?" she asked her mother.

"Roy suspected the person wanted you out of the way. He became obsessed with finding out more and collected these clippings and other evidence." Her tone made it clear she'd never understood her husband's obsession.

Addie buried her face in her hands. "Who am I?" Gideon pushed his cold nose against her cheek. When she lifted her head to stare at Mr. Driscoll, the pity on his face stirred her. "What do you want from me?"

"I want to reunite you with your family." He hesitated. "Henry searched for weeks, desperate to find you and Laura. He'll be overjoyed to find you alive."

The thought that her real father had loved her stirred Addie out of her pain. A gust of wind and rain rattled the panes in the window, and she raised her voice over the din. "Reunite us? You mean you want me to go with you?"

He flexed his swollen fingers. "I hadn't thought of that. Perhaps you should stay here until I find out who paid to keep you away, and why."

"I need to help my mother." *My mother*. The familiar words mocked her, but surely the devil she knew was better than the one she didn't.

"That's right," Josephine said. "I depend on your assistance."

Mr. Driscoll looked at Josephine. "I suspect you

have milked every drop of sweat possible from the poor child over the years. You deserve nothing more from her."

Though his words made sense, Addie shied away from the idea of leaving the life she knew. "I'd rather not face them until I know they want me."

He studied her face. "I can't introduce you as Julia until I get more proof. I don't want to subject you to possible scrutiny until we're sure."

She picked up the metal box. "The things in here don't prove it?" She skimmed through the articles about the shipwreck. One article mentioned the Eaton family's desperate search for Laura Eaton and her child, Julia.

He shook his head. "Your father collected articles about the shipwreck, but that's hardly proof of your identity. It's enough for me when I see the locket and look at your face, but Henry will demand more than that."

She slumped back against the chair. "Why wouldn't he see the resemblance as you do?"

"Henry Eaton is wealthy beyond your imagination. Better men than I have tried to hoodwink him without success. He is skeptical of any unproven claim."

She lifted her necklace. "But the locket?"

He chewed his lip. "Yes, he might believe the locket." He glanced at Josephine. "Where was it found?"

25

"It was around Addie's neck when Roy rescued her."

He nodded. "There are many questions about how you came to be here and why. Henry will want a logical explanation of how this happened. I'd like to have something more to prove your claim. When he realizes you're his darling Julia, you'll be showered with love and material possessions."

"I don't really care about money." Loneliness had dogged her all her life. The lighthouse stood on a rocky cliff that was an island most of the time. The only access to the mainland was an isthmus at low tide. Even then, her parents had rarely allowed her to go to town, and she'd longed to fit in, to find friends to laugh with and share with.

Addie stared at him with fresh eyes. Pain etched his mouth and left pallor on his face, but his blue eyes held keen determination. How had he gathered her true need so completely no longer than he'd been here? "Is the Eaton family large?" she asked. "Have I any siblings?"

"Not living," he said. "Your sister, Katherine, died in a streetcar accident three years ago. She was your half sister. Closer, really. After Laura died, Henry married our sister, Clara."

"Can you tell me more about the family?"

"There were three of us. Clara and I have the same mother. Our mother died in childbirth when Clara was born. Laura is the daughter of our father's second wife, so she was our half sister."

"So you're the oldest, then Clara, and my mother was the youngest?"

He nodded. "There are three years between Clara and me, and two years between her and your mother."

Addie's eyes filled. An entire lifetime of belonging had slipped from her fingers. "Katherine was my only sibling?"

He nodded. "But you have a nephew. Edward. He's five."

"A nephew! Do we look alike in any regard?"

"More than a bit," he said. "I have a thought. I can't just take you into Eaton Manor and announce you are Julia. However, Edward's father, John, has mentioned his need of a governess for Edward. Henry is raging about it. He dotes on the boy—being his only grandchild—and has had the care of him since Katherine was killed."

For the first time she was tempted to actually do this thing—to go to this family where Mr. Driscoll claimed she belonged. "Why hasn't Edward been with John?"

"Henry persuaded him that the boy needed his grandmother as he worked through the grieving process. Besides, John is a naval officer and was out to sea when Katherine died."

"The poor child. I would become his governess?"

He nodded. "If your education passes muster."

"I love studies. I obtained a degree through correspondence."

"So you wish to accompany me?"

Did she? She chewed her lip, then slowly nodded. "I'll come."

"You will not!" her mother said.

Mr. Driscoll fixed her with a cold stare. "You have no say in this." He turned his attention back to Addie. "You'll enter the household as my ward, the daughter of a friend. That way you'll be part of the family."

"Then what?"

"I plan to hire a Pinkerton investigator in San Francisco. I'll have him talk to this attorney and ferret out who hired him and why."

Addie hadn't been thinking about the faceless person who had contrived to keep her out of the family. "Why would someone do that?"

"It's something we must discover. Henry hasn't risen to prominence without making many enemies along the way. I have several people in mind."

"Who?"

He rose. "A couple of years before Laura's death, there was some scandal about one of Henry's rivals. When he went broke, his son committed suicide. Perhaps he sought to exact revenge. A child for a child."

She gulped in air. "This person might be dangerous. Are you sure of my identity?"

"Read the papers in the box, Addie. You'll see there is no doubt." He went toward the steps. "I'll

28

leave you alone to absorb this news, my dear. I'm utterly exhausted, and my arm is a misery." His shoulders were stooped as he climbed the stairs.

There was no sound in the living room except the hiss of the gaslight. Addie stared at her mother. No, not her mother. Josephine Sullivan. Addie wasn't a Sullivan. Her entire identity had been stripped away.

Josephine sipped her tea. "You're about to be dropped into the lap of luxury. I expect you could send money to help me out from time to time."

"Did you ever love me at all?" Addie said, her voice barely audible.

"Let's not talk anymore tonight." Josephine moved from the fireplace and went up the stairs.

Addie sat frozen on the chair with the metal box in her lap. She dropped it to the floor, and the papers scattered. With a cry, she fell to her knees and buried her face in her dog's warm coat.

THREE

THE OFFICES OF Mercy Steamboats squatted on the corner of Main and Redwood. A three-story brick building, it presented an austere front to the world. Naval Lieutenant John North paused at the door long enough to remove his hat, then stepped into the entry.

"Good afternoon, Lieutenant North." Mrs. O'Donnell smiled from behind her typewriter.

"Mr. Eaton is in his office. He asked me to send you in when you got here."

John walked down the tiled hall to the first door on the left. The imposing walnut door was closed. He gave a brisk rap on the polished surface. He'd slept little on the steamer from San Francisco, and his eyes burned.

"Come," Henry's voice called.

He'd rather go. John entered and closed the door behind him. "Good afternoon, Henry." When John had married Katherine, she'd insisted he call her parents Mother and Father, but it had never been natural for him. After she was gone, he'd been glad to revert. He suspected Henry felt the same way.

Henry regarded John over the top of his spectacles. "The ferry was late?"

"A few lingering storm swells slowed us down."

John settled in a chair and studied his father-in-law for clues to his mood. Henry's expression was as dark as the clouds rolling in from the west. A tall man, he had a thick head of brown hair that held only a few streaks of gray in spite of being in his midfifties. His brown suit—impeccably cut, of course—fit his muscular frame perfectly. His waxed mustache suited his angular face.

"Have you been to see Edward yet?"

John shook his head. "That's my next stop. I'll set the nurse to packing his things."

Henry leaned forward. "What the devil are you

thinking to yank him from the place he's been secure?"

"Henry, you knew all along this arrangement was temporary. I appreciate all you've done, but Edward is my son. Not yours. Not Clara's. He belongs with me."

Henry banged his fist on the desk. "You were happy enough to leave him with us when Katherine died."

"That's rubbish and you know it. I had no choice. I *do* have a choice now. My new assignment is at a desk, and Edward can be with me."

"You have no one to care for him."

"Actually, I do. Walter rang me, and the daughter of a good friend of his is seeking a position. He is bringing her in today to see if she will suit."

Henry's mouth grew pinched. "Can't the child at least stay until after my birthday ball? You too. You're on leave for a month. There's time to ease him into new arrangements."

Perhaps it would be best to let Edward get used to the idea, used to his father and the new governess. The last thing John wanted was to inflict more trauma on his boy. "Very well. But let's not argue about it anymore, Henry. It's bad for Edward."

"You don't care about what's best for the boy or you wouldn't be yanking him away from us. In the city, people might make fun of him. He's known and loved here. Have you ever thought of resigning, son?"

Henry's genial tone warned John to be on his guard. "The navy is my life."

"Mercy Falls is a charming town. Edward is happy here. I saw a house that would be perfect for you and Edward."

"The navy is all I know."

"You've managed naval supplies for years. You're detailed and organized. I'd put you over my companies without a qualm. Perhaps you could pull the steamboat business out of its slump."

"Henry, the steamboat travel is faltering all over the country. The train is more convenient. You need to be prepared for the coming decline. Perhaps invest in a train."

Henry held up his hand. "You know how I feel about the trains. Noisy and smelly."

"But profitable. You can't hide your head in the sand, Henry. The world is changing."

"Not in my lifetime." He wagged a finger at John. "I see what you are doing. Changing the subject. Think about Edward. Considering his challenges, he'll do so much better here than in the city."

Heat rose along John's neck. "Edward is very bright. He'll have no trouble with school or with adjusting to a new place."

"He has fits, John. We must do whatever we can to help him."

"His epilepsy won't hold him back. He has spunk."

The last comment brought the faintest twitch of

a smile to Henry's face. "Let's put aside our differences and think of the boy. I want to show you my new automobile, so I'll run you home."

If only Henry would take his own advice and think of Edward. Henry believed his solution was the only possible choice, and it wasn't one John was willing to consider.

The stage passed a picturesque lighthouse on the coast. "Who mans it?" Addie asked Mr. Driscoll. He hadn't spoken since they'd boarded the stage. She and Driscoll were the only passengers since the last stop north in Trinidad.

"I believe it's unmanned at the moment. They're looking for a new lightkeeper, according to the paper."

The coach left the seaside and traveled up the hill. The vehicle rounded a curve and began to slow as it neared a town. Addie craned her head out the window at the charming valley. Milk cows grazed on the hillsides until the redwood forest encroached again. The stage rolled through Mercy Falls slowly, and she took in the small shops and brick buildings of the bustling town.

She gathered her valise from the floor by her feet. "Are they expecting me?" she asked.

"I called John. As I thought, he was only too happy to have help finding someone suitable. He's expected from the city on the afternoon ferry. May already be here by now."

"And my father?" She was unable to keep the eagerness from her voice.

"He knows as well. But remember, say nothing. I sent a telegram to a Pinkerton agent in San Francisco, and he is investigating. Once I have proof, we'll talk to your father."

Gideon laid his muzzle on her shoe. She rubbed her temple. The stage jerked to a stop. Moments later, the driver opened the door. Mr. Driscoll disembarked first, then extended his hand and helped her alight. She'd just completed the pale-green dress she wore, and the boots were new, a gift from Mr. Driscoll. Her hat, decorated with tulle, was a concoction she'd created to give herself courage, though she found it failing now.

Placing her hand on her dog's head, she stared up and down the sidewalk and smiled at several passersby. Such an interesting town.

"Shall we walk, or is there a carriage to greet us?" she asked Mr. Driscoll.

"The carriage is there." He indicated a grand brougham across the street. "But I need to run in to see Henry a moment. Will you be all right by yourself?"

"Of course." She watched him walk away, then glanced up and down the busy street. Through the open windows of the building to her right, she heard the familiar clatter of sewing machines. Gideon growled and strained at his leash.

"Is something wrong, boy?" She allowed the dog

to lead her toward the sounds of sewing. The austere brick building sat on the corner. She peeked inside the open door and saw rows of sewing machines. Women bent over their machines, and their feet pumped the pedals furiously. Addie had never seen machines sew so fast. How did they manage to keep their fingers unharmed?

Gideon led her to a small, sobbing girl. She stood to one side of her machine and held her left hand in her right. Addie saw the child's finger welling with blood. Gideon nudged the little girl's leg and whined. The child leaned against the dog.

"Honey, are you hurt?" Addie asked, hurrying to reach her.

A man in suspenders over his short-sleeved shirt approached. He gripped the girl's shoulders roughly. "You're being ridiculous, Brigitte! Get back to work or I'll have to dock your wages." He thrust the child toward the vacant sewing machine.

She couldn't have been more than eight. She wore a rough dress made from a flour sack. Her dark-blonde hair hung in strings around her face, and she had a smudge on her cheek. Who knew when she'd last been bathed?

"What's going on here?" Addie asked. "Where is this child's mother? She needs attention."

The man narrowed his eyes at her well-made dress and black shoes. "You're not one of my workers."

Most of the machines had slowed or stopped,

and Addie realized she had the attention of all the workers. "No, I certainly am not. This child is much too young to be working with a sewing machine. She belongs in school."

The man put his fists on his hips. "Look, lady, this is none of your business. Run along and let me tend to my workers."

"Where is this child's mother? I want to speak to her."

"My mama is sick," the little girl said. Her tears had stopped, and her eyes were big as her gaze traveled from the foreman to Addie. She had one arm looped around Gideon's neck.

Addie squatted in front of her. "Where do you live, honey?"

"Across the street on the top floor," the child said. She leaned forward and whispered, "My mom has consumption."

Addie winced at the family's lot in life. She well knew the pain of the illness. "What's your name?"

"Brigitte."

"That's a pretty name. Where is your sister?"

Brigitte pointed. "She's over there."

Addie saw another child only slightly older than this one. "How old is she?"

"She's nine. I'm eight."

Much too young to be working here, both of them. Addie inched closer and held out her palm. "I'd like to look at your hand."

The foreman grabbed the girl and drew her away

from Addie. "Lady, this is not your business. I'm going to call the owner if you don't get out of here."

Addie stood. "Why don't you do that? Let's talk to the owner of this place and see what excuse he has to offer for forcing a child to do an adult's job."

"Mr. Eaton is across the street," the foreman said. "I'll go get him, and he'll toss you to the street."

Addie barely restrained her gasp. "Mr. Eaton?"

The foreman's cocky grin straightened. "You know him?"

She held out her hand again. "I'm taking this child with me. Her sister too. What's her name, Brigitte?"

"Doria."

Her skirts swishing, Addie marched between the rows of sewing machines to the little girl. "Come with me, Doria," Addie said.

The child's brow wrinkled. "I'll lose my job, miss. We can't afford to lose our jobs."

"I'll talk to the owner." She held out her hand. "Come along."

Doria took her hand, and Addie led her to where the foreman stood with Brigitte. "I'm taking these children home."

"If you go with her, girls, don't bother coming back." He nodded toward the front of the building. "Here comes Mr. Eaton's brother-in-law now. We'll let him sort it out."

Addie turned to see her uncle coming in the door. A man in a navy uniform was with him. Mr. Driscoll wore a thunderous frown that only darkened when his gaze clashed with hers. She straightened her shoulders and set her jaw.

"What is going on here?" Mr. Driscoll asked.

Addie tipped her chin higher. "Are you aware this business employs children who should not be near these machines?"

He blinked. "I have little to do with this place. It's one of Mr. Eaton's pet projects." He frowned at the girls. "These children work here? They surely don't run a machine, do they?"

"They do. Look at Brigitte's hand. She injured it under the needle."

The uniformed man stared at the foreman. "Is this true?"

He shrugged. "Mr. Eaton arranged it. We have about ten kids, some from the orphanage and some from the community."

"I'll have a word with him," the man said. "Did you care for the child's injury?"

"It's just a little prick. She'll be fine."

"Her fingers are bloody," Addie said. "It's still bleeding. With your permission," she asked her uncle, "I'd like to clean her up."

Mr. Driscoll nodded. "By all means."

"Where is the ladies' room?" she asked.

The foreman jerked a dirty thumb behind him. "In the back."

"Where are first-aid supplies to be found?" she asked.

"I'll get them," he said grudgingly. He stalked off toward a small office that had a window facing the work floor.

She eyed the navy man. Her uncle had mentioned that her new employer was an officer. If this was that man, she might find herself out of a job before she started.

FOUR

JOHN STOOD IN the shop and watched the workers disappear when the quitting whistle blew. "Who is that young woman?" he asked Driscoll. While her beauty had stunned him, her fire and compassion impressed him even more.

"Edward's new governess."

Aware his mouth had dropped open, John shut it. "Miss Adeline Sullivan?"

"Indeed. I do wish she hadn't gotten involved in this. Henry will be livid."

"Someone should have gotten involved long ago."

The foreman had vanished into his office after handing Addie the first-aid box and didn't return. John glanced at the other little girl. Doria stood off to one side with her hands clasped. Her lips quivered and she stared at the floor.

He saw a movement. "Here they come now."

John watched Miss Sullivan and Brigitte weave through the sewing machines and tables of fabric. The child chattered to Addie, who seemed to be paying grave attention to the little girl. He studied her neat attire and the fiery lights in her hair.

"Ready to go?" Driscoll said when she reached them.

"I'd like to explain to their mother what happened," Addie said, her voice pleading for Driscoll's understanding. "She lives just across the street."

The husky, feminine voice had a confident quality that gave John pause. Her auburn hair glowed with vitality. Her eyes caught his, and he nearly gasped. Thick lashes framed eyes as green as a lily pad, and the flecks of gold in their depths lit them from within. Or maybe it was the compassion that shimmered there. Such purity, such empathy.

"Miss Sullivan? I'm Lieutenant John North."

She put her hand to her mouth. "My employer? I suspected as much. I'm afraid I'm not making the best first impression on you."

"On the contrary. I'm quite taken with your desire to help these children." He held the door open for them, then stepped into the slanting light of the sun. "It's good of you to care." Katherine had never noticed the poor around her. And why was he comparing Miss Sullivan to his dead wife? "You needn't trouble yourself," he told Driscoll. "I'll handle this."

Buggies clattered down the cobblestone street, and he waited for an opening before guiding the governess and the children to the other side. The five-story tenement was down a dark alley. Mortar had chipped from between some of the bricks, and one of the chimneys lay on its side on the roof. The faded paint and gouges in the door attested to the building's age and lack of upkeep.

He held the door open for Miss Sullivan and the children. Though he didn't say anything, he frowned. Addie shrugged and went past him up the stairs littered with paper and dried mud. The place stank of body odor, tobacco, and stale food. The banister wobbled when he touched it, and he opted to ascend without its assistance.

Brigitte and Doria scampered up the stairs like squirrels. Brigitte kept turning to see where the adults were, then dashing ahead a few more steps.

"How far?" he called.

"One more floor. We're on the top," Brigitte said.

He shouldn't be winded climbing five floors, but the stairwell had no ventilation, and the odors intensified as they rose. The last few steps left him breathless and longing for the cleansing coolness of the redwood forest.

The stench of cooked cabbage hung in the air. Doria's face grew pinched as she approached the first door on the left. The latch plate was bent, and he wondered if someone had kicked in the door. It wasn't locked, and the knob turned when the child laid her hand on it.

"Mama?" Doria called. "I have visitors." She held open the door. Her sister had grabbed Addie's hand and clung to it as they paused on the threshold.

He took Brigitte's hand and brushed past Miss Sullivan but left the door open. This place needed all the fresh air it could get. She followed with the dog, who rushed past her to the parlor.

Doria beckoned to him. Her face brightened when he stepped into the tiny parlor. "Mama's getting up. She was in the bedroom."

He glanced around the room. Sparse, threadbare furnishings, no decorations, paint that was streaked with soot. He heard a sound and turned to see a gaunt woman hurrying toward him. She wore a dressing gown that might have been white once but was now a blotchy gray. Her hair hung untidily from her bun, and she shoved it out of her face as she came.

The dog padded forward to greet her and licked her hand. She patted his head. "Is Brigitte all right?" she asked in a tremulous voice.

"She had a puncture from the needle," he said. "Please don't trouble yourself. Brigitte said you'd been ill. I'm sorry. I didn't introduce myself. I'm John North."

"I'm Nann Whittaker. Thank you for bringing my girls home, Lieutenant North." Her gaze went past him to Miss Sullivan, who had retrieved her dog's leash.

"I'm Addie Sullivan," the young woman said. "I tended to Brigitte's wound. It's quite minor. The iodine should stave off any infection."

"You're too kind," Mrs. Whittaker murmured.

He put his hand on the child's head. "They're much too young to be working on machines."

Mrs. Whittaker's smile faded. "If there were any way to put food on the table without them working, I'd take it. My husband was killed in a logging accident last year. We got by okay with my job at the sewing factory, but then I took sick."

"Consumption, Brigitte said?" Miss Sullivan put in.

The thin woman nodded. "The doctor says I need to get into the country, but that's not possible. I've got three other children, all younger than Brigitte."

Five children and no husband. The knowledge pained him. "Both girls are polite and hardworking. You should be proud of them."

"Oh, I am!" The woman pressed her trembling lips together. "I'll go back to the shop myself just as soon as I'm able, and they can go back to school. They are so smart."

"I can see that," John said, noticing Brigitte's bright, curious eyes.

"Brigitte made top grades in school." Mrs. Whittaker's hand made a sweeping motion toward

43

the room. "I want more for my children than . . . this."

John nodded, unable to speak past the boulder in his throat. What chance did this family have? He wished there was something he could do, but he hesitated to bring her into his own house. She might pass her disease on to Edward.

He saw Miss Sullivan's eyes swimming with tears. He had to help. He dug into his pocket and pressed all the cash he had into her hand. Fifty dollars. "I'll see what I can find for the girls that isn't so dangerous," he said.

"God bless you," she whispered, her voice hoarse. "I had no food in the house."

"Can I pick up something for you?"

She shook her head. "The girls will fetch groceries for me."

"I must go," he told Mrs. Whittaker. "Good-bye, girls." He fled the stink of sickness.

Miss Sullivan and her dog followed him down the stairs. He noticed she was still fighting tears. "There's no choice but to let the girls work in that shop," he said, "but I'll talk to Henry about finding a job that doesn't involve the sewing machine. Mrs. Whittaker needs a good sanatorium for a few months. She might be able to work once she's stronger, but she'll never get well breathing in this air."

Addie kept her hand on the dog's head. "God is always sufficient. We must pray for them."

"I fear God isn't listening much of the time," he said.

"God is always listening. Sometimes things don't turn out the way we want. But even when they don't, God is always sufficient."

When they reached the first floor, she quickened her steps to exit the tenement, and he watched her draw in a lungful of air devoid of the smells permeating the building. The alley held other structures just like this one. How many other heartbreaking situations resided on the floors of these dwellings?

Mr. Driscoll met them on the sidewalk. Addie gauged his expression and realized he wasn't angry, just distracted.

"Everything is arranged?" he asked.

Lieutenant North shrugged. "Not really. It's a sad situation."

Mr. Driscoll turned toward the carriage. "Might I offer you a ride to the manor?"

His dark eyes never left Addie. "Thank you, but no. I have business at the bank to attend to before I leave town. Henry offered me a ride." He tipped his hat to her. "I'm sure we'll get a chance to get better acquainted tonight," he told her.

"Of course," she said faintly. She watched him walk away and wished she could stop him. Nothing in her life had prepared her for the onslaught of emotion that churned inside her from the first moment she'd seen him.

Mr. Driscoll offered his arm, and she took it. The streets were a muddy quagmire after the rain, and she lifted her skirt to clear the muck. A driver helped her into the carriage. She let herself imagine she was Elizabeth Barrett Browning about to embark on a journey. Or maybe Alice Roosevelt. She so admired the president's courageous daughter. Someday she wanted to see far-off places like Alice did, and dig her bare toes into distant sands. In her daydream, the man at her side matched the man who had just left her.

Josephine had worked to squelch Addie's romanticism, but Addie couldn't help it anymore than she could help the color of her eyes. "How far to the estate?" she asked Mr. Driscoll.

"At the edge of town. Five minutes," he said, settling onto the leather seat beside her. He cast a doubtful glance at Gideon. "You should have left that dog behind. I don't know how I'll explain it to Henry."

She tipped up her chin. "I wouldn't come without him."

"Which is the only reason I finally agreed. But it was most unfortunate. Henry is sure to be put off."

"I thought Lieutenant North was my employer."

"He is, but Henry's wishes are generally considered."

She watched the scenery as the carriage rolled through town. A drugstore and ice-cream shop looked interesting. She noticed a sign that said

46

Mercy Stagecoach Company. Before she could ask, Mr. Driscoll pointed it out as belonging to her father. There were several dress shops and haberdasheries in town.

"Henry owns half the town," Driscoll said. "The bank, the creamery too."

Addie shrank back against her seat. "I fear I'll be out of place."

"You'll be fine. As my ward, you'll be treated like one of the family."

The carriage slowed at two large stone columns that anchored a wall taller than Addie's head. A massive iron gate barred the way. The vehicle stopped until the guard opened the gate, then it turned into a long driveway.

"Why is it gated?" she asked. "Are they in danger?"

He laughed. "You have much to learn, Adeline. The Eatons don't mingle with the lower class other than to employ them. It's better that way."

"Better for whom?"

His smile faltered and he turned away. "There's your new home."

Addie caught her breath at the sight of the mansion. Three stories high, it rambled in so many directions she had to crane her neck to take it all in. Five or six colors of paint emphasized the architecture's features. The porch encased two sides of the manor, and the railing made her think of toy blocks. The red trim accented the medium gray-green siding. The door and shutters were black. The home had so many gables and dormers, it made her dizzy to take them all in. Numerous outbuildings peeked from the coastal redwoods that shaded the yard. The forest began barely ten feet from the back corner of the house.

"It's quite lovely," she said.

"Henry attends to every detail," Mr. Driscoll said. "You'll see many homes such as these in town. We call them butterfat palaces, since most were constructed from money made from dairying. Henry's is the grandest by far."

"Did Mr. Eaton make his money in dairying too?"

"In the beginning. He owns many other businesses now, as I mentioned." He stepped from the carriage and helped her down. "Remember, mention nothing to anyone. It might be dangerous to reveal your identity."

"Dangerous?"

"Someone took great care to keep you from Henry. Whoever did this must hate him very much. That level of hatred might be dangerous. If Henry finds out who has done this, that person's life would be ruined. Henry would see to that."

"My father sounds formidable."

"He doesn't suffer fools gladly, and he expects those around him to be loyal."

She accepted the arm he offered, and they walked past banks of blooming goldenrod and salvia. Gideon followed at her heels. "How about you, Mr. Driscoll? How do you feel about Mr. Eaton?"

"He's a loyal friend to those he trusts. He's been good to me for my sisters' sakes, and I've made my home in the manor for many years." They reached the front door. He opened it and motioned for her to enter. "Stay," he told the dog.

She repeated the command and stepped into the entry. The first thing she noticed was the scent of something baking. A berry pie, perhaps. Then she saw the opulence of the hall. Her mouth dropped as she took in polished walnut floors and woodwork, richly colored wallpaper, and an Oriental runner down the entry and up the six-foot-wide staircase. Through a doorway lay a parlor with lovely red upholstered furniture and fine pictures.

She craned her head to look at the art that lined the walls. A woman's portrait caught her eye. "My mother? I'd like to know more about her."

"That's not her. It's your grandmother Vera."

She clutched her necklace. "The one in my locket. She's much older in this portrait."

"Yes."

She glanced at her shoes and realized she was tracking mud on the carpet. "Oh, dear me," she muttered. She quickly retraced her steps to the porch and removed her shoes. "Might I have a rag to clean up the mess?"

"Molly shall get it. Come along," Mr. Driscoll

commanded. "I'll show you to your room, then introduce you to your charge."

Her pulse leaped at the thought that her new life was about to begin.

FIVE

ADDIE STEPPED INTO the room at the end of the long hall. The tiny space held only a dresser and a single bed covered with a blue and yellow quilt. A bowl and pitcher had been placed atop the doily on the dresser. Beside the bed lay a plain rag rug on the oak floors. The scent of beeswax hung in the air. Pleasant. And lavish compared to her stark bedroom at the lighthouse. The window in this room looked out into the deep shadows of red-wood forest, and she shivered at their imposing height.

She dropped her valise on the floor. "What about my trunk?"

"The driver will bring it up. Will this suit?"

"Of course. Where is my charge's room?"

"Across the hall. I shall show you." Mr. Driscoll stood aside for her to exit, then stepped in front of her and led the way. Her slippers sank into the plush runner in the hall. The green wallpaper appeared new. Portraits of people lined the walls, and she longed to linger over the images to see if she could find a woman with red curls.

He motioned to her, and she followed him into

the room opposite hers. Tin soldiers, a wooden train, and a stack of books on a small shelf proclaimed the space to be a child's room. A small table with two chairs was under the window. The other furnishings included a cot, a chest of drawers, and a chifforobe. This room had wallpaper in a tiny blue print that matched the blue quilt on the bed. A rug covered the unpainted floor.

"He's not here" she said.

"He's likely in the side yard with his nurse." He motioned to her and exited the room.

She hurried to fall into step. "If he has a nurse, does he really need me?"

"He's five. It's time he began to receive instruction in reading and sums. Come along, my dear." His clipped words urged her to hurry.

She quickened her pace. So many new relationships to learn. After a lifetime of loneliness, she was about to discover a family. Her pulse stuttered, and she wasn't sure if it was fear or anticipation. She followed him down the steps.

Gideon greeted her on the porch and pressed his cold nose against her hand. She rubbed his ears. "What about Gideon? He's used to sleeping with me."

"Gideon will sleep in the barn. It's clean and dry."

"Yes, sir." She stepped across the spongy grass to the side yard. A small boy gripped a baseball bat in his hands and squinted into the sun. An older woman in a gray dress prepared to pitch a baseball at him.

Addie drank in the curly dark hair and his quite adorable cowlick. He was a miniature version of his striking father. He wore knickers and a white shirt. He bit his tongue as he concentrated on the nurse preparing to pitch the ball. She wanted to run to him and scoop him into her arms. She longed to hear him call her Auntie. After a lifetime of wanting a large family, here was part of all she'd longed for.

The child saw Gideon. "A dog!" He dropped the bat and called the dog to him.

Gideon trotted forward, and the boy rubbed his ears. "He likes me," Edward said, his voice eager.

"Of course he does," Addie said. She knelt beside him. Her fingers itched to bury themselves in his curls. She wanted to put her nose in his neck and smell his little-boy scent. He was adorable, and she was already in love.

"Does he like to play ball?" he asked.

"I'm sure he'd like that very much," she said. She stood and watched the boy throw the ball to Gideon for a few minutes. Then Edward dropped the ball and stood staring. "Edward, are you all right?" she asked.

Gideon lunged toward the boy. When he reached him, he grasped Edward's sleeve in his teeth. "Gideon, down," Addie called, starting after him. The dog tugged the child down to the grass. She gasped and put on an extra burst of speed. She'd never known her dog to attack. He was the most mild-mannered canine. Edward slumped to the ground. His limbs began to twitch.

The nurse reached him. "He's having a seizure!" She pulled a hankie from her pocket, rolled it up, then thrust it between the child's teeth as though she'd done it before. "He has the falling sickness," she said, peering up at Addie.

"Epilepsy," Mr. Driscoll said, his tone sharply corrective.

The nurse inclined her head and glanced at Gideon. "What a blessing your dog pulled Edward down so he didn't fall, Miss."

"I have never seen him act that way," Addie said. "It was almost as if he knew what was coming."

"Nonsense," Mr. Driscoll said. "He was practically attacking the boy."

"Gideon has never attacked anyone." Addie petted the dog's head. "Look at him, Mr. Driscoll. He's worried about Edward." Gideon lay near the child. His dark eyes never left Edward's face. He whined and licked Edward's cheek.

The man studied dog and boy. "Nonsense," he said again, but his tone lacked conviction.

A *putt-putt* from behind caused her to turn. A most unusual contraption came rolling up the drive. It resembled a buggy, but there was no horse pulling it. The sun glimmered on shiny red paint and black leather seats. The wheels turned around red spokes. An oily stink roiled from it. The man in the seat behind the wheel wore a leather coat and beret, and a scarf around his neck. And a huge smile. Beside him sat a familiar set of wide shoulders encased in a navy uniform.

"Is that my father?" she whispered.

"It most certainly is. In his new Cadillac."

Henry. Her father. Her legs twitched and adrenaline surged, but she forced herself to remain still and watch him maneuver the vehicle over the potholes until it stopped with a final *putt*. Lieutenant North leaped out, then the automobile rolled on to the carriage house. Neither of the men noticed the boy on the ground.

John spotted Miss Sullivan the moment he dismounted the automobile. She stood to one side with Driscoll, and he caught a gleam of auburn hair under her large hat. She was just as attractive as she'd been in town and inspired the same leap in his pulse. He'd hoped his reaction had been a temporary insanity.

She and Driscoll and Edward's nurse, Yvonne, faced a form on the ground, and it took a moment for the scene to register. When he recognized his son, he ran toward his boy. "Edward!" He knelt beside him.

The boy's eyelids moved, but he didn't awaken. At least no seizure contorted his features. "He had a seizure?" he asked, glancing up at Yvonne. She nodded. He touched Edward's forehead. "Edward. Wake up, son."

There was still no response and likely wouldn't be for a few more minutes. Edward would be tired for hours. John clenched his fists. If only he could fix this for his son. He took a deep breath, then smoothed his son's hair. "It's all right, Edward. I'm here."

"He collapsed so quickly," Miss Sullivan said in that compelling, husky voice.

He rose and nodded. "Were you here when Edward's attack occurred?"

"Yes, Lieutenant North." Her worried eyes never left the boy. "We'd just come out to meet him when he fell."

He lifted his son in his arms and carried him toward the house. The young woman fell into step beside him. The dog started to follow her, and she made a hand gesture that stopped it in its tracks.

"Is there anything I can do? If I'm going to be with him most of the day, I need to know how to handle this when it happens."

At least she wasn't flustered by the incident. She'd taken charge here the same way she'd done in the sweatshop. His deceased wife had dissolved into hysterics every time Edward had a "fit," as she called it. She'd never reconciled herself to the idea that her son had a chronic problem.

"Come with me," he told her.

He carried his son into the house and up the staircase to his bedroom. He laid the boy on top of the quilt and stood staring down at him. He ached to take the ailment on himself, but all he could do was stand by.

Miss Sullivan stepped closer to the bed. "Why isn't he waking?"

"He'll be up and around soon. But he'll be tired. He had a seizure."

"What can be done to help him?"

"I've had him to the best neurologists in the country, but there is no treatment for it."

"So he'll always have to deal with this?" Her gaze softened even more.

He nodded. "The main thing to remember when he has a seizure is that he needs to be kept safe. Help him to lie down, and put something soft between his teeth so he doesn't bite his tongue, then wait it out."

She caressed Edward's hair. "Poor child."

John warmed to her empathy. He thought it was sincere. "He's a good lad. Never lets it get him down." He folded his hands across his chest. "You were most confident in the sewing factory. I think it would be difficult for anything to get the better of you. I liked that."

Color stained her cheeks. "Thank you, sir. I was thankful for your protection."

"You're much younger than I expected." *And prettier*, he could have added.

Her green eyes held a challenge. "I'm nearly twenty-five."

"I merely remarked on your youth. If Walter thinks you are suitable, I'm sure that's the case."

She dropped her gaze to the floor, and her cheeks went rosier. "I'm sorry for my tone, Lieutenant North."

It wasn't his fault he liked her appearance entirely more than was proper. "Forgive me, Miss Sullivan. I don't mean to make you feel uncomfortable in your position. Take care of my son, and teach him well, and you'll hear no complaints from me."

"I will do my very best," she said. She turned toward the bed. "He's awakening."

Edward yawned, and his eyelids fluttered, then opened. "Papa? I did it again."

John sat on the edge of the bed and slipped his arm under his son's head. "It's all right, little man. You're fine now."

Edward bolted upright. "Where's the doggy?"

"What dog?"

"The one that helped me," the boy asked Miss Sullivan. "Was it your dog?"

"Yes. That's Gideon."

"He knew I was getting sick and helped me sit down."

John hid his smile. And his skepticism. "What did he do?"

"He jerked on my arm until I sat," Edward said.

John glanced at the woman. Her expression was soft as she stared at his son. "Did you know the seizure was coming?"

Edward shook his head. "I was going to toss the ball for him. Can the dog sleep on my bed?"

"You know your grandfather doesn't allow dogs in the house."

"But this is a special dog. He helped me. I'll ask Granddad myself." Edward scooted to the edge of the bed. He staggered when he gained his feet but quickly straightened.

"You're the only one Granddad might listen to," John muttered after his son disappeared through the doorway.

Glancing at the new governess, he wished he would quit feeling as though the undertow were carrying him out to sea.

SIX

ADDIE COUNTED EVERY tread as she walked back to the entry. Twenty-one. She kept track of every time she put her foot down on the entry and porch, and on each of the front steps. Thirty. And she prayed. The austere man she'd glimpsed sitting in the automobile next to the lieutenant wasn't what she'd expected.

The yard was empty except for Gideon and Edward. Smiling, she approached the boy and dog. "He likes you, Edward." She couldn't resist touching his hair again. The soft locks curled around her finger.

"Can I have him?" The question was asked with the innocence of a child who had never been denied.

Addie inhaled as she tried to decide how to answer. She'd raised Gideon from a puppy and would never give him up. "I'll be happy to share him," she said finally. "But he's my dog."

Edward's lip thrust out. "I want him to be *my* dog." He began to sob.

Addie wanted to gather him in her arms and soothe his cries, but she knew it wasn't wise to give in to every demand.

"How did you get him to do that?" a gruff voice demanded from behind her. "The dog, I mean. Yvonne informed me the canine appeared to have anticipated my grandson's fit."

She turned to see Henry Eaton approaching. He'd removed his cap and scarf. Flecks of mud dulled the sheen of his boots. "I don't know, Mr. Eaton. I've never seen him do anything like this before."

Edward had his arms around Gideon's neck. "He seemed quite attuned to the lad," Mr. Eaton said.

"He's always been intuitive. Whenever a ship-wreck occurred at our lighthouse, he knew before we did. He would have plunged into the raging sea if I had allowed him to do so."

"He must stay with my grandson at all times,"

Mr. Eaton said. "You're the new governess, is that right?"

"Yes, sir," she said, raising her voice above Edward's hiccupping sobs.

He studied the dog again. "We should breed him. His pups might have his magical ability as well. I'll find a female at once. Where did you find him?"

"In Crescent City. My father bought him from a neighbor."

"Give me his name, and I'll see if he has any other dogs with this one's ability. What's the dog's name?"

"Gideon."

"This is a lucky day for us, young lady. We must do all in our power to make sure you and the dog stay with us."

The note of approval in his voice brought the truth to the front of her tongue. How much greater would his welcome be if he knew she was his daughter? She had to get away before she blurted out the story. "I believe God brought me here for a reason, Mr. Eaton. I'll do my part to follow the Lord's guidance in all ways."

"Such simple faith," he said. "Very quaint."

His condescending tone squared her shoulders. "If you'll excuse me, I need to unpack."

The intensity of his demeanor softened. "I've come on too strong with you. Please accept my apology, Miss Sullivan. We all indulge the child too much. It's his af-affliction, you see."

His heartfelt stammer tugged at her heart. "No

need to apologize. I've already fallen in love with Edward myself. I'll protect him with my life. After all, God has arranged this for Edward's benefit."

Eaton tipped his head to the side. "You look familiar. Have we met?"

She turned her head. "I don't remember meeting you, sir. I grew up much north of here."

"Strange," he muttered. He put his large hand on Edward's head. "Enough of these histrionics, Edward. The dog will be here for you. Miss Sullivan has graciously agreed to share the animal with you. Stop the wailing."

Her charge sniffled, then swiped the back of his hand across his wet face. "Can he sleep with me, Granddad?"

"You know I quite dislike animals in the house, boy," his grandfather said.

"But he helped me!" Tears filled Edward's eyes.

Eaton sighed. "Very well. But keep him out from under my feet. And out of the kitchen, you hear? It will be your job every morning to put him out for the day. He's not to lie around on the rugs."

Edward's eyes began to shine. "Yes, sir!"

Addie hid a smile at the boy's deft manipulation. She would have her hands full with him. He'd been coddled all his life. While she pitied him his affliction, it would be her job to see that he developed into a man, not a namby-pamby without backbone. At least her father showed love and compassion.

A movement caught her attention, and she

watched Lieutenant North approach from the carriage house where the automobile was stowed. Warmth crept into her skin. When they'd talked over Edward's bed, she'd had the most peculiar sensation, as if something inside her had recognized him—the timbre of his voice, the way he looked at her as if he really saw her. He possessed everything she'd dreamed of when she read Elizabeth Barrett Browning's poetry: wide shoulders that tapered to a trim waist, unruly black hair, and dark brown eyes that pierced right through her defenses. She'd read about love at first sight and assumed it was the stuff of dime novels, but when she held this man's gaze, she could almost believe in it.

Her gaze went to her dog. Had he really sensed Edward's approaching seizure? Often she'd thought Gideon could sense pain and despair. He'd proven it again today when he'd led her to the garment factory. What if he possessed some innate ability to predict the seizures? He could be a great boon to the child.

She told herself not to be so silly. It was a childish fancy that had taken Edward. He'd soon outgrow it and move on to a new obsession. Children always did. She turned toward the driveway as a carriage turned in at the gate.

John turned his back on Miss Sullivan and approached his mother-in-law's carriage as it rolled to a stop. He extended his hand to help her alight. Would Katherine have aged as well as Clara? Her creamy skin was unlined, though he knew she had to be fifty or a little older by now. The smile he greeted her with was genuine. "Clara, it's good to see you."

She touched a gloved finger to his cheek. "John, when did you arrive? You look quite handsome with that tan."

He brushed his lips across her cheek and inhaled her rose perfume. "Just this afternoon."

"Fetch my parcels from the driver, would you? I am perishing for tea." She swayed off toward the house without waiting for his answer.

John shrugged and did as he was told. Henry never begrudged her any of the funds she spent on her fripperies. Katherine might have paupered him in following her mother's example. Carrying the parcels, he strode to the house, where he handed off the purchases to Molly, then followed the sound of voices to the parlor.

Miss Sullivan stood with her back to the wall and her hands clutched in front of her green dress. She faced his mother-in-law. Driscoll stood off to one side with Edward.

"Yes, ma'am," she said. "I studied three years of Latin, though I don't think Edward is quite ready for another language."

"I agree, Miss Sullivan." Clara made a sweeping survey of the younger woman. "Your dress is quite well made. Where did you find it?"

"I made it, ma'am."

"How refreshing to find such an industrious young woman. How did you learn to sew such a stylish garment?" Clara stepped nearer and examined the waist of the dress. "The way the waist dips is very becoming. And the stitches are invisible."

The young woman shifted, and the color leached from her cheeks. "My mother taught me to sew when I was a child. She thought the income would help the family, but I discovered a real love for textiles and design."

To John the dress appeared ordinary, but then, what did he know of style? He noticed how long Miss Sullivan's lashes were and averted his gaze. She was his employee.

Miss Sullivan touched Clara's hand. "Are you feeling all right, Mrs. Eaton? A headache perhaps?"

Clara pressed her other hand hard on her forehead. "My head does ache. How did you know?"

"I saw it in your eyes. Let me rub it for you," Miss Sullivan said. "I have some peppermint oil that will help ease the pain."

"What a dear you are," Clara said. "We have a few minutes before dinner, and anything you might do to help would be most welcome."

"I'm sure it will comfort you," Miss Sullivan said.

"Over our meal I wish to know more about your dressmaking skills. I'm planning a ball for Henry's birthday in two weeks, and I must have a new dress. I have an idea in my mind's eye, and perhaps you can bring it to life."

"I'll be happy to do whatever I can, Mrs. Eaton," Miss Sullivan said. "But I need to start immediately if I'm to have time to complete it."

John glanced at the young woman, then at his mother-in-law. Both of them were smiling. "What about Edward?" he asked. "Miss Sullivan was hired to teach my son."

Clara tapped her closed fan on her son-in-law's arm. "Don't be such a stickler, John. I'll make sure my dress doesn't cut into Edward's lesson time. Come along, my dear. Get your oil, and meet me in my salon."

John's mouth dropped as Clara took Addie's arm and escorted her out of the room. He'd never known the older woman to bother with those she deemed beneath her. After a falling-out with Walter over the young man's shenanigans of drinking and gambling, their father had bequeathed to her one of the most lucrative logging operations in the West. She seldom let anyone forget that she came from power and money. She must have been inordinately impressed with Miss Sullivan.

He called Yvonne and had her take Edward for his meal. When the boy protested, John stepped to the front door and called the dog in. Gideon's nails clicked across the wood floor, then he went up the stairs after the boy and his nurse, and John made his way to the dining room, where he found Walter pouring himself a glass of claret.

Walter set the decanter back onto the sideboard. "I hope Miss Sullivan is to your satisfaction."

"She appears competent." John noticed Walter's sling. "You never mentioned what you did to your arm."

"I sprained it in a fall down some steps. Near Crescent City. I shall dispense with the sling in a day or two." Walter turned to pour another glass of claret. "Miss Sullivan is a lovely girl, is she not? Edward is crazy about her dog. Hauling all her books here nearly broke my back."

John grinned. "I doubt you carried them yourself with your injury."

Walter smiled back. "You caught me. She's quite the scholar though." He went to his place at the table as the ladies joined them.

Clara seated Miss Sullivan beside John. The young woman's eyes took in the gleaming silverware and china, then the napkin ring holding the linen. She'd likely never seen a place set with twenty-four pieces of silverware. She bowed her head and closed her eyes. Her lips moved. Was she praying? The rest of the family gave her but momentary notice, then turned back to their plates. When she raised her head, she kept her hands in her lap. John nudged her discreetly, then slipped the ring off the napkin and placed it in his lap. A faint smile curved her lips, and she imitated his action. When the servants brought in the first course of raw oysters, he selected the proper fork.

She took only one oyster from the footman's tray, and he noticed her pale when she managed to gulp it down. "It's not my favorite either," he whispered. "But soup is coming too."

Henry appeared not to have noticed Miss Sullivan's discomfort. "I stole my cook from the Vanderbilts," he said. "I went to one of their parties, and after dinner, I slipped back to the kitchen and promised Mrs. Biddle double the salary and her own house on the grounds. She's been with us for three years."

John had never heard the story, but he could well believe it. When the footman brought the next dish, broiled salmon, he again deliberately selected the fish fork. Miss Sullivan was a quick study and selected the proper one as well. She took a larger portion of the fish from the tray and ate daintily as the conversation flowed about his new assignment at the base and the places he'd been with the navy. By the time the spring chicken arrived, she barely picked at the meat with the proper fork. At the salad course, she managed only a few bites, though he hid a smile as he noticed how quickly the bonbons disappeared when the footman brought them around.

All through the meal, Walter kept a sharp eye on Miss Sullivan. The longer the meal went on, the more his attention irritated John. Walter was much too old for an innocent girl like the new governess. John sprang to his feet when the meal finally came to a close two hours later.

Miss Sullivan rose as well. "Thank you for a wonderful meal, Mrs. Eaton," she said. "I'm blessed and honored to be here with you."

Clara colored. "What a lovely thing to say, Adeline. We shall enjoy having you join us at every meal."

How did Miss Sullivan do it? Any other governess would have been ignored at the end of the table. She drew everyone with her charm and naïveté. He found he didn't mind the thought of staying at the manor for the next three weeks.

SEVEN

ADDIE RUBBED HER tired eyes. All she wanted was to fall into bed, though she'd required the assistance of a chambermaid to find the way back to her room after dinner.

"Here you be, Miss," Sally said. She appeared to be about Addie's age. Combs held her wispy blonde hair to her head under the white cap.

"Thank you, Sally. This place is so big and intimidating. So are the people. Have you enjoyed working for the Eaton family? I'm not sure what to expect."

Sally ducked her head. "They be nice enough. Generous too."

"How long have you been here?"

"Two years, Miss."

"Do you have time off? I'm not sure how much to request. This is my first employment experience."

"Thursdays be my day off. So you'll be a servant, Miss? Not a guest?"

"I'm Edward's new governess."

"A working woman like you, you should come to the suffrage meeting next week!" Sally smiled as she warmed to her subject. "We be so close to getting the vote!"

Addie hadn't heard much of political issues at the lighthouse. "I might do that." Lieutenant North's penetrating gaze seared her memory. "Do you see much of Lieutenant North?"

Sally shook her head. "He be gone most of the time on his ship." A smile played at her lips, "Lawdy, he be handsome. Those eyes." She sighed. "But don't be setting your cap for him, Miss. Mr. Eaton discourages mingling between the family and the likes of us."

Addie nodded, but her mind churned. Maybe when her real identity came out, her father would look kindly on a match. If the handsome lieutenant would deign to notice her.

Addie worked to feel more at home in the first two days. The meals still baffled her, but Edward was a delightful boy, inquisitive and energetic, though a trifle spoiled. He responded well to correction and had a quick mind. They hadn't started lessons, as she wanted to assess his needs. The real problem was his father. Addie admitted to herself that she was more intrigued with getting to know her employer than with her real reason for coming here. She needed to focus on the goal.

And yet, Mr. Driscoll had told her his Pinkerton agent was on the case. They'd soon have proof enough to tell the family of her true identity. Addie longed to see her father's reaction to her reappearance, but she had to remind herself that patience was a virtue God was cultivating in her.

After lunch Wednesday, while the nurse took charge of Edward for his nap, Addie grabbed a book from her room, then slipped outside with Gideon. The mighty coastal redwoods towered over the impressive mansion. She picked up her skirts and ran for their cool serenity behind the manor. Moss clung to the rocks along the path that led into the dimness of the forest, and she breathed in the moist freshness.

She paused where a shaft of sunlight slanted through the canopy of giant trees. A faint impression in the moss and vegetation led her along, and she began to hear the sound of running water. She followed it and came to a waterfall. This must be the Mercy Falls that the town was named for. The falls towered a hundred feet over her head, then thundered into the clear pool.

Breathtaking. Gideon immediately plunged into the water.

A flat rock called to her, and she sank onto its gray surface. Prayer would calm her. She let the beauty of the waterfall and forest surround her and lifted her spirit to the Lord. She murmured the words to the Twenty-third Psalm, and peace reigned over the chaos she'd been feeling.

Her calm restored, she flipped open her book of Elizabeth Barrett Browning poetry. The pages fell open to "A Man's Requirements." Though she'd read it many times, this time she understood the words. She pondered the first stanza.

> Love me Sweet, with all thou art,
> Feeling, thinking, seeing;
> Love me in the lightest part,
> Love me in full being.

It explained exactly how she'd felt the moment she saw John North. Every innermost thought of her heart had been ready to spill from her soul into his ears. Every moment of the past two days that she'd spent in his presence had deepened her fascination with him. She found herself watching for him every moment and waiting for him to arrive home when he was gone. When his dark eyes turned her way, heat enveloped her.

Her head ached, and she took the combs from her hair and shook it loose to her shoulders. She uncapped her fountain pen and jotted some thoughts in the margin. They were the silly thoughts of a romantic girl, but she couldn't help her mooning over him.

"There you are."

She peered through the gloom to see Lieutenant North walking toward her. Her book fell into the ferns as she scrambled to her feet, smoothing her dress. She grabbed for her hair combs, but there was no time to make herself more presentable. "Is Edward awake already, sir?"

He stopped three feet from her. "He's napping. You can easily become lost in this forest. Every tree looks alike, and the lighting is poor."

She felt through the ferns for her book, and her hair fell forward to obscure her face. "I don't have a very good sense of direction, but I have Gideon."

"Lost something?"

"My book." Her cheeks burned when he reached into the ferns and retrieved it.

"Browning?" He flipped it open.

She caught her breath. If he saw what she'd written . . . She held out her hand for the book.

He shut it and handed it back to her. "I haven't read her since I was in school."

Her fingers closed around the book, and she clutched it to her chest. Now he'd think her a hopeless romantic and even less capable of caring for his son.

"I also came to discuss Edward's education with you. How is he doing?"

"Quite well. He's very bright."

"Are you going to have the time to devote to him and also see to Clara's new dress?"

She caught a whiff of his cologne. Something spicy. "Edward is my first priority."

"Unless Clara begins to demand more of your time."

Before she could think how to answer his concerns, she heard a scream from the direction of the house. Lieutenant North turned and sprinted back toward the manor, and Addie followed him. The terror in the shriek gave wings to her feet, and she had no trouble keeping up with the man.

A branch from a shrub slapped her in the face, and she shoved it out of the way, but it slowed her down. Lieutenant North disappeared ahead of her. She put on an extra burst of speed but still saw no sign of his back. The scream came again, and the sound galvanized her even more.

She leaped over a rock in her way, but instead of landing on her feet on the other end, something hard hit her back. Her breath whooshed out of her. Her arms pinwheeled out, but the heavy weight bore her to the ground. Her head plowed into the ferns, then her face pressed into moist moss. The fecund scent of the forest filled her head, and she struggled against the weight squeezing the breath from her lungs. A burlap sack smelling of oranges came around her head, and the suffocating darkness gave her new reason to fight. She flailed until someone grabbed her arms.

"Don't move," a voice hissed in her ear.

A cold blade touched her throat, and she froze. She didn't recognize the voice behind the threatening tone. It was a man, but that was all she knew. Calloused hands roped her wrists together behind her back, then the pressure atop her was gone. She heard steps swish through the vegetation. The normal sounds of the forest resumed—birds chirping in the trees and insects humming. She rolled to her back, then sat up. With her hands tied, she had to make two attempts before she gained her feet. The burlap sack was still over her head. She stumbled to a tree, then moved her head against the rough bark until she managed to rub off the offending burlap.

The scent of the forest washed the orange aroma from her nose. She would need help getting the rope off. And what about the scream she'd heard? Gathering her strength, she ran for the house.

The rope chafed her wrists, and Addie was near tears by the time she emerged from the shadows of the redwoods. She stood blinking in the brilliant wash of light until her eyes adjusted, then she started toward the back door of the house. She hurried in case her attacker was still watching.

Was someone else hurt? The scream she'd heard reverberated in her head.

"Lieutenant North?" she called.

The backyard appeared empty, but she called again. She longed to have her hands free again and to feel safe. A woodpecker's *rat-a-tat-tat* echoed in the open yard. The sound unnerved her, and she broke into a run. Perspiration moistened her forehead as she rounded the side yard and saw Mr. Driscoll lying on the ground. Mrs. Eaton stood nearby, wringing her hands. Lieutenant North knelt beside Driscoll on his right, and Mr. Eaton was on his knees on Driscoll's other side. Several servants with pale faces clustered on the porch.

"Lieutenant North?" she said in a faltering voice. "What's happened?"

Lieutenant North glanced up. "There has been a vicious attack on Walter," he said. "Someone struck him in the head, then vanished."

"Will he be all right?"

"The doctor is on his way."

She drew nearer. "I was also attacked."

"You are unharmed?"

"Yes, though my hands are tied." She turned around so he could see her bonds, then faced him again.

Lieutenant North had her turn around, and he struggled with the knot at her wrists. His hands were cool and dry, but her skin tingled where he touched her. Her gaze lingered on Driscoll. The poor man lay motionless and pale on his side. His eyes were closed. She saw no blood, so perhaps the blow was only enough to render him unconscious. Moments later, the rope fell to the ground by Addie's feet.

"Thank you," Addie said. She rubbed her wrists and turned back toward the group huddled around Mr. Driscoll. "How badly is he hurt?"

"He hasn't moved," Mr. Eaton said.

She inspected Driscoll's pale face. "Is there anything I can do?"

"Not unless you hold a medical degree," Lieutenant North said.

"I've often tended to shipwreck victims until the doctor arrived," she said. "I'm quite competent."

He moved back. "Very well, then."

She pushed past him and knelt beside the older man. When she touched his face, she found it cold. "He needs a blanket," she said.

"I'll get it," Mrs. Eaton said, rushing for the door as if eager to flee the scene.

She felt along Mr. Driscoll's head. "There is a lump here," she said, probing the spot. "He's bleeding." She wiped the blood on her fingers onto the grass.

Mr. Driscoll stirred, and she realized he likely felt the pain of having the wound depressed. He moaned and tried to push himself erect.

"Please lie still, sir," she said.

Mrs. Eaton returned with a quilt in her arms. She

tucked it around her brother, then backed away. "Oh dear, where is the doctor?" she muttered.

A horse neighed, and Addie saw a carriage come rushing up the drive. "Is that the doctor?"

"Yes." Lieutenant North waved to the white-haired man holding the reins. "Here, Dr. Lambertson."

The man leaped from the seat with a black bag in his hand before the buggy had fully stopped. He wore black pants and a white shirt under a vest. His bowler was askew as if he'd grabbed it and jammed it on his head without looking. "Mr. Driscoll was attacked?"

"He's unconscious. We didn't move him."

The doctor's expression grew more sober as he knelt beside his patient. "A good decision, but I'm going to have to roll him over to tend to his injury. I shall require your assistance. Slide your hands under his buttocks, and I'll do the same with his shoulders."

Lieutenant North complied, and the men gently rolled Mr. Driscoll onto his stomach. The large lump on the back of his head oozed blood, and his hair was matted with it. She heard a sigh and and turned to see Mrs. Eaton crumple.

Addie sprang forward but was too late to catch her aunt. "Bring me a wet handkerchief," she called to Molly. The maid nodded and rushed for the house.

Addie pulled Mrs. Eaton's head onto her lap.

"Mrs. Eaton?" she whispered, stroking her hair. Poor woman. Molly returned with the wet hankie, and Addie dampened the prostrate woman's pale face with it.

Mrs. Eaton's eyelids fluttered, then she opened them. "My brother," she murmured. "Is he dead?"

"No, no. The doctor is tending to him." Addie stroked the wet cloth across Mrs. Eaton's forehead again. The doctor worked at staunching her uncle's blood.

Maybe she shouldn't have come. She already cared about her new family, and the last thing she wanted was to thrust them all into danger. Someone wanted to keep her away, and it appeared that person was dangerous.

EIGHT

THE SUN HAD touched the tops of the redwoods by the time the doctor announced that Mr. Driscoll could be moved inside. After John assisted his uncle-in-law to a four-poster bed, he strode down the sweeping staircase in search of Miss Sullivan. Two attacks in one day disturbed him.

He found her in the solarium by Clara's prize azaleas. The greenery framed her and complemented the red glints in her thick hair, now sedately contained with pins and combs. Her face was turned toward the window, and he stood a moment and studied her. There was more to her arrival than he'd been told. Unidentifiable currents pulsed between her and Driscoll. He couldn't get past the thought that she might be Driscoll's doxy even though he couldn't quite see this fresh-faced girl in the demure gown on Driscoll's arm. Nor could he see the straitlaced Driscoll carrying on with such a young woman. The pharmacist took pains to conduct himself respectably in the community.

She put down the book in her hand. "Lieutenant North," she said, her voice wary. "How is Mr. Driscoll?"

"Resting." He dropped into the wicker chair opposite her settee. "I wanted to find out more about the attack on you. What happened after I left you?"

"I started back toward the manor right behind you. Someone tackled me from behind and jammed a burlap sack over my head so I couldn't see."

"A man?"

She nodded. "It was a man's voice."

"What did he say?"

"He told me not to move. When he put a knife blade against my neck, I obeyed."

John frowned and leaned forward to look at the ivory skin above her blouse. "He cut you?"

She shook her head. "No. He merely tied me up, then ran off."

"Seems strange two attackers would be on the property at the same time," he muttered.

"Perhaps it was the same person. He struck Mr.

Driscoll, then ran into the woods and attacked me."

He nodded. "Likely scenario. But for what reason?" He studied the curve of her cheeks and that lustrous hair. He wondered what it would feel like.

"There you are," Eaton's jovial voice broke into their conversation. "How is Walter?"

"Recovering, with Clara's solicitous attention," John said.

Eaton pulled up another wicker chair. He glanced from John to Addie. "Is something wrong?"

"Miss Sullivan was attacked today as well."

Eaton's eyes widened. "You are all right?"

"Yes, sir. He encased my head in a burlap bag, then tied my hands." She held them out. A faint red line still showed on the translucent skin.

John noticed the color had drained from her cheeks. "Are you frightened, Miss Sullivan?"

She tilted up her chin. "Not exactly afraid, Lieutenant North. I am concerned for Edward, though, if there is even the remote possibility something dangerous is going on."

"I've been considering that myself. Perhaps we should go home, where we have close neighbors and the police are within minutes of the house."

"Where is home?" she asked.

"Near the naval base in San Francisco. I'm only staying until after Henry's birthday in order to allow my son to adjust to the changes."

"I'll be leaving with you?"

Why did she sound dismayed? He studied her downcast face. "Of course. It would be difficult to teach Edward from here."

"Mr. Driscoll didn't mention it," she said.

"I don't think we should assume there is any ongoing danger," Eaton said. "There's no need for you to take Edward and leave. It might simply have been a robber who attacked Walter. When he fled, he ran into Miss Sullivan."

John frowned at his father-in-law. "We have no way of knowing what really happened. I'm not sure I want to run the risk to my son."

Eaton picked up a paperweight and tossed it from hand to hand. "There is no need to react and change plans at this late date. Walter is injured. I'll need your assistance more than ever. Besides, Miss Sullivan is needed to help Clara with her gown for the ball."

"That's hardly my concern," John said. "Edward is my priority."

"As he is mine. I want only the best for my grandson. That includes having him here where I can care for him."

"Whatever you decide is fine, Lieutenant North," Miss Sullivan said.

He wondered again about her relationship with Walter. "Very well, Henry, I'll stay for now. But if anything else out of the ordinary happens, I will pack up Edward and take him home." He kept eye contact with Eaton.

Eaton's jaw clenched, but he didn't remark on John's tone. "Fair enough," he said, rising from the chair. The sound of his footsteps faded on the red-wood floors.

John turned his attention back to Addie. She glanced out the window at the dark yard. "I'd hoped to retrieve my book from the woods. It's too dark now."

She was still pale. Her wide eyes revealed her stress. "The book will survive the night. You should get some rest."

"Mr. Eaton seems more concerned that you might leave than he was about Mr. Driscoll's injuries."

"He does love the boy," he said. "Even if his condition embarrasses him at times."

"The epilepsy is not Edward's fault!"

"No, but that doesn't mean he doesn't wish his grandson were whole and normal."

She winced. "I wish I could help him."

"So do I."

She locked eyes with him. "I'd like us to be friends. A team committed to doing what's best for Edward."

He smiled at the innocence of her remark. While he sensed something more going on than what he knew now, he didn't doubt her naïveté. "A friend is always welcome," he said.

When had he ever heard a woman be so open with her feelings? He couldn't help it. He liked Miss Adeline Sullivan.

• • •

A smile hovered on Addie's lips when she left Lieutenant North. He might not completely trust her, but she would prove herself to him. She rubbed her sore wrists, and her smile faded as she looked at the red marks still on the pale skin.

She hadn't had time to consider the assault and what it meant. Nor the attack on Mr. Driscoll. Could her father's enemy have recognized her already and be trying to drive her away? And to silence Mr. Driscoll? She sighed and opened the door to her room, but the empty space repelled her. Gideon didn't come to greet her with his wet nose. Retreating, she retraced her footsteps down the hall to Edward's room. The lad lay on top of the covers in his nightshirt. She pulled the sheet over him and beckoned her dog.

Gideon rose from his post on the rug by the bed. He yawned, then trotted to her side. She petted him until they were both soothed, then tiptoed out. Mr. Driscoll's door was open when she passed, and she peeked inside to see him propped on pillows.

He gestured for her to come in. "I just sent the maid to ask you to come see me."

"Is everything all right?" she asked.

"Come closer so I don't have to raise my voice."

She peered down the hall, then stepped into the bedroom. Logs had been laid in the fireplace but weren't lit. She seated herself on the chair beside the hissing gaslight. She folded her hands in her lap and prayed for this to be over so she could retire. She was unutterably weary.

"I heard someone attacked you also, child. Is this true?"

"Yes, sir. In the woods. He put a burlap bag over my head and tied my hands." She showed him her wrists.

He fingered his temple. "He didn't hit you?"

"No."

"What did he say?"

"He said, 'Don't move.' But he put a knife blade to my neck."

"That's all?"

She turned up the wick on the gaslight so she could see better. "I suspect it was the same man who attacked you, and he happened to stumble into me. I believe he wanted only to slow me down so he could escape."

Mr. Driscoll blinked, and his hands dropped back to the sheet. "Have you talked to anyone at all about your past?"

"No, sir. When would I have had time?"

"The attacks must be related," he said.

"Is this normally a safe area?"

"Very safe. We've never had a break-in at Eaton Manor."

"Did your attacker take your wallet or anything else?"

He shook his head. "It's all accounted for."

Addie studied his pallid face. He could easily

have been killed. "Do you have any idea what was behind the attack?"

He pointed to the glass on the bedside table. "May I have a drink?"

Was he stalling having to answer her? "Of course." She lifted the glass to his lips and let him take a sip.

"Thanks." His head fell back against the pillow. "I didn't tell Henry, but I think the attacker intended murder. He had a knife, as you know."

She put her hand to her throat. "How did you escape him?"

"I kicked the knife out of his hand. He shoved me, and I fell back into the tree. Clara came out onto the porch and began to scream as he came toward me. I think her presence prevented him from finishing the job. He grabbed his knife and ran off into the forest."

"You think the attacker wanted to kill you because you brought me here?"

His intent gaze held hers. "I'm a pharmacist and well liked. No one has so much as held up my drugstore."

"Why didn't the man try to kill me, too, then?" she asked, her head spinning with questions. "He merely threatened me until he could tie me up. I was an easy mark if he intended murder."

He picked at the sheet. "I don't know," he said after a long pause. "Maybe he thought it would cause the police to dig into your background and the truth would come out."

"There's nothing to be found if someone investigates me. Even those in Crescent City know me as the lightkeeper's daughter." She rubbed her eyes. "Have you heard from your investigator yet?"

"I received a call this morning. The attorney's office that processed the funds sent to your parents was destroyed by the Great Fire. All records were lost, so my investigator can't find out anything by examining them. I'd hoped he could bribe someone to let him look at the records without involving the attorney."

"Oh no! Will we be able to find any proof?"

"If he can locate the attorney, my agent might be able to persuade him to reveal the story, but that's a long shot. If not, the locket and your resemblance will have to do."

"What resemblance?"

He pointed to a painting over the fireplace that she'd paid little attention to. "Look at that picture of Laura."

She rose and stepped to the painting. Her mother. Addie had longed to see what she looked like, but she hadn't yet found a photograph. She drank it in. "Her hair is redder than mine. And she has green eyes." The woman's demure smile said she knew she was beautiful. And she was. Lustrous red hair lay coiled at the nape of her neck. The turquoise gown she wore accentuated the depth of her eyes.

Some dim memory struggled to bubble to the forefront of her memory. Soft hands, a sweet voice. Words of love. "She's much more beautiful than I," Addie whispered.

"Look beyond her more vivid coloring. Notice the shape of her nose, the fullness of her lips, the dimple in her right cheek. The similarities are subtle, but they're there if one knows where to look."

"Many people have dimples." Her fingers pressed the outline of the locket under her bodice.

"Perhaps it's easier for me to see because I loved Laura. You have her smile."

"But why would anyone want to prevent me from being united with my father?" She could look into the woman's laughing eyes no longer. She went back to the chair. "Do you have any idea who would have paid for my upkeep? You mentioned one of my father's rivals. Is there anyone else?"

Mr. Driscoll sipped his water. "I have some ideas."

"Such as?"

"You are nearly twenty-five, correct?"

She nodded. "My mother said I was about two when my father rescued me."

"I suspected Clara in the beginning. She met Henry first, and he sought her hand until he met your mother."

Addie liked her aunt, and the thought she might be behind her situation disturbed her. "Clara? What would be her reason to keep me away?"

"She might have wanted to wipe away all traces of Laura and her relationship with Henry."

She leaned back in the chair. "That seems so Shakespearean."

"He wrote about human nature. Jealousy is a powerful motivator."

"I suppose. What about an inheritance?" she asked.

Driscoll pursed his lips. "Laura's grandfather Francis died about two years ago. You are the beneficiary in his will. The will dictated the estate would go to you on your twenty-fifth birthday. In the event of your death, it would go to Clara, who intends it to be Edward's."

"Why Clara? This wouldn't be her grandfather, right? You and Clara had a different maternal grandmother."

He nodded. "That's right. But Laura was his only living relative at the time he drew up the will. He liked Clara, and when the attorney recommended a contingency bequest, Francis decided to leave his estate to her. I believe Henry forgot about the inheritance until recently. When he realized the passing of ownership was due to take place, he realized he had to have you declared dead."

"Just me? What about my mother?"

"He had her declared dead before he married Clara. I assume he thought it wasn't necessary for a child."

"And maybe he thought my great-grandfather would change his will."

He nodded. "The legal step has taken some time, and it's not yet completed. When that happens, the land will pass to Clara, who has drawn up papers for Edward to receive it."

"A great-grandfather." Addie clasped her hands together. "I always wished for grandparents."

"He was a remarkable man. He doted on you."

Yearning tugged at her heart. She'd missed out on so much love. "But all this still doesn't tell us who had anything to gain by keeping my presence a secret all these years."

Mr. Driscoll set his glass of water back on the bed stand. "We need to find out."

"What difference does it make now? I don't want anything from the Eaton estate. All I want is to make my father love me."

"I mentioned I feared for Henry's safety. The other possibility in today's attack is that he was the intended target, and the assailant didn't try very hard to hurt me when he realized he had the wrong man."

"I see," she said slowly. "You think whoever paid for me to be kept away is now about to move against Mr. Eaton."

"And perhaps you."

She gulped. The sensation of cold metal against her throat had been terrifying. But nothing was enough to drive her from the family she was just coming to know.

NINE

ADDIE SLEPT POORLY, startling awake at the slightest creak of a floorboard or the hoot of an owl outside her window. When she finally pulled back the curtains, the sun had crested the tops of the redwood trees and streamed through her back bedroom window. From the other window to the front, she could almost see past the town to the ocean's waves.

She'd thought leaving the lighthouse would be exciting, romantic. Now she longed for the roar of the waves outside her window and the cry of a seagull diving for a fish. The familiar held more appeal than she'd ever imagined.

Turning from the view, she washed at the pitcher and bowl on her dresser, then pinched a bit of color into her cheeks. She selected a white blouse detailed with tucks, and a gray skirt. When she stepped out of her room, her nose caught the aroma of sausage. She could just hurry down the back stairway and find her book before breakfast. Once she got back, she'd braid her hair and put shoes on, but for now, she wanted to talk with the Lord and dangle her toes in the water at the falls. It would almost be like standing at the ocean's edge. If she went down the back way, no one would know.

On the way out, she checked Edward's room and found it empty, then went down the back staircase to the first floor. Where was the rear door? The manor easily comprised forty rooms, and the labyrinth of halls and doorways confused her. It would take weeks before she could find her way easily. She went toward the back of the hall and found the smell of food stronger. Following her nose, she walked past a study, another drawing room, a ladies' lounge, and a library before seeing Mrs. Eaton in her study.

The kitchen had to be nearby. That's where the back door would be. She started past the study, but Mrs. Eaton called to her. Addie turned. "Yes, ma'am?"

Mrs. Eaton sat on a chair, with her gray silk skirt spread around her. "Come in, dear."

Addie looked down and spied her bare feet. Maybe Mrs. Eaton wouldn't notice if she scooted slowly into the room so her feet didn't show. She entered the room. Various needlepoint projects lay on a table, and smaller furniture pieces matched a female's size. She tucked her feet under her skirt as she sank onto a pink brocade chair beside a plant stand that held a fern.

Mrs. Eaton laid down her needlepoint. "I would like to discuss the ball with you." She pointed at Addie. "That blouse. Did you make it, Adeline?"

"Yes, ma'am."

Mrs. Eaton slipped her glasses onto her nose and inspected the garment. "The pin tucks and embroidery are quite lovely. You're very talented."

"Thank you, Mrs. Eaton. How might I help you?"

"What ideas have you come up with for my gown?"

Addie gulped. Sally had mentioned that the woman had already tossed aside one gown made by a top dressmaker. Mrs. Eaton had said no more about the dress in the last couple of days, and Addie hoped she'd abandoned the idea. "What if you hate it, Mrs. Eaton? I want to please you, but I admit I'm fearful."

The woman's brows rose. "Are you saying I'm hard to please, Adeline?"

"We met only days ago, and I have no way of knowing that," Addie said.

Mrs. Eaton laughed. "You certainly speak your mind, child. I rather like that."

"My father always told me I was the light-keeper's daughter. God's child. And only truth would do." She winced at the words. Her father hadn't followed his own advice.

Mrs. Eaton picked up her needlepoint again. "You listen to him. The world could use more honesty. Now, what about that dress?"

"If I know clearly what you want and start right away, I can get it done. Provided I can find the proper material," she added.

Pink bloomed in the matron's cheeks, and her eyes sparkled. "I'd like something in chiffon. Very elegant and flowing, with lace framing my face. Maybe in white."

Addie feared she knew exactly what Mrs. Eaton was talking about. "You wouldn't prefer something in brocade or silk?" Something more suited to her age.

Mrs. Eaton shook her head. "I want the latest fashion. Brocade is so matronly." She picked up a magazine and thumbed through it. "Like this."

Addie rose and took the magazine from her employer's hand. It was as she suspected—something much more suited to her age than to Mrs. Eaton's.

Truth. The truth in love. "Ma'am, I fear this would not suit you well. Would you give me leave to try a pattern I saw in the latest *Godey's*? It's quite elegant, and no one else in town would have anything approaching its magnificence. It has a matching turban that's all the rage in Paris."

"Paris?"

"It would highlight your splendid eyes," Addie said. "They are a beautiful shade of green. I've never seen such lovely eyes."

The older woman preened. "Very well, Adeline. I'll trust your judgment. Don't disappoint me."

"I'll do my best," she said.

The work would be constant. Addie had very little experience with frills and lace. Her designs tended toward good lines and quality fabrics, not lavish trim and ruffles.

She rose. "I need to run to the falls and find my book. I dropped it yesterday."

"Very well. Breakfast will be ready in a quarter hour. And do put up your hair and come in shoes."

Addie hurried from the room. She had to find the book, get back, and finish her toilette in fifteen minutes.

A mother quail and her babies ran through the morning fog across John's path. He waited for them to pass, brushed aside the towering ferns, and entered the redwood forest. The air smelled heavy with the scent of vegetation and pine. Birds chattered overhead, and insects hummed by his ears. He strode toward where he'd left Miss Sullivan yesterday to see if any evidence of her ordeal remained.

He reached the roaring Mercy Falls and peered through the mist curling around the water. There, the matted grass showed their path back to the manor. He followed the faint trail until it widened into a more flattened area. This must be where she'd been tackled. A burlap sack lay near a tree. He picked it up and caught the scent of oranges. Using his foot, he prodded the vegetation for anything else that might illuminate the incident.

The toe of his shoe struck something in the weeds. He parted the greenery and saw a book on the ground. Miss Sullivan's book of poetry. When he picked it up, it fell open, and his gaze was drawn to the scrawled words in the margin of a poem called, "A Man's Requirements."

John North. What a strong name. I was lost the moment I gazed into his eyes. So dark. So compelling. As if he knew me and I knew him. Is that not strange? Did Elizabeth Barrett Browning feel this pounding in her blood the first time she saw Robert? Must pray and see what God would say about this.

He blinked and read the words again. His first inclination was to laugh at her naïveté. So innocent and childlike. Then he read the words of the poem.

> Love me Sweet, with all thou art,
> Feeling, thinking, seeing;
> Love me in the lightest part,
> Love me in full being.

Something in the words stirred him. Had he ever been the focus of a heartfelt longing? Not even Katherine had thought of him as her hero, nor, for that matter, had wanted to share her innermost thoughts. She certainly hadn't loved him with all her being. What might it be like to be loved like that?

Something rustled in the grass behind him, and he whirled with the book in his hand. Addie stepped into his line of vision, with her dog tagging along. She was singing "When the Red, Red Robin Comes Bob-Bob-Bobbing Along" in a clear, sweet voice. Her bare toes peeked from under the gray skirt she wore. He couldn't look away from her long hair, which caught a shaft of light that slanted through the leaves.

Her smile came as soon as she saw him. And dimmed when she spotted the book in his hand. The open book.

Pink rushed to her cheeks. "You found my book."

He shut it and held it out to her. "I stumbled across it when I was looking for clues that might point to your attacker."

Her fingers closed around the book, and she clasped it to her chest. She didn't meet his gaze, and her color heightened. He was sure she wondered if he'd seen her notes. The truth would embarrass her further.

Her gaze finally rose to his face. "You read it, didn't you? I can see it in your eyes."

"You're very direct," he said. His own face burned, a sensation he didn't think he'd ever felt before.

She lowered her lids and twisted a long curl through her fingers. "I'm sorry. It's not very lady-like to say what I think, is it? You must forgive me. I grew up with only my parents for company."

"Your honesty is refreshing," he said. If she didn't ask again whether he'd read her note, he wasn't going to offer up the information. "Is Edward up yet?"

She nodded. "He's having his breakfast, and I

came out to find my book." She fell silent and bit her lip. "I should explain about the note."

He held up his hand. "Please don't. It might dilute the pleasure I took in knowing you find me somewhat attractive."

Her face turned a brighter shade of pink. "You're mocking me," she said in a choked voice.

"That's not my intention," he said before falling silent.

How could he clear the air between them? Right now he'd like to ask her to dinner and the nickelodeon. He suspected most women who flirted with him at a social event were more interested in his bank account or the fact he was a naval officer. Women found the role strangely dashing and romantic, but few really saw him for who he was. No one had ever remarked on his eyes. He studied her downturned face. She was no more capable of subterfuge than the moss under his feet was.

He removed his bowler and rubbed his thick thatch of hair. "Can we start over? You mentioned earlier you'd like to be my friend. I'd like that too."

She stared at the ground, and he followed her gaze to her bare toes. He'd never seen a woman's bare feet except for Katherine's, in the privacy of their bedroom. The young woman was unlike any he'd ever met. He wanted to find out more about her, hear her views.

"Please?" he said, putting a plea into his voice.

She smiled, a timid curve of her lips. Her long

lashes swept up, and those green eyes smiled too. "Do you promise never to bring up this book again?"

"I promise," he said.

She rested her chin on two fingers, and her dimple flashed. "If you break your promise, you have to jump in the waterfall."

"Deal."

But he was talking to the wind in the trees. She had turned and fled the way she'd come, her auburn hair flying behind her.

Addie pumped cold water over her feet. What was she thinking to have gone out without her shoes and with her hair down? This wasn't the beach. There were standards here she needed to abide by. She sat on the edge of the rock garden and dried her feet with the hem of her dress. The ugly wet spots on the fabric looked terrible. Now she'd have to change her skirt as well.

"Addie?"

She glanced up to see Mr. Driscoll approaching. "Good morning, Mr. Driscoll," she said.

He'd discarded his sling and wore a gray jacket and waistcoat. "You're out and about early."

She held up her book. "I dropped this in the forest yesterday after that man knocked me down."

"I'm glad you found it."

She noticed his eyes shone, and a smile tugged at his lips. "Do you have news?"

"You're a very bright girl," he said. "I do indeed.

I received a call from my investigator. He's located the attorney."

She held her breath. "And?"

"The lawyer refuses to reveal his client, but he told my agent where the money is located. My agent managed to discover that there's quite a sum in the bank in San Francisco."

"I told you I don't care about the money. Ma—Josephine can have it." In spite of her word choice, Addie realized she still thought of Josephine as her mother.

His smile flickered and went out. "She cannot, Adeline. It's not right. That money belongs to you, and I mean to see you get it."

She stood and shook out her skirt. "I just want the proof so we can tell my father the truth."

"I want that as well. And we're getting close. Another couple of days, I suspect."

"I want to know more about my mother and the rest of my family. It's hard to ask questions without appearing nosy."

"Check out the attic. Some of her old dresses are probably packed away in trunks. Maybe pictures and diaries as well. There are traces of Laura around."

Addie wanted to run straight to the attic and see what treasures it contained, but she restrained herself. She was expected at the breakfast table. "Won't the family wonder what I'm doing poking around in the attic?"

"I doubt they'll notice. No one but the servants ever goes up there."

"I'll find a time to slip up there, then. What about the attack on you? Any word from the police?"

"No." He offered his arm, and she took it. He led her toward the back door. "I discovered the name of Henry's rival. The one whose son committed suicide. Samuel Tuttle. He lives in Crescent City now."

She stopped just shy of the door. "Near our light-house. Is it mere coincidence, or something more?"

"My question too. I think I'll travel up to speak to Mr. Tuttle personally. He might be the culprit."

Addie shuddered. "Revenge is so pointless. It can't bring his son back."

Mr. Driscoll held open the door for her. "Revenge can be sweet if the offense was grave enough. At least that's what I've heard. Maybe that's Tuttle's view as well."

"If he'll admit it, at least we'd have our proof." And her family would welcome her with open arms.

TEN

BACK IN HER room, a smile lifted Addie's lips as she braided her hair. While she might be naïve of the ways of men, John clearly had not been offended by her ridiculous note about him. What had possessed her to write such a thing? Anyone might have seen it. She pulled on socks and shoes and coiled her braid around her head, then hurried down the steps. After she checked on Gideon, who waited patiently on the porch, she started toward the dining room.

She went down the hall past the salon where she'd talked with Mrs. Eaton. The dining room was down another hallway. She passed a large, airy room. Its bay window looked out onto a formal garden with clipped hedges, a labyrinth, and several fountains. Exploration would have to wait until later, but she was eager to see what delights the garden held.

She stepped into the dining room and approached the long table. "Good morning." The handsome lieutenant's eyes still held the warmth she'd seen in the forest. She'd never thanked him for his kindness in showing her which utensil to use the first night she'd arrived.

"Come sit by me." Mrs. Eaton indicated the seat to the right of her at the far head of the table.

Addie walked through the gauntlet of stares. Things were much more formal here than she was accustomed to. She didn't think she would ever get used to this lifestyle. She slid into the chair and picked up the linen napkin. She swallowed hard and prayed she wouldn't embarrass herself by clinking her fork on her plate or spilling her tea. This time, John couldn't easily show her how to proceed.

Mrs. Eaton passed her a bowl of fluffy scrambled eggs. "How are you adjusting, my dear? Are you sleeping well?"

"It's a strange place, Clara. Of course she doesn't sleep well yet," Mr. Eaton said.

Addie's smile faded at his tense tone. She turned to face Mr. Driscoll. "How are you feeling, sir?" She should have asked him outside.

Mr. Driscoll spooned scrambled eggs onto his plate. "Other than a slight headache, I am none the worse for wear."

"I told him he should have stayed in bed, but he insisted on getting up," Mrs. Eaton said. "His arm heals, but then he's nearly killed by an intruder."

"I need to open the drugstore," he said.

Addie took a bite of egg, but she barely tasted it. Mr. Driscoll was attacking his food with gusto.

"How are you, Adeline?" Mrs. Eaton asked. "I neglected to inquire after your health when we spoke earlier."

"I'm fine, ma'am."

"Not sore or bruised?"

"Perhaps a bit. But I feel nothing a long walk along the beach wouldn't cure."

John glanced at his pocket watch. "I would have time to take you and Edward to the beach if you'd like. He could use some exercise."

"There are bicycles in the carriage house," Mr. Eaton said. "You're welcome to use them."

Addie put her hands to her cheeks. "You have

bicycles? I've always wanted to learn to ride one."

"Bicycles are out for today, then," John said. "Tonight I'll give you a lesson. You'll need to be able to get around at your leisure."

"Does Edward have a bicycle? Once I learn, we might go together. It would be excellent exercise for him." The family grew silent, and a rock formed in her belly when she realized her gaffe. "Oh, of course not. What was I thinking?" Her face burned, and she fixed her attention on her plate.

"Edward does have . . . challenges," Mrs. Eaton said. "But there is much he is able to do."

"Of course." Addie put her napkin down. "If I might be excused, I'll get Edward ready for our excursion."

"I'll direct the cook to prepare a lunch for you," Mrs. Eaton said. "And I'll send Wilson to fetch you around two. Would that suit?"

"That's perfect," Addie said.

John rose as well. Addie followed him out. "I'll only be a moment," she said. "Thank you for your offer."

His smile and easy manner returned. "My pleasure. I assume you want to take the dog?"

"Oh yes. Edward will have great fun with him at the water." Dressed in a navy blue sack coat and matching trousers, the lieutenant was just as handsome as he'd been in his navy uniform. "You have nothing else to do today?"

He shook his head. "I'm on leave for a month.

It's been much too long since I had the opportunity to play with my son." He took his bowler from the hall tree and donned it. "I'll have the buckboard ready." He exited through the front door.

She took the stairs two at a time with a smile on her face. A day at the water and a drive with John, followed by lunch at the beach! She wanted to dance, but she forced herself to assume a sedate pace. She stopped off in her room to change into her bathing costume, tights, and bathing shoes. When she fetched Edward, she nearly danced into the room. She changed him into his bathing costume, then packed his sailboat, pail, and shovel in a bag.

"I forgot my hat," she said. "You take your things out to the buckboard, and I'll be right there."

Edward skipped off, and she darted into her room. When she returned to the hall, she found Mr. Driscoll waiting for her. His somber expression wiped the smile from her face.

"Is something wrong?" she asked.

"You seem very chummy with John."

"We are related," she reminded him.

"By marriage only. Don't let your guard down around him. For all we know, he's the one who arranged for the attack on you and me."

"That's impossible," she said. "He was with me in the woods when you were attacked."

"He could have paid someone."

"For what reason?"

"Addie, you must use your head. If your identity becomes known, his son will no longer be Henry's immediate heir. He has the most to lose of anyone."

She found it difficult to breathe. "I believe he's an honorable man."

"The women all like him. I should have guessed you would be taken in by his good looks. He never stays with any woman long. Katherine was going to leave him."

"For seeing other women?" Bile burned her throat.

Mr. Driscoll patted her shoulder. "The reasons are too numerous to go into. But hold him at arm's length, my dear." He walked off.

Addie swallowed hard. Had she been duped by John's smile and dark eyes? She didn't want to believe it.

A stone lodged somewhere in Addie's midsection as John helped her down from the buckboard. The sea breeze tugged at her hair, and she lifted her face to the salty tang on the wind. The temperature along the northern California coast ranged from fifty-five degrees in the winter to sixty-eight in the summer, but the sun heated the sand under her feet even on the coolest day. Today the air was close to seventy.

Edward raced after Gideon, who ran into the white caps rolling to the shore. Could Mr. Driscoll be right? She didn't want to believe John might have orchestrated the attack on them, but it made sense. Who else stood to lose so much if her identity became known? But how could he possibly know?

She chose not to believe it. Not until she could verify his lack of integrity.

John retrieved the basket of food, the quilt, and the toys from the back of the buckboard. "You're wearing a serious frown," he said. "Is everything all right?"

"Are you a philanderer, Lieutenant North?"

His brows rose, and he laughed. "You're a constant surprise, Addie. What a question. Is this a joke?"

"I'm quite serious," she said, grabbing her hat when the wind threatened to send it tumbling across the sand.

His grin faded. "Why would you ask such an insulting question?"

She dug the toe of her shoe into the sand. "I meant no insult. I have no experience with men. I thought perhaps . . ."

"You thought I was toying with your emotions."

She nodded. The dark intensity in his eyes made her shiver. This was no cold, passionless man, but one who felt things deeply. His lips flattened, and his nostrils flared. His eyes sparked with some emotion she couldn't name. Then it winked out as his control tightened.

When he smiled, it was a cold grimace. "I like you, Miss Sullivan. Do you think I play with your emotions because I want to become better acquainted?" he asked.

"Not unless your intentions are less than honorable."

He shifted the basket in his hand. "Less than honorable. I doubt you even know what it means for a man to behave dishonorably toward a woman."

She tipped her chin up. "My knowledge of such things might be a bit vague, but there's no need to mock me. I grew up around animals. I know what should be reserved for marriage."

The darkness behind his eyes lightened, and his lips curved in a genuine smile. A bark of laughter escaped. "We don't dare turn you loose in town. You'll tell the mayor he's too fat."

"Is he?"

He grinned. "He weights four hundred pounds or more."

"Maybe someone should tell him."

All trace of anger was gone from his face. "You're one of a kind, Miss Adeline Sullivan. The Eaton family may never be the same after your sojourn with us. No one says what they mean in that house. I'm afraid I've become accustomed to it." He glanced toward his son, who was throwing a ball for the dog. "Let's get our things settled." He turned his back on her and strode across the sand with his burden.

The wind tore the hat from his head and sent it sailing straight at Addie. She snagged it in midair. He slipped in the sand, then his legs flew out from under him, and he landed on his backside. The items he carried scattered in a circle around him. She gasped and ran to help. A seagull cawed overhead, and a white blob dropped. It landed squarely on the shoulder of John's jacket.

Addie stopped, observing first the mess on his suit, then the sand on his pants. His face reddened, but she wasn't sure if it was from embarrassment or anger. His lip curled when he spied the bird droppings on his jacket.

A giggle erupted from Addie's lips. And another one. "I'm sorry," she gasped through her laughter. "But if you could see your face. Such disgust. It's only a little offering from the gull to show his affection."

He stood before she reached him and bent to brush the sand from his trousers. "I think you were more deserving of that deposit from the gull."

Her giggles rose again, and she squelched them. She pulled her hankie from the inside of her sleeve at her wrist and stood on tiptoe while she dabbed at the gunk on his jacket.

His fingers caught hers. His intense gaze held her in place. "I should like to take you to dinner one night. Would that be acceptable?"

"Yes," she said, struggling to maintain her composure. "I would like that very much."

His grip tightened. "They'll try to change you, Addie. I should dislike to see that happen."

"Who will?"

"The Eaton family. Society. They'll shush you when you speak your mind." His hand went to a loose curl hanging down her back. "They'll tell you it's more proper to put your hair up."

"Mrs. Eaton already suggested I wear my hair up when she saw me with it down." Warmth gathered in her midsection at his touch. "I'm sure there are many things I need to learn."

He leaned close enough for his breath to mingle with the salt air that caressed her skin. "I like you just the way you are." His hand trailed from her hair to her cheek. "Promise me you won't change."

"How can I promise such a thing? God wants each of us to grow."

"Let's have a talk with him and ask him not to mess with perfection."

She managed to find enough moisture in her mouth to swallow. If he didn't take his hand from her cheek, she was going to throw herself into his arms. If there wasn't such a thing as love at first sight, she was in so much trouble.

ELEVEN

ADDIE'S HANDKERCHIEF DID little to remove the gull doo on John's jacket. He'd long since removed his jacket and rolled up his shirtsleeves. Popcorn clouds filled the blue bowl of sky overhead. He reclined on the blanket and watched Addie splash through the whitecaps with Edward in her arms, both of them squealing at the cold waves. The dog chased them both.

"Come in with us," she called.

The moist sea air caused her auburn locks to curl. The thought that there might be an opportunity to kiss that smiling pink mouth nearly prompted him to obey. The slim tights of her swimming costume showed off the shape of her legs, and he couldn't take his eyes off her.

She put Edward down, then stood with her hands on her hips. "Roll up your trousers. At least let the waves break at your ankles."

"I didn't bring a swimsuit," John said. He grinned. "Besides, don't you know that sailors drown in an inch of water?"

"Coward!" She staggered out of the sea, then paused to wring the water from her skirt.

He stood as she neared. She smelled enticingly of brine and seaweed, an intoxicating scent to a man who loved the sea. It was all he could do not to nuzzle his face in her neck and kiss her smooth skin.

"I'm quite starving," she said. "What do we have for lunch?"

He forced himself to step to the lunch hamper and peer inside. "Egg salad sandwiches, cranberry scones, and apples. A veritable feast."

She dropped onto the blanket. "I might eat the whole thing."

Edward and Gideon frolicked on the sand. Edward kicked a ball, and the dog ran to pounce on it. She lifted the plates of sandwiches wrapped in wax paper. The kitchen maid had packed enough scones to feed an army.

"Edward, your luncheon is ready," she called.

Had John ever seen Edward so happy and carefree? The boy's curls were tousled, and his cheeks were as red as the apples Addie was lifting from the basket. She'd been good for his son. The dog had helped too. It was amazing how confident they all felt in the dog's presence. If not for Gideon, John would have been fearful of allowing Edward in the water.

He could do worse than courting Addie. The thought came out of the blue, but he quickly realized he was getting ahead of himself. But he acknowledged his willingness to go where this relationship might lead.

Henry and Clara would be gone tonight. When Edward was in bed, John might be able to get to know the intriguing Adeline Sullivan a little better. When was the last time he'd been this interested in a woman? Not since Katherine, he realized. And maybe that should be a warning to him.

But no. His relationship with Katherine had been a very different situation. She'd flirted, then backed off, then flirted and backed off again. She'd played a cat-and-mouse game that led to marriage before he realized what was happening. She'd offered her family name and beauty to escape an older suitor her father had selected, and John snapped it up because he thought she really loved him. Reality had soon set in.

This young woman was different. He bit into his sandwich. "There is no subterfuge in you, Miss Adeline. Why is that?"

Color came and went in her cheeks. "Everyone has layers. Even me."

He leaned closer as his son neared and allowed a curl to wrap his finger. "I look forward to peeling back those layers."

Her blush was charming. What would she think of living on a naval base?

Addie glanced at John a few times as the buggy pulled away from the beach. Edward and Gideon slept as they traveled back toward town. "Thank you for a lovely day," she said.

"The pleasure was all mine."

Lassitude encased her limbs, and her eyes were heavy. The next thing she knew, she heard voices call and the rumble of more buggies. She opened her eyes to find her head resting on John's shoulder as the buggy rolled through Mercy Falls.

"I'm so sorry!" she said, startled. After she jerked upright, she brushed her hair out of her face.

He smiled at her. "I didn't mind."

Heat seared her cheeks, and she turned, pretending to scrutinize the stores and shops they passed rather than his amused eyes. Ahead, Mr. Driscoll stepped from the darkness of an alley onto the street and approached a woman who was holding a baby. "There's Mr. Driscoll," she said. She called out to him and waved. He flinched at the sound of his name but waved back when he caught sight of them.

"He should take care in that neighborhood," John said. "If a fellow is going to get mugged, it would be there. Thugs and gamblers haunt these streets."

"He's probably delivering medicine to someone," she said.

"It's no place for a woman and infant. He should escort her home."

They left town and entered the coolness of the forest. She smelled wildflowers and the scent of deep woods. The trees were so high and the trunks so big that all she could do was stare. She would never get used to it. "Is this virgin forest?" she asked.

"Yep. One of the last tracts left."

The beauty and serenity of the place drew her.

The branches nearly touched the blue sky. "Why is it still unlogged?"

"Laura's grandfather left it to her daughter, Julia. When the child died, it went to Clara, and she signed it over to Edward. So this will be Edward's as soon as the paperwork declaring Julia deceased comes through."

Addie's throat convulsed. He was talking about her. This land belonged to her. She couldn't take it in. "So it belongs to Edward now? Or will soon?"

He nodded. "I intend to use it to increase Edward's net worth."

"What are you going to do with it?"

He hesitated. "I haven't decided. I've had a lucrative offer from a logging company, but it seems a shame to destroy something so beautiful."

In her mind's eye, Addie saw a lovely home for tuberculosis patients in a grove surrounded by clean air and nature. For someone like Nann Whittaker. If Roy Sullivan hadn't had the stress of the lighthouse, he might have recovered from his illness in a place like she envisioned, with paths for the patients to walk and babbling streams to nap beside. Such a pipe dream. Where would she find money for something like that?

"I would hate for it to be ruined," she said.

"I must be practical." He picked up the reins again. "We'd better be getting home."

"What time is it?" She tried to gauge the sun, but it was behind clouds.

He pulled out a gold pocket watch. "Nearly three."

Addie held to the side of the seat as the buggy made a turn onto the paved road. "Is Henry's birthday ball terribly exciting?"

John slapped the reins on the horse's rump, and the animal broke into a trot. "It's the most boring affair of the year, but Henry likes the illusion of a happy family gathered to celebrate."

"You sound as though you don't like him."

A muscle twitched in his jaw. "I admire him, and he's been good to me. But his demands can be hard to deal with."

"Demands? About Edward?"

"He thinks he owns my son." He slanted a smile her way. "I'm sure you've seen it."

She laid her gloved hand on top of his. "It's already clear to me that no one owns you, Lieutenant. You are the kind of man a woman can depend on with her life."

"I haven't had very good luck with relationships," he said. "Women seem to put a lot of stock in money and property. I'm not very good at figuring out the gold diggers."

"I don't care about money." But would he believe that when he learned the land he wanted for Edward belonged to her? She might give it back to him, but not if he would sell it. There were bigger and better things to do with it. She studied him. "Your wife, Katherine," she said. "How long has she been gone?"

His shoulders tensed. "About three years. She was struck by a streetcar in San Francisco. Typical Katherine, she was trying to beat the vehicle across the street."

"I'm so sorry. She was shopping?" She knew the question was out of line the minute she saw his fingers tighten on the reins.

"So she said," was his only response.

Addie pondered the cryptic answer. Had Katherine lied to him about what she was doing? Or had he disapproved of the money she spent? She couldn't decipher the undercurrents.

He sighed. "You'll hear the rumor soon enough, so I might as well tell you. She was leaving me. Running off with some fellow who was teaching her to golf."

Addie smoothed the curls away from Edward's face. "She was leaving her son too?"

He nodded. "His illness was more than she could handle."

She wanted to pick up the child and hold him close. "It's not his fault."

"She thought it was mine," he said grimly.

Addie knew better than to probe that wound, but oh, how she wanted to heal it.

Addie's feet barely touched the floor after the day at the beach. When they reached the manor, she turned Edward over to his nurse for a bath while John took the motorcycle to the bank. The house seemed quiet without the very large presence of her father and Clara. She paused in the hallway outside Mr. Eaton's office.

No one would know if she slipped inside to look for pictures of her mother. The only one she'd seen was the one in Mr. Driscoll's bedroom. If Mr. Eaton loved her and her mother so much, surely he would keep some memento of their lives in his private domain. Glancing down the hall to make sure no servants were prowling about, she stepped into the office and closed the door behind her.

The late-afternoon sun slanted through the bay windows flanked by floor-to-ceiling bookcases. The chandelier over the desk sparkled with crystal, and heavy velvet drapes hung at the two windows. A spittoon was in a corner by the heavy chair, and a row of pipes was on one corner of the desk. A frame stood on the other corner, its back to her. It was a man's room, thick with the scent of tobacco. The gleaming redwood desk was clear of papers. She stepped around to the other side and frowned to see the picture was of Clara and another woman. Katherine perhaps? What had she been expecting? Of course Mr. Eaton would have his wife and daughter on his desk. He had no idea Julia still lived.

Addie picked up the picture and stared into the smiling face of the beautiful young woman. Katherine's hair was blonde and elegant. She had her mother's patrician nose and full lips, and the gown she wore must have cost the earth. Addie's bubble of happiness burst. John couldn't possibly be interested in her after having been married to the lovely girl in the photograph. She set the frame back onto the polished surface, then turned her attention to the bookcases. The shelves held gleaming leather books, and she wondered if she might be allowed to choose some to read. But she found no other photographs.

She turned back toward the door and stared at the drawers on the desk. Might he have any mementos tucked away from Clara? The thought of rummaging through his private papers held no appeal, but she longed to know more of her mother and the little girl once known as Julia. She wanted to find something that showed the love her family had once showered upon her. After a slight hesitation, she settled in the chair and pulled out the top drawer. It held a stack of papers. When she lifted them, a note fell from between the pages. She picked it up and saw several words in a feminine scrawl.

Only a payment of ten thousand dollars will prevent me from telling the world about your child.

Addie studied the note. There was no name to identify the author, and she wasn't certain Henry was the intended recipient. Maybe it had nothing to do with Henry, but if not, how had it come to be in his possession? She dropped it back into place and closed the drawer before going on to the next.

It was only when she pulled open the lap drawer that she found what she'd hoped to discover. She lifted a small scrapbook from the drawer and laid it on the desk. The leather cover was tattered and torn, but the photographs inside made her throat close. The beautiful woman she'd seen in the portrait stared into the camera. In her arms was an infant. Addie recognized the child as herself. In the next photograph she appeared to be about a year old and stood next to her mother. They were both dressed in white.

Her vision blurred, and a sob lodged in her throat. If only she could snatch the faint trace of memory lingering in her mind. Every time she strained to grasp it, it sifted through her fingers.

She finished flipping through the scrapbook. The last image was the same one she'd seen in the metal box at the lighthouse. Her life as an Eaton had been brief. She closed the book and replaced it, then shut the drawer when she heard John's motorcycle rumbling up the drive.

TWELVE

TWILIGHT WAS FAST approaching. John sat on the porch and watched his son play with the dog. He smiled at the camaraderie between the boy and Gideon. The dog barked and ran after the ball.

The day at the beach had left him more relaxed than he'd been in a long time.

The dog changed directions and raced toward the front porch. John turned to see Addie exiting the house. She stood poised on the top step with an expectant expression. She'd changed from her bathing costume into a shimmery green dress. Her thick hair was wound on top of her head again. He much preferred it down.

"Have you come to call us to dinner?"

She nodded. "Mrs. Biddle said it would be on the table in five minutes."

"I haven't seen Driscoll. I think it might just be us."

"He mentioned he had to make a trip up the coast." She approached with graceful steps, pausing only to pet the dog and direct him back to Edward. "When would you like to go over Edward's lesson plans?" she asked when she reached John. "I'd like to ensure I'm doing what you expect."

He waved Edward over and told him to go get washed up for dinner. When the boy complained, then finally ran off to the house, John gestured to the wicker lawn furniture. "Have a seat and we can talk about it."

She gathered her skirt and sank onto the chair. Her clear green eyes focused on his face. "Edward is very bright. Is there a reason he is not attending school?"

"I would think it is obvious," he said.

Her eyebrows winged up. "His affliction? But surely that doesn't prevent him from school attendance."

"Kids can be cruel. I don't want him laughed at or ostracized."

"You sound as though you know this from personal experience."

He shied away from the memories of kids mocking his English accent when his family had first immigrated. He'd worked hard to overcome it. "Doesn't everyone?"

"I wouldn't know. I've never been to school," she said, her tone wistful.

"Never?"

She shook her head. "My father taught me, and I obtained a degree by correspondence."

"Admirable." He meant it. Not many women cared so much about education.

Her cheeks bloomed with delicate color. "Edward has to learn to live in the real world. Better now than to coddle him so much he doesn't know how to face adversity as an adult."

"He's five years old. There's plenty of time for him to face the hard knocks of life."

She inclined her head. "He's making great progress in just a few days on his numbers and letters."

"Excellent." He found himself watching her as conversation lagged. She was so innocent and sheltered, yet intelligence and fortitude glimmered in her eyes. He'd told her more about his feelings for his son than he'd even discussed with Katherine. Interesting. His wife's tactic had always been avoidance and tears.

Addie's slipper-clad feet, peeking out from under her green dress, moved in a rhythmic way, and she was humming "Maple Leaf Rag." A carriage rolled down the driveway. The groom rushed to help with the horse, and John watched Lord Carrington clamber down and toss the reins to the groomsman. John rose to greet him and noticed the arrival had caught Addie's attention as well.

"That's Lord Thomas Carrington, one of Henry's friends from England. I haven't seen him in quite some time."

A bowler perched atop his head. Once upon a time, a black, curly beard had burst furiously from his cheeks and nearly encased his nose and mouth. John had often wanted to suggest Carrington follow the newer fashion and become smooth shaven, if only to see what lay beneath that mass of dark hair. Someone must have told him, because he'd shaved the beard into a trim mustache.

Carrington nodded as he passed. "John." He stopped when his gaze landed on Addie.

John extended his arm to Addie and waited until she took it. "Miss Sullivan, this is Lord Carrington. Thomas, Miss Sullivan is a friend of the family and has arrived to take charge of Edward's education."

The big man moved closer. "Delighted to meet you, Miss Sullivan," he boomed. "I hope you'll forgive me for remarking on how fresh and pretty you look this evening."

Addie blushed. "Thank you, Lord Carrington." She withdrew her hand from John's arm. "I'd better make sure Edward gets his hands clean. If you'll excuse me." She stepped through the front door.

Both men watched the graceful sway of her skirt. "Pretty girl. Yours?" Carrington asked.

"Of course not," John said.

Carrington bared his teeth in a smile. "Excellent. I have a mind to call on her."

"She's thirty years your junior, Carrington!"

"And pretty and fresh as a flower."

John barely managed to hold his temper. "If you're here to see Henry, he's gone to a concert."

"A fine reason to call again tomorrow." Carrington tipped his hat and strode to the buggy.

John stood slack jawed, emotions reeling. That man couldn't be allowed to get his hands on her.

Addie eyed the bicycle John rolled from the carriage house. "Are you sure I can do this?"

"Of course. It just takes practice."

"Can I ride too?" Edward asked. He sat with the dog on the grass, watching them.

"Not tonight, little man," John said.

It pained her to see the light go out of Edward's

eyes. She ran her hand down the gleaming paint. The metal warmed to her touch. "It's lovely. What do I do first?"

"Put your, uh, right lower limb through to the other side and perch on the seat. I'll hold the bike steady."

She lifted her skirt just enough to stick her leg through the opening, then sat. Just gripping the handlebars made it seem more real that she was about to have her first lesson on riding a bicycle. She was conscious of John's nearness as he held the vehicle steady.

"Now put your feet on the pedals," he instructed.

She propped her shoes on the platforms. "Do I move them?"

He nodded. "Let's go. Don't go so fast I can't keep up."

She began to push. John ran beside her on the brick drive, his breath warming her ear. A grin stretched across her face as the wind lifted her hair. "I love this!"

She rode up and down the driveway with John jogging beside her. At the top of the drive, she circled and began to pedal back toward the house. The bicycle rolled and maneuvered as if it were a part of her. She turned her head to tell John again how much she enjoyed the experience and realized he wasn't beside her anymore. She was balancing by herself. Her initial reaction was to jerk the handlebars, and the bike wobbled, but she regained control and pedaled on down the drive-way. She made the final approach to the house on a sweeping curve.

It came more quickly than she'd mentally pre-pared for. She swerved too far, too fast. The bicycle rocked, and she jerked on the handlebars again to straighten it out. The cycle tipped, and she and the bicycle went down in a tangle of limbs and metal. Addie felt no pain at first, just the shock of taking a tumble. Then her elbow throbbed to inform her that she'd scraped it. Her forearm too. She pushed herself upright as John came running toward her.

"Miss Addie!" Edward, too, rushed to her side, but Gideon reached her first and pranced around her.

"I'm all right," she said as John arrived.

He knelt beside her and slipped his arm around her. "Are you injured?"

She had no idea of her true condition with him so close. Assessing the pain level, she leaned her head against his shoulder. His presence was the best medicine. "I-I don't think so."

Edward threw himself atop her, and she pulled him onto her lap when she realized he was cry-ing. "It's okay, darling."

"You're bleeding," the child wailed.

John moved away, and she hugged Edward, relishing the little-boy scent of grass and dog. "It's merely a scratch, Edward. Proof of valor." John was still near enough that she could smell his bay rum hair tonic.

"I should call the doctor," John said. He placed his hand on her shoulder.

"No, no, I think I can get up with your assistance." Aware she was showing more of her leg than was seemly, Addie flipped her skirt into place. She brushed a kiss across Edward's cheek and scooted him onto the grass. "Papa's going to help me up." She grasped John's arm and allowed him to lift her to her feet.

"Does anything hurt?" he asked.

She smiled into his face. "Only my pride."

"Let's get you inside."

She glanced at the heap of wheels and metal. "No, I want to get back on the bicycle."

His mouth gaped. "You aren't afraid?"

"I'm terrified. But if I don't get back on now, I might never do it. The fall will expand in my mind. I want to learn this."

She released his arm and stepped away, though she preferred to stay close to him. "The bicycle appears unharmed."

"But you're not. You're bleeding."

She bent her elbow up to have a look. "As I said, it's merely a scratch." She straddled the bicycle again. "I believe I need your assistance."

"Against my better judgment." He steadied the bicycle.

She put her feet on the pedals and began to

move up the driveway, though her chest was tight and her breathing labored. Chances were, she wouldn't fall again. Even if she did, she meant to master this skill. She loved the freedom she felt on the conveyance.

John ran beside her again, and she knew he wouldn't let go unless she forced him. Maybe it was safer to ride with his assistance. But no, playing it safe wouldn't help her learn to ride by herself.

"You can let go now," she said, keeping up a steady pressure on the pedal though her pulse began to thump.

He stepped back, and his hands dropped away. "You can do it!" he shouted after her as the bicycle picked up speed on the slope toward the house.

Addie gained confidence as the wheels turned easily and the bicycle handled well. She was beginning to understand how to handle it, and her balance didn't waver. She reached the front steps and braked. When the bicycle rolled to a stop, she put her feet down and sighed. She'd done it.

"Bravo!" John said, running to her side. "Your form was excellent. Now try to start it by yourself, without my assistance."

She smiled back into his animated face. What was this relationship that was developing between them? He'd never answered her question about philandering. Maybe he treated every woman as if she were special. Mr. Driscoll had warned her to be careful, but it was hard to think of such things when she looked into John's face.

His smile faded when she didn't move. "Miss Adeline? Are you all right?" he asked.

"Fine," she said, hastily putting one foot on a pedal.

She gave the bike a push with her right foot, then put her foot on the pedal and began to rotate the wheel. Her balance became steadier as the bicycle picked up speed. She was doing this alone! When she reached the top of the driveway, she turned in a circle and rode back to the house.

Her cheeks were warm from the ride. "I'll put the bicycle in the carriage house. Thank you for teaching me to ride. It was most exhilarating."

"One of the stablemen will do it." When she dismounted, he leaned the bicycle against the porch. "I should put some iodine on your scrapes."

"I can do it."

"It's hard to do by yourself. You can barely see if it's clean." He caught her arm and steered her toward the house, then down the hall to the parlor. "Wait here. I'll get water and iodine."

She rolled up her sleeve while he went to get the iodine. When had anyone tended to her so lovingly?

Dirt caked her elbow and arm where she'd grazed it on the driveway. Blood oozed from the abrasion. When John returned, he knelt and set the basin of warm water on the floor. Wringing out the washcloth, he touched it to the blood. She didn't flinch.

"Nasty scrape," he said. He washed the area as gently as he could.

"I can't see it well."

"As I said." He smiled and set about cleaning the injury. The only time she winced was when he applied the iodine. "Sorry," he said.

"The sting will ease in a moment."

He rose and stepped back. "I wouldn't hurt you if I could help it," he said.

Addie's eyes flickered, and she sobered. "You never answered my question at the beach," she said. "About your intentions. Were you avoiding a straight answer?"

He grinned. "You are so direct." He grew serious and held her gaze. "No, I'm not a philanderer, though Henry believes I need a new wife. He's been on a crusade to find me one."

"What do you think about it?"

"I have no desire to enter the matrimonial state again. Or at least I didn't."

"What does that mean?" she asked, her voice soft.

"There is something between us, Miss Adeline. I don't know what it is, or where it will lead."

"I don't either."

"I would like to find out," he said. "In fair disclosure, let me mention that I've been seeing a young woman in the city. My commander's daughter, Margaret. But I give you my word that I won't be seeing her again."

She bit her lip. "Have you been dating her long?"

He hesitated, then shrugged. "We've gone out four times."

Her expression softened. "Oh, Lieutenant North. That poor woman. What will she think when you don't ask her out again?"

"She's beautiful and sought after. I'm sure there are many men who will be glad to step into my shoes. I shall call her tomorrow and inform her of my interest in you."

Her eyes shimmered with moisture. "I don't like that she'll be hurt."

He laughed. "Miss Adeline, there isn't a woman alive who would find it in her heart to empathize with a rival as you do." That's what drew people to her, he decided, the compassion that emanated from her. Was it the result of her faith or something else?

"Did you love Katherine too much to replace her?"

He smiled. "What a romantic you are, my dear. Our marriage was less than warm."

"I'm sorry," she said, resting her hand on her chin. "I saw a photograph of her. She was very beautiful."

"And spoiled." John's smile faltered. "Edward embarrassed her. I fear at times I embarrassed her more."

Addie appeared so small in the large chair as she propped her chin on her hand. "You?" she asked.

Her tone implied it was beyond her comprehension that anyone wouldn't be honored to be on his arm. No one in his life had ever treated him with so much respect. No wonder she intrigued him.

"I didn't have enough ambition. Or perhaps I had the wrong kind." Such an honest woman as Addie deserved the truth from him. "And I know I wasn't the husband I should have been. I was away often, working hard to be the man she could look up to. I didn't handle the stress well. We drifted so far apart that we were strangers in the same house."

Addie shuddered. "I'm so sorry. Poor Edward, to lose his mother at such a young age."

If she only knew how much better off his son was without the mother who hardly acknowledged his existence. "He barely knew her. She avoided him when she could."

Her eyes glistened again, and she blinked quickly. "Poor child." She rose. "Thank you for tending to my wounds."

"My pleasure. Good night."

"Good night," she echoed.

He watched her walk away, her gown swishing with every step. Something about her made him want to be better than he was. When he saw the admiration and respect in her eyes, he could feel himself straighten and walk taller. Not many women caused that kind of reaction in a man.

So many women simpered and danced around the truth. Addie was exactly what she seemed. Being around someone so honest was a refreshing experience.

THIRTEEN

MONDAY MORNING, ADDIE surveyed her domain again. The schoolroom lacked a proper desk. The existing chair and table were too small for Edward. Such circumstances gave her the perfect excuse to go to the attic. She'd been itching to find more of her mother's possessions.

She touched the lad's head. "Edward, you practice writing your *A*. I'll be right back."

The boy put his arm around the dog's neck. "What about Gideon?"

"He can stay with you."

She told Gideon to guard the boy, then went in search of Molly and found her scrubbing a bathroom. "Molly, I hate to disturb you, but would there happen to be any school desks in the manor?"

Molly pushed a tendril of damp hair that had escaped her cap out of the way and leaned back on her haunches. "I'm not sure, miss, but there might be something in the attic. I could check for you." She started to get to her feet.

"Oh, don't get up. I'll do it if you direct me to the attic access."

"It's the door at the end of the hall by your bedroom."

"Thank you." Addie walked briskly through the labyrinth of halls and doorways, then found the attic door where Molly had indicated.

Light from the dormer windows shone dimly down the steep stairway. A lantern would help her see better, but she was in no mood to retrace her steps and bother Molly again. Perhaps there was a gaslight. She gathered her courage along with her skirts and ascended the stairs.

More light was the first thing she sought. Too many shadows dominated the space. She found a gaslight on a table, along with matches. When its hiss filled her ears, the warm glow from its globe made the attic appear less unfriendly. She glanced around and saw dressers, tables, trunks, and chifforobes. In another corner lay rolls of rugs. The other side held several desks and showed promise for what she needed. She picked her way through the jumbled furniture.

How would she know what furniture had belonged to her mother? She recognized the value of several lovely pieces under their drop cloths. She went through a stack of portraits but found none of her mother. In the back of the stack, she paused at the sight of a child, then realized it was too old to have been of her two-year-old self. The little one had long blonde curls and appeared to be about four. Perhaps it was Clara?

Addie left the paintings and began to look over the desks. Most of them were beautiful but built for a man, not a five-year-old boy. She removed protective covers from several pieces until she uncovered a woman's desk. The desk was so lovely an exclamation escaped her lips. A white pastoral scene was painted on the doors that hid the drawers. She admired the delicate turned legs and the scrollwork on the front and top.

She had to see inside the dainty piece. The doors refused to open, and she realized it was locked. The key must be here somewhere. Kneeling, she ran her fingers over the legs, then under the desk. A key had been taped to the back edge. She peeled it off, then fitted the key into the keyhole. The hardware clicked, and she opened two doors to reveal two shelves and three drawers in a pale wood tone.

She wished she could claim it for her own. Never had she wanted something so badly. She touched the smooth wood, then pulled open the drawers. The two on top were empty. The bottom one ran the width of the desk and held bundles of letters in a woman's script. Her hand hovered over one letter that was loose from the rest. Would reading this be prying? But surely whoever owned this didn't care, not if she'd left the letters in the desk.

Addie decided to take a peek and see whom this exquisite desk had belonged to. The paper was heavy and stiff in her fingers. She unfolded the letter and made note of the address.

Dear Laura,

A gasp escaped her throat. Her mother's letters? Her gaze roamed the desk. Did all these letters belong to her mother? She scooped them up and stuffed them into the waistband of her skirts. Once she reached the privacy of her room, she would read them. Perhaps they would reveal who was behind the events that had shaped her life.

She heard a creak on the steps and whirled to see John's dark head appearing through the floor opening. She feared he could read the guilt stamped there and turned back to the desk.

"You startled me, Lieutenant North." She closed the doors on the desk and placed the cloth back over it.

He stepped onto the attic floor. "What are you doing?"

"Trying to find a desk for Edward. The table is much too small."

He joined her. "Will this work?" he asked, pointing to a desk.

She examined it and nodded. "It's much like the one I used at the lighthouse."

He gave the attic a quick appraisal. "Lots of useless stuff up here."

"Beautiful things," she said. "Did you notice the desk I covered up? It's so lovely."

"I didn't see it." He lifted its cloth. "A woman's desk," he said. "I don't remember Katherine using it. But then, she didn't want anything old."

Addie ran her hand over the painted front. "It's exquisite."

"I'm sure no one would object if you used it while you're here."

"Oh, I couldn't." She took a step back. "I'm sure it's very valuable."

He shrugged. "It's just an old desk. I'll have one of the servants bring it down with this one for Edward. Do you want it in your room?"

"I'd rather use it in the schoolroom. Shouldn't we ask permission first?"

"I'll check with Clara, but I'm sure it's fine." He offered her his arm. "Lunch is in an hour. Henry will be back soon. I overheard you tell Sally you were itching to try the grand piano, and I'd like to hear you play."

She put her hand on his arm. She could get used to attention from this man.

Addie sat on the bench at the grand piano. The ragtime music that poured from the instrument made John tap his foot. Edward cavorted with the dog on the wood floors, and John was of half a mind to join them.

"Who taught you how to play?" he called.

Her pensive smile faded. "My father taught me. He studied music and had thought to be a concert pianist before consumption changed his plans."

Her mouth grew pinched, and he wondered

about the relationship with her mother. There was pain there. He stood and walked over to lean on the piano lid. Before he could ask more questions, he heard a bellow behind him. The music tinkled to a stop and faded to an echo of its vibrant energy.

Henry's broad form filled the doorway. "What is the meaning of this?" he shouted.

Addie's hands still lay on the keys, and she turned to face Eaton, her green eyes wide. "I was told I would be allowed to play the piano," she said.

"Not trash like that. This isn't a bordello." Henry's face reddened. "Pardon me for mentioning something so indelicate to a lady, but Miss Sullivan, that kind of music is most unsuitable for my grandson and for anyone to hear echoing from the Eaton house."

She paled even more. "I meant no harm, sir. My father paid for lessons, and these are the tunes I learned. To me, they express the joy I find in the Lord."

Henry's feigned smile was more of a grimace. "Well, you must unlearn them. Hymns will do more to connect you to God than that drivel can. There is suitable sheet music in the piano bench." He turned and stomped out.

Watching Addie's stricken face, John realized she was already feeling the pressure to conform, as he'd feared. He extended his hand. "I believe luncheon should be ready. Shall we go?"

She took his hand and rose, releasing it once she was on her feet. "I didn't mean to offend him."

"He'll get over it." The scent of Addie's honeysuckle cologne smelled better than the aroma of roast beef, which grew stronger as they approached the dining room. He stopped in the doorway when he saw Carrington at the sideboard, dishing compote onto his plate. If John had realized the man had been invited for lunch, he would have made his excuses. He'd respected Carrington until his attention to Addie had commenced.

When they were seated, he turned to Clara. "Miss Adeline and I were in the attic looking for a desk for Edward."

Clara stirred sugar into her tea. "Adeline? You've moved to first names?"

"A slip of the tongue," he said hastily.

Her gaze slid to Carrington, who was obviously besotted. "You appear to have some competition, John."

He resisted the impulse to tug on his tie. "About the desk?"

She took a sip of her tea. "Did you find one? There should be something suitable up there."

"Yes, we did. We also stumbled across a writing desk. I told Miss Sullivan I saw no reason she couldn't use it."

She stilled. "A white one? With a painted scene on the front?"

"That's the one."

She directed a gaze at Henry on the other side of the table. "Henry, dear. Adeline would like to use Laura's old desk that's in the attic. That's quite all right, isn't it?"

Laura's desk? John heard the taunting tone of her voice under the sugary sweetness that lay over it. He glanced at Henry and wasn't surprised to see red running up the older man's neck.

"Of course she can use it. Might as well get some good out of that old thing," Henry said in an overly hearty voice.

Addie's expression was stricken, and John knew she had caught the undertones too. It was clear to him that Clara had always known she was Henry's second choice. Pictures of Laura and baby Julia were in Henry's study somewhere, and he still wore the cuff links Laura had given him as a wedding present.

"I'll have one of the servants bring it down," John said. He noticed the Englishman was about to engage Addie in conversation again. "Miss Sullivan, since you're finished with lunch, I wonder if I might have a word with you. About Edward," he added when he saw a frown gather on Carrington's face.

"Of course." She put down her napkin and rose. "It's been a pleasure, Lord Carrington."

Carrington half rose. He took her hand and kissed it. "I look forward to seeing you again, Miss Sullivan."

She withdrew her hand and moved away from the table. John wanted to believe it was relief he saw on her face. He'd like to think she was too smart to be taken in by Carrington. She took his arm, and they stepped out of the dining room. Once the clink of silverware was behind them, he stopped in the hall.

"Is something wrong, Lieutenant North?"

"Beware of Carrington," he said.

"Mr. Carrington was very kind," she said. "He made no untoward remarks."

"He's already got you lined up in his mind as his next wife. He's buried one already."

Her breath came fast, and spots of color lodged in her cheeks. "What happened to his other wife?"

Surely she wasn't interested! "She died in child-birth."

"Recently?"

He dropped his gaze. "No," he muttered, struggling to maintain his temper. "About ten years ago."

"The poor man," she murmured. She removed her hand from John's arm. "But I'm not interested in becoming wife number two."

"I'm relieved to hear it," he said.

She tipped her head. "Are you? Why would that concern you?"

"He's much too old for you," he said.

She smiled, and her dimple appeared. "Surely he's not more than fifty."

"As I said. An old man." He put her hand on his

arm and steered her to the staircase. "I'm sure Edward is finished with his lunch by now. I'll arrange to have the desk brought to you."

Her impish smile faded. "I thought Mr. Eaton seemed not at all fond of the idea."

"He said it was fine."

She swept up the stairs beside him. "It was what he didn't say that concerns me. It belonged to his first wife?"

"Clara's half-sister."

"Clara seemed somewhat jealous."

"She always has been. Have you noticed the pictures of a beautiful redhead around the manor? That was Laura. Henry would be wise to take them down. Everywhere Clara turns, she sees the reminders of Laura."

"I've only seen one."

He stopped and thought. "You're right," he said, nodding. "Clara must have succeeded in relegating them to the attic."

"He must have loved his first wife a great deal," Addie said.

"It seemed quite the grand passion." They reached the top of the staircase, and he turned her toward the schoolroom. "Katherine was always curious about the daughter, Julia. She'd wanted a sibling."

"Julia," she said, her voice strangled.

John hadn't missed the change in her voice. "Is something wrong?"

She shook her head violently. "You were saying?"

"She was around two. She and Laura went down in a shipwreck. I heard Henry didn't eat or sleep for days. He searched for them for weeks, but there was never any sign of them. There were no survivors."

"How sad," she whispered.

He touched her chin and turned her liquid eyes toward him. "Don't cry. It happened a long time ago. I'm sure Henry is over it all by now."

"Love like that never dies."

He smiled. "Such romanticism. No wonder you read poetry."

"Does he ever talk about them?"

He released her chin and shook his head. "Clara would be in tears if he did. The servants tell how he raved like a madman when he heard the news. Molly said she'd never heard a grown man cry like that."

Her fingers tightened on his arm as they moved toward the schoolroom. "Don't talk about it anymore or I shall cry myself. It's too sad for words." Her voice broke.

"As you wish. I was just answering your questions." He led her down the hall.

Edward's empty plate lay on the table in the schoolroom. John stepped to the window and looked down into the side yard. "He's tossing a ball to Gideon."

"They'll both burn off some energy."

He turned toward her. "You haven't asked how my call to Margaret went."

She smiled. "*Now* who is very direct?"

He raised his brows. "You're rubbing off on me."

"I hope not. You'll be reprimanded like me."

"Someone has reprimanded you?"

She waved her hand. "Nothing serious. Mrs. Eaton told me not to be so forthcoming about where I am from. That I must maintain the position."

He put his hands on her shoulders. "I told you not to let them change you." Her scent filled his head.

Her dimple appeared. "I promise not to change too much." She gazed up into his face. "What about your call to Margaret?"

He shrugged and let his hands fall back to his side. "It was fine."

"Did you tell her you wouldn't be calling on her again?"

"I did. She took it graciously, then asked when I would return to the city. I told her it would be several weeks."

Color stained her cheeks. "Do you intend to see her again?" she asked, her voice low. She turned toward the window.

He turned her back to face him. "No, Miss Sullivan, I do not. I should not have mentioned her question, but I must admit I wondered if you cared enough to be jealous. My remark was quite ungentlemanly."

Her expression warmed. "I care entirely too much, Lieutenant North."

No, he was the one who was smitten, and it was much too soon to be so taken with her.

FOURTEEN

ADDIE FOUGHT TEARS all afternoon. Hearing how her father had searched for her and her mother had done something to the fences she'd put up around her emotions.

"You did a wonderful job on your letters today, Edward," she told her charge.

His small face brightened. "Can I take Gideon out to play ball as a reward?"

"It's nearly time for your dinner."

His face puckered. "I don't like lessons when I have to stay inside. Gideon has been waiting for me to play all afternoon."

She glanced at her dog, who stared back at her with hopeful eyes as though he understood. And he probably did. *Play* was his favorite word. "Very well," she said. "I'll go down with you."

It was a sacrifice, because she wanted nothing more than to shut her door and go through the letters she'd stuffed under the mattress. What might she discover in those pages? The identity of the man who had attacked her? The reason behind the events that had changed her life?

She took Edward's small hand and led him and Gideon outside. Clouds swirled overhead, and a drop of rain plopped onto her face. "We won't be able to stay long," she warned. "It's going to rain."

She settled on the wicker chair and watched the boy throw the ball to her dog. Gideon was enjoying it as much as Edward was. The dog wasn't used to being cramped up in the house. He'd roamed the island at their last station all day, then wandered home at night. The stress of the day had taken its toll, and her eyes drooped. A cacophony of wild barking opened them again, and she leaped from her chair to see Gideon crouched and barking at Edward. The dog lunged forward and grabbed the boy's arm. Was he attacking the child?

"Gideon!" she shouted, rushing to intervene.

The dog succeeded in tugging Edward to a sitting position. The boy's staring eyes did not respond to Gideon's agitation. The child swayed where he sat, then he toppled onto his back. Gideon pranced around the boy.

She knelt beside the boy. "Good boy, Gideon," she crooned as she checked out the lad. "You saw what was happening to Edward, didn't you?"

Addie pulled Edward onto her lap and held him. He jerked, and his eyes rolled back in his head. She pulled her handkerchief from the sleeve of her dress, rolled it up, then thrust it between his teeth.

Someone else needed to know about this. "Help! Lieutenant North, someone. Please help!"

At first she thought no one had heard her, then the door opened and a figure stepped onto the porch. She recognized John and waved to attract his attention in case he didn't see her in the twilight. As he started toward her, the heavens opened up with a gush of rain. She huddled over Edward and tried to protect him from the worst of the water.

John reached them. "An attack of epilepsy?" he shouted over the pounding of the rain hitting the trees.

She nodded. "Is it safe to move him?"

"Yes. Here, let me." He lifted his son from her lap and rushed with him toward the house.

She splashed through the widening mud puddles. Gideon loped along beside her. When they reached the porch, she snapped her fingers at her dog. Mrs. Eaton would go into vapors if Addie let the muddy dog onto her redwood floors.

"Stay, Gideon," she said. The dog whimpered but lay down. "I'll get some rags to dry you and come back," she promised.

When she stepped inside, she found the household in an uproar. Both grandparents hovered over the unconscious boy. John had laid him on the leather sofa in the smoking room.

Clara wrung her hands. "Oh, why does this happen to our sweet lad?" she moaned. She caught sight of Addie. "What happened, Adeline? Was he upset?"

Addie shook her head. "He had a good day of studies. I gave him permission to toss the ball to Gideon, and he was having a good time."

"Maybe he got too hot," Mr. Eaton said.

"I don't think so," Addie said. "Gideon was doing the running. I heard the dog bark and saw Edward standing still, just staring. Gideon grabbed his shirtsleeve and pulled him down. A few seconds later he fell back."

John glanced up from his vigil beside his son. "The dog sensed it before it happened? Just like the day you arrived?"

"I think so. I watched it with my own eyes."

"Amazing," Mr. Eaton said. "Edward claimed it was so from the very first." He fixed his gaze on Addie. "What magic is this, Miss Sullivan?"

"Gideon seems to sense these things," she admitted. "He has often led me to injured animals or children."

"Did he lead you to the child in the garment factory?" John asked in a low voice.

She nodded. "He's a remarkable dog."

"We must breed him and see if this trait can be duplicated. I did some checking with a neighbor who has a shepherd. She'll have a female in heat in a few weeks. With her permission, I'd like to see what kind of pups we might get." Addie's cheeks went red, and Mr. Eaton stuttered. "Pardon me, Miss Sullivan. I should not be discussing something so indelicate. Have I your permission to, uh, mate Gideon?"

"Please do, sir," she said. "I'd love to have some little Gideons running around."

John was thinking more about a little girl with Addie's magnificent eyes.

Addie leaned against her closed door and let the pent-up air escape from her lungs. Every moment in the handsome lieutenant's presence left her more infatuated. When should she tell him about her identity? She longed to reveal it to him. As soon as Mr. Driscoll returned, she planned to inform him she couldn't keep the truth from John. She loved his name. Such a strong, manly sound encompassed by that one-syllable word.

She turned on the gas lamp, closed her curtains, then slipped into her white nightgown. In Gideon's absence, the room echoed with emptiness. He was so necessary to Edward, but she missed her companion. If the puppies were found to have his innate sense of compassion, Edward could have his own puppy.

They were much alike, she and Gideon. Ever since she could remember, she'd been able to sense another person's pain. When her father had a headache, Addie knew where to rub. When her mother broke her ankle, Addie's had throbbed as well. This was the first time in her life that she knew the right thing to do was to gift her dog to the child, but she couldn't quite summon the will.

Adrenaline still raged through her. The letters under her mattress awaited discovery. Standing by the gaslight, she realized she hadn't prayed in two days. No wonder her day hadn't gone well. That was usually her first thought, and the realization it had been her last thought struck her hard. She dropped to her knees by the bed and poured out her distress to the Lord. The agitation faded, and peace warmed her like a blanket.

It would be all too easy in this environment to forget her roots. To lay aside what was truly important. She had to be on her guard.

While she was on her knees, she thrust her hand under the mattress and found the bundle of letters. She rose and carried them to the chair by the lamp. Her hands trembled as she held them under the warm glow of light and tried to decide which letter to read first. Chronologically made the most sense. She sorted them by postmark. Some had the bold slash of a man's handwriting.

Once they were sorted, she laid the stack on the table and lifted the first one. It was addressed to her mother in a delicate handwriting.

Laura,

You simply must come to tea next week. Wednesday at 2:00 p.m.? Bring Clara if necessary, but come! Mr. Henry Eaton has confessed that he is quite smitten with you. He says Clara knows they are friends only. He asked me to intercede on his behalf.

Most warmly,
Inez

Addie noticed the date. October 19, 1875. The first meeting between her parents. She could imagine how it played out: her father, slimmer and with his hair still dark, bowing over her mother's hand. Was it love at first sight? And what about Clara? Had she known Henry felt nothing for her but friendship?

She picked up the next letter and saw a man's bold scrawl. From her father perhaps? She opened it and held it under the light.

My dearest Laura,

I am the happiest man on earth now that you know my feelings. Your face, your form, haunt my dreams. I am a man obsessed. Would you honor me with your presence on a ride along the shore next Saturday? I will be sure to bring a carriage with enough room for Clara if she could be persuaded to act as chaperone.

Your humble servant,
Henry

Addie drew the back of her hand across her damp eyes. The love her father felt was clear. She suspected her mother had the same experience. Reading their exchanges was like reading an Elizabeth Barrett Browning love poem. Totally enthralled with the relationship unfolding in the letters, she picked up the next one.

Laura,
   I'm thrilled things are so wonderful between you and Henry. I'd be honored to be your bridesmaid for the wedding in June. I completely understand that your stepmother would insist that Clara be the maid of honor.
                    Warm regards,
                    Inez

Addie gave a blissful sigh. John's face flashed through her mind, but she pushed it away and picked up another envelope. The next five letters were all invitations to different parties and teas. The last was addressed in her mother's handwriting. It was in an unaddressed envelope with only the name Henry slashed across the front.

My dearest Henry,
   I know you do not understand, but I must be gone for a few weeks. I still love you very much, but when I overheard the awful truth, it was more than I could bear. I will be in

touch when I'm settled in the hotel. Don't try to make me come home yet. I need some time.

Laura

Addie folded the letter and put it back in its envelope. "Awful truth," her mother had said. What would cause a wife who was clearly devoted to her husband to flee with her daughter? Addie needed to talk to Mr. Driscoll. He'd said he would be home tonight. Maybe he was in his room. She snatched up her dressing gown.

FIFTEEN

JOHN TUCKED THE sheet around his sleeping son, then stepped over the dog and tiptoed out of the room. He started across the hall to his own bedroom and heard the murmur of voices. A man and a woman were arguing. Or at least it sounded like an argument. In case the woman was in distress, he followed the sound around the corner to the other wing of rooms. As he neared, the voices became clear enough to identify.

Driscoll and Addie. They were in the school-room.

He stopped before he turned into the final hallway. He'd listen a minute to make sure things were all right, then head to his bed. If she needed him, he wanted to be there.

"Why would she leave so suddenly?" Addie asked, her voice raised.

"You should have told me before you read the letters," Driscoll said.

"I have to know the truth."

Frowning, John sidled nearer while staying hidden around the corner.

"And we'll find out the truth," Driscoll said. "But we have to work together, Addie."

"I want to find out what happened," she said. "Who I am."

Driscoll cleared his throat. "You should have told me the minute you found the letters."

"You've been gone, Mr. Driscoll. Did you discover anything?"

"Unfortunately no, child. Tuttle died six months ago."

"He still might have been the one behind it." Desperation tinged her words.

"The money would have stopped."

"Unless he made arrangements for it to carry on in the event of his death. I want to tell Mr. Eaton now. And John."

John's gut clenched at the way her tone went soft when she said his name. At least keeping the secret from him hadn't been easy for her. Whatever it was.

"We have to be careful, Adeline. Someone has already attacked you. You're making yourself a target if we announce why you're here."

"I think it would be worth it. I'm tired of the charade." Her voice dropped to a near whisper.

"I advise patience."

"My whole life has been turned upside down since you appeared on our doorstep, Mr. Driscoll. It's easy enough for you to advise patience when you're not the one whose future hangs in the balance."

"I'm sorry, Addie." Driscoll's voice grew gentle. "I know this has been hard for you. Get some sleep. Let's talk about it tomorrow."

"Very well. I can see you are not going to budge. Good night, Mr. Driscoll."

"Good night, my dear."

Driscoll's footsteps neared, and John slipped into an empty guest room until the noise of his passage faded down the hall. Driscoll had brought Addie here for a reason, but the import of it escaped John. The rock in his gut grew heavier. The discussion John had overheard made one thing clear. Addie wasn't the innocent he thought. Just as much pretense ran through her veins as through all the other women he'd known. He'd been sure she was different. He'd been ready to pursue her. He'd even stepped away from a good match because of her. Addie's directness had been all a front. How very clever of her.

When he stepped back into the hall, he nearly ran down Addie. He caught her before she stumbled back against the wall.

"You startled me," she said. Her bare feet peeked out from under her green dressing gown, and her hair was down.

A visceral emotion hit John in the gut. His fingers itched to plunge into that thick mane of auburn hair, to examine the red tints in the firelight. He imagined lifting that heavy curtain to place a kiss on the warm skin of her neck. Resisting the liquid warmth of her eyes, he released her arm and thrust his hands in his pockets.

Neither spoke for a long moment. A blush colored her cheeks, and he eyed it. Figuring out how to blush on command must have taken some training and practice. It gave her an innocent air that had completely fooled him.

"Is something wrong?" she asked, clutching the neck of her dressing gown.

Would she tell him the truth if he asked why she was really here? He could tell her he'd overheard her conversation with Driscoll.

"No, nothing," he said abruptly. "You're up late. Can I help you with something?"

Her dimple flashed. "I couldn't sleep and thought I'd get some warm milk."

"You're going the wrong way."

"I get so turned around in this big place."

More lies? Probably an excuse to explain her presence.

He led her down the hall until it teed to the

right, then to the end of the next hallway. "Careful, the stairs are steep."

He went down the steps ahead of her. Even in the kitchen stairway, the Eatons had spared no expense. Flocked wallpaper covered the walls, and the stairs and handrail were redwood. John and Addie emerged in the large kitchen. The wooden counters were clean and ready to be used in the morning.

He took a glass down from the cupboard and went to the ice chest. "Would you care to have it warmed?"

She held out her hand for the glass of milk. "You don't need to wait on me. I don't want to keep you from your bed."

He handed it over and watched as she poured hot water from the kettle on the woodstove into a bowl, then set the glass of milk in it to warm. "I'm a little hungry. Would you care for some jam and bread?"

Her smile came. "I admit I'm a bit peckish myself. Let me get it. Sit down."

He sat at the kitchen table and watched her cut thick slices of bread and spread them with jam and butter. The intimacy of the moment swamped his resolve not to look at her hair.

He had to remember she had a secret agenda.

The warmth John had shown for days was replaced by a chill demeanor that tightened his lips and hooded his eyes. As Addie layered on the top-pings, she cast her mind back over the day and couldn't think of anything she might have done to offend him.

She placed the food on a plate and slid it in front of him. She slipped into the seat across from him and propped her chin in her hand. "I fear I was too honest about my feelings, Lieutenant. I've frightened you with my boldness, perhaps?"

"Candor is never misplaced, Miss Sullivan. Falsehood, on the other hand, is something I despise."

"Falsehood? Surely you know me well enough by now to know I say what I think."

"The problem is not what you say but what you *don't* say."

She studied his cold, dark eyes when he finally raised them. "You know," she whispered. "I wanted to tell you right from the start, but Mr. Driscoll forbade me to say anything."

"I heard you talking to him a few moments ago."

She thought about that conversation. Nothing had been said about her identity. All he knew was that she had some purpose for being here, but she couldn't endure his coldness. "You don't know all of the story, but I want to tell you."

"Will it be the truth?"

"Have I ever lied to you, Lieutenant?"

"Right now, I'm not really certain. I thought you were the clearest pool of honesty I'd ever peered into. I admit I'm most disappointed in you."

She winced. "I'm exactly what you see. The only thing I haven't revealed is my purpose in coming here."

"I thought it was to teach Edward. Or is that a lie as well?"

"The moment I heard about Edward, I wanted to meet him," she said. "He's very important to me, and I loved him from the first."

His eyes softened only a fraction at the mention his son's name. "So what other purpose brought you here?"

"I want to discover my heritage."

He frowned. "I don't understand. How could coming here help you learn that?"

"I was born here. To Laura Eaton." She waited until the light began to dawn in his eyes. "I believe I'm Julia Eaton."

"That's impossible! She drowned years ago."

She pulled her locket out from under her dressing gown and opened it. "Then explain this."

He leaned over and peered at the picture in the locket. His fingers grazed hers when he cradled the necklace in his hand. She shivered with the over-powering urge to touch his hair. If he didn't move, she wouldn't be able to resist. When he finally leaned back, she was able to breathe again.

"It's Vera," he said. "Where did you get it?"

"I think I must have been around five when my father gave it to me. When Mr. Driscoll showed up, my mother admitted it was around my neck when my father found me on the shore. I was about two."

"Julia's age when the shipwreck occurred."

"Yes." She willed him to believe her. "My mother showed me a metal box full of clippings my father had collected about the shipwreck. And someone paid my parents for my upkeep all these years. They were instructed not to turn me over to the authorities but to tell everyone I was their natural child. They were able to do that because my father had just taken the post at Battery Point a few days before the shipwreck. My mother hadn't joined him yet but arrived a few days later."

The coldness began to fade from his face. "You're really Julia Eaton?" He rubbed his forehead. "Does Henry know?"

She rubbed the warm metal of her locket. "Not yet. Mr. Driscoll is searching for more conclusive evidence."

"What role does Walter play in this?"

"A friend of his took a picture of me at the lighthouse, and he happened to see it. Something about my appearance made him think of my mother, so he came to see for himself. When he saw the locket, he knew for sure."

"It might have washed ashore and had nothing to do with you. And your resemblance isn't overt."

She pushed her hair back from her face. "That's why he's searching for more proof. If he can find out who paid for my upkeep, he'll go to Mr. Eaton then."

"Why would someone want to keep you from your family?"

"That's what we want to know."

He reached over and took her hand. "The attacks on you and Walter might be related to this."

The press of his fingers comforted her. "That's what Mr. Driscoll fears. He's hired an investigator, but the records of the attorney who paid the stipend were burned, and so far the attorney is not revealing his client."

"Henry will want proof, though the locket will have an impact. Still, it's not conclusive."

"Perhaps I should tell Mr. Eaton anyway. If we all work together, we may discover the truth."

"I'm not so sure," he said. "Someone had a powerful reason to keep you away from him. What if that's who attacked you and Walter?"

"If the truth comes out, that person won't have any reason for another attack."

"Or it might force him into a more desperate move."

"Or her," she said before she could stop the words.

"Her?"

"Mr. Driscoll suspects Mrs. Eaton."

"I can't see Clara involved in this."

"Jealousy? She was in love with Mr. Eaton before he dropped her for her my mother."

"I have heard that story," he said slowly. He pushed his half-eaten bread away. "We should retire, Miss Sullivan. This will take mulling over."

She rose when he did. When he avoided her gaze, she laid her hand on his arm. "Are you angry with me?"

"Maybe. When we drove past the property, you knew then all the plans I had for it would come to nothing, didn't you?"

She willed him to see the truth in her eyes. "You can keep the land. Money isn't the reason I came. Please don't hate me for it. I couldn't bear it."

His warm fingers lifted her chin, and he stared into her face. "I fear I could never stay angry with you for long." He brushed the back of his hand along her cheek, then stepped to the stairs.

SIXTEEN

LAST NIGHT'S LITTLE tête-à-tête was the first thing Addie thought of when she awoke. They'd eaten their bread and she'd drunk her milk by the dim glow of the gaslight. How strange to think that a few weeks ago she didn't even know John. Now he was all she could think about. The dear man had been understanding when she revealed her identity. She rubbed her eyes and yawned. She'd worked on Mrs. Eaton's dress until after midnight every night.

A knock came at her door, and she leaped from

the bed. "Yes?" she called, grabbing for her dress-ing gown.

"Miss?" Molly said from the other side of the door. "A telegram has come for you."

Addie unlocked the door and opened it. Molly held out a silver tray with an envelope on the lace doily. Addie hesitated to pick it up.

"Miss?" Molly asked.

Addie collected herself and picked up the enve-lope. "Thank you, Molly. Is Edward awake?"

"Yes, miss. He has had his breakfast and is out back on the swing."

"Alone? Or is his nurse with him?"

"She's poorly this morning and stayed in bed. He wanted your dog to go, but Gideon refused to budge from your door." She pointed to the dog lying on the floor in the hall.

"Oh dear, Gideon should have gone with him. I'll be right there." She thanked the maid and called Gideon to her. She gave him a quick pat, then hurried back into the room.

Selecting a white lace blouse and a black skirt, she quickly dressed. On her way down the back stairway, she tore open the envelope and scanned it. She froze on the middle step when she realized it was from Josephine.

Have taken position at Mercy Falls Lighthouse. Stop. Will be there today. Stop. Want to see you. Stop.

Addie's first instinct was to rush to the light-house and embrace her mother, but she knew it would be fruitless. She'd tried to earn Josephine's love for twenty-three years and had never succeeded. Still, what was behind the summons? She stuffed the note in her pocket and stepped into the warm kitchen with the dog on her heels. Oatmeal bubbled from a pot on the stove, and the scent of bacon hung in the air. Her stomach growled, but she didn't have time for a real breakfast, not with Edward outside alone.

She stepped to the back door. "Go find Edward, Gideon." After the dog glanced up at her, then slowly went out, she shut the door behind him.

"Breakfast?" the cook asked.

"Might I take a few pieces of bacon with me? I need to be caring for Edward."

"But sure, let me get that for you." The cook forked four pieces of bacon onto a thick slice of bread and put it on a plate.

Addie scooped off the sandwich and left the plate. She thanked the cook, then hurried into the backyard. Nibbling on her sandwich, she scanned the yard for the boy, but the swing hung empty. Maybe he was in the front yard. She hurried around the back. No Edward. She shouted for Gideon, and he came running back to her side.

Maybe Edward had gone back inside through the front door. She took the last bite of her sandwich, then stepped into the front hall. "Have you seen Edward?" she asked the butler.

"No, miss. Not since he went outside."

She checked with the cook, and Edward hadn't come in the back door. Trying not to panic, she went back to the front. Still no Edward.

John came down the steps. "Is something wrong?"

"I can't find Edward." Aware her voice was rising, she made a conscious effort to modulate her tone. "I checked outside, and all around the house. Is there anywhere else he might have gone?"

John reached her side. "There's the falls. I've told him never to go there alone, though. And another pond that's a little closer. Let's try there first." He held open the door for her, then hurried down the steps. "This way."

She and Gideon followed John along a brick path through the large redwood trees. Trunks big enough to drive a buggy through reached for the sky on both sides of the path and blocked out the sun. Insects hummed around her ears, and she heard the sound of trickling water.

John strode ahead of her but paused long enough to point out their destination. "It's in the grove ahead."

As she quickened her steps, she prayed they'd find the boy happily skipping rocks. They broke through the towering trees into a clearing where water lilies floated on a clear pool. Wildflowers formed a blanket and perfumed the air.

"He's not here," John said, an edge to his voice. "How did he get outside without you or his nurse?"

"He went out before I was out of my room, and his nurse is ill," she said evenly. "We need to instruct the servants not to allow him outside without supervision."

"My fault," he said. "I should already have done that. I didn't take the attacks on you and Walter seriously enough." He raised his voice. "Edward!"

Gideon bristled, and a low growl rumbled from his chest. "What is it, boy?" Addie placed a hand on his head.

His ruff stood at attention, and he focused on a patch of bushes on the far side of the pond. She saw the vegetation flutter.

"It's probably just a deer or a squirrel," John said. He shouted for his son again.

Gideon's growl intensified. "I don't think it's an animal," Addie whispered. "He's not typically alarmed at animals."

"Could Edward be playing hide-and-seek?"

The back of her neck prickled. "He wouldn't growl at Edward."

Gideon walked on stiff legs toward the thick vegetation. She and John followed. The green leaves went into violent movement. A man with Edward under his arm broke from the cover of shrubs. A muffled shriek came from Edward, who had a rag in his mouth.

"Get him!" Addie shouted to Gideon.

The dog broke into a run and reached the fleeing man in seconds. He leaped onto the back of the criminal and knocked him to the ground. Edward rolled away, and the dog jumped between the man and boy. Baring his teeth, Gideon stood guard over Edward.

John rushed toward his son and the would-be kidnapper, but before he reached them, the man leaped to his feet and vanished into the forest. John dropped to his son's side and snatched the gag from Edward's mouth as Addie reached them. She knelt beside them as Edward burst into noisy sobs and flung his arms around his father's neck.

She exchanged a grim glance with John. None of this made sense to her.

The army of servants had been called together and questioned, but no one had seen anything. Though John had threatened to remove himself and his son back to San Francisco, he was reluctant to do so. If the kidnapper had penetrated the Eaton estate, how easily could he bridge the defenses of John's house? He had only a housekeeper and cook to defend his son while he was at work. Both were middle-aged women. Though he could take Addie with him, he wasn't sure if her arrival had plunged all of them into the fire with her.

What could Edward have to do with Addie's true identity? There was no clear connection he could see.

Henry had called a family meeting in the drawing room. Beside him on the sofa, Clara dabbed her eyes with a hankie. Addie stood by the window to the formal garden. Driscoll was in the easy chair by the fireplace, and John dropped into the matching seat.

Henry took out a cigar and chewed on it. "I'm going to hire a Pinkerton agent to investigate this," he announced. "They've a branch right here in Mercy Falls, and plenty of guards for hire."

"I'd feel immensely better if they were here," Clara said. "Abraham Lincoln employed Pinkerton's for his own protection. Did you know that?"

"I'll secure some guards to stand watch around the property," Henry continued. "I intend to find out who dared touch my grandson."

"What about enemies, Henry?" John asked. "Are there any pending acquisitions or touchy contracts that could be at the root of this?"

"If you mean someone who might kidnap my grandson to force me into a position I've refused, then no," Henry said. "Things are going remarkably well in the office. What about you, John?"

"Me?" John shook his head. "I'm a navy man. I simply carry out my duties day to day."

Henry's eyes narrowed. "Could this have been an attempt to kidnap Edward and demand a ransom?"

"I considered that, but it doesn't explain the attack on Walter. Or Miss Sullivan," John said.

The sun from the window highlighted the young

woman's slim figure. The dog wasn't with her but was with Edward as he rested from his ordeal. John needed to protect her as well as his son.

Molly appeared in the doorway. "Sir, Lord Carrington is here."

"Send him in. Maybe he can make sense of this," Henry said.

A few moments later, Carrington strode into the room. His smile faded when he glimpsed their somber faces. "Has there been a death?"

Henry pointed to a chair. "Have a seat, Carrington. Someone tried to kidnap my grandson. The dog foiled the attempt."

Carrington's jaw dropped, and he sank into the chair. "Who was it?"

"If we knew that, he would already be in jail," Henry said with an edge to his voice.

"Ransom?" Carrington suggested.

"That's what we were just discussing. It seems to make the most sense," John said. He was unable to stop the instinctive roil in his gut when Carrington's eyes raked over Addie.

"I'm surprised nothing like this has ever happened before," Carrington said. "The recession has made men desperate, and it's well-known that you control the wealthy in northern California."

Clara fanned herself. "What's next? A holdup on my way to town? You must do something, Henry."

"I am," he said sharply. "As I said, I will hire Pinkerton's. They're as numerous as the redwoods.

You can have one for your own carriage if you like." Henry sat back in his chair. "What are you doing here, Carrington? I didn't expect you today."

"I came to see if Miss Sullivan would care to go for a drive," Carrington said, turning hopeful eyes toward Addie.

Her cheeks grew pink. "I'm flattered, Mr. Carrington, but I'm sorry to say I must decline. Edward needs me, and I have other work I must attend to."

Carrington huffed and turned to John. "You surely aren't going to work Miss Sullivan all the time, young man."

"Of course not. She's welcome to take off any afternoon she pleases, and one whole day a week," John said, glancing at Addie. "Just please clear it with me, Miss Sullivan."

"You're very generous," Addie said, standing. "Thank you for your offer, Lord Carrington, but I'm going to be much too busy for the next few weeks for a social life. I need to devote all my free time to Mrs. Eaton's wardrobe. Now, if you'll excuse me, I need to tend to Edward."

Was that an appeal in the gaze she sent John's way? He rose and stepped to the door.

"I'll go with you," John said. He followed her out of the room and down the hall, where she stopped before they ascended the staircase. "Running from Carrington?"

She put her hands on her cheeks. "I'm sure he's

a very nice man, but I have no interest in seeing him socially."

"He's considered a very good catch," John said before he could stop himself. He stood close enough to smell her honeysuckle cologne.

Her quick intake of breath told him he'd offended her. "I'm sorry. That was uncalled-for." He preceded her up the stairs. When he reached the landing, he turned and saw tears in her eyes. "I never thanked you for protecting Edward," he said.

She grasped his hand. "I already love Edward."

It was sheer force of will that kept him from showing his emotion. Her fingers tightened on his, and he could feel calluses on her palms before she pulled away and stepped into the schoolroom. She was no soft society princess, but a woman who knew what work was. So very different from Katherine.

SEVENTEEN

THE LATE-AFTERNOON SUN slanted through the windows and heated the schoolroom enough that Addie raised both windows to get a cross breeze. She was used to being outside more and being cooped up indoors so much made her long to be able to take a walk in the forest.

"Look, Miss Addie, I made an *E*," Edward said, holding up his paper. He still clutched the fat pencil. Gideon woofed his approval.

"Very good, Edward," she said. "You're doing an excellent job. I'm very proud of you." She touched his dark hair, so like his father's. It was soft and silky. Would John's feel the same?

"Make me three more of them," she said. She turned at a tap on the door and saw Molly standing there. "Good morning," Addie said, smiling at the woman.

"I brought a bit of food for you and the lad," Molly said. She carried in a tray loaded with boiled eggs, cheese, and tea.

"You're so thoughtful, Molly, thank you." Addie cleared a spot on the table, and Molly set down the tray. "How long have you worked here? I know so little about this place."

"Thirty years, miss. I came as a girl of sixteen."

"Goodness, you've been here all your adult life!"

Molly nodded. "That I have, miss. The Eatons have been good to me."

"You knew the first Mrs. Eaton," Addie said, deciding to throw out the question.

Molly stilled and took a step toward the door. "I were her personal maid when she married Mr. Eaton."

"So you knew her better than anyone else in the house," Addie said. "Who was her friend Inez?"

Molly's dark eyes looked Addie over. "How are you knowing these things, miss?"

Addie wished she could reveal it all, but did she dare? She'd felt a kindred spirit in Molly, but

171

would the maid be quick to run to Mr. Eaton with the news?

"I found a letter in the desk," she said finally. "From Inez."

Molly's palpable tension eased. "Mrs. Inez Russell. They was best friends."

"Does Mrs. Russell still live here?" Addie asked, a plan beginning to form.

"That she does. Her husband is the haberdasher, and they live on Ferndale Street. She doesn't come here no more, but I sometimes see her at the market, and she always says hello."

"I saw a picture of Laura Eaton. She was lovely."

"She was, miss. And just as lovely inside. Always laughing and quick to help others. She volunteered at the hospital two days a week, even over Mr. Eaton's objections." She put her hand to her mouth. "I'm talking too much." She started toward the door.

"Please don't go, Molly. I'm very interested."

The woman stopped and turned back to Addie. "It don't matter now. Miss Laura has been dead and gone nearly twenty-three years."

Addie bit back the confession that bubbled up. "She had a child, didn't she?"

Molly nodded. "Little Julia. She were the sweetest baby ever borned. Red curls, dimples. Hardly never cried."

"Did you care for her?"

"Miss Laura hardly let anyone touch that child.

No wet nurse, no nanny. She doted on that baby."

The hollow space in Addie's chest grew. The dim memory of soft hands and a sweet voice singing a lullaby was all she had. "She sounds quite lovely."

"Miss Laura didn't deserve—" Molly bit her lip and turned toward the door.

"Didn't deserve what, Molly? To die?"

"Don't say nothing to Mr. Eaton about my big mouth," Molly said in a low voice. "He'd fire me on the spot for gossiping like this." She stepped into the hall and pulled the door shut behind her.

What had Molly meant to say? It would have been easy enough to say Laura didn't deserve to die, but Addie sensed the maid's words had nothing to do with Laura Eaton's death. If only she had more letters. Addie had checked every drawer, and all were now empty.

Edward tugged on her sleeve. "Teacher?"

She smiled at the child. "Are you hungry, Edward?"

He shook his head. "I have to go potty."

"All right. Wash your hands when you're done, and I'll fix you a snack."

He nodded and tugged the heavy door open by himself. Addie studied the desk. She'd heard of such things as hidden drawers. Could this little desk have something like that? She pulled out the chair and seated herself in front of the desk, then opened the cabinet doors to reveal the drawers. No matter how much she pressed and tugged, the top drawers contained nothing but the velvet lining. She took out each one and checked to see that the bottom of the inside matched up with the outside. No hiding spaces here.

The remaining large drawer was what it seemed as well. She pulled it out and examined the bottom. Nothing. Before she put it away, she peered inside the cavity, but it was too dark to see much but the back. She ran her hand into the opening and traced the shape of it with her fingertips. She touched a small slit. She caught her breath and leaned forward to try to see better. If only she had more light. She managed to wedge a fingernail into the crack and tugged. It flexed but didn't open. She needed a letter opener or something with more leverage. There was nothing useful in the schoolroom, but she'd seen a letter opener in Mr. Eaton's den.

She heard Edward coming back down the hall, so she quickly slid the drawer back into place and shut the desk doors. It would be hours before she could check this again.

John paused outside the Pinkerton's branch office on the corner of Ocean Boulevard and Ferndale Street. He'd never hired a detective before, and he wasn't eager to have to do it now. He squared his shoulder and pulled open the door.

A man stood at a set of filing cabinets. A large desk took up most of the rest of the space in the room. "Good afternoon," he said. "May I help you?"

"I certainly hope so," John said, closing the door behind him.

The place smelled of cigars. He put his hands in his pockets. "I need an investigation run on a young woman."

The man shook his hand. "Nathan Everest," he said. "Have a seat." He indicated the wood chair across from the desk.

"John North." John released Everest's hand and seated himself on the chair.

"Ah, Mr. Eaton's son-in-law." Everest moved to the other side of the desk and sat down. He pulled a sheet of paper to him and picked up a fountain pen. "Let me just get some information. The subject's name?"

Addie's face flashed into his mind. Was this the right thing to do? His instincts indicated she'd told him the truth about why she was here, but if he was going to protect her and Edward, he had to know more.

"Sir? The name?"

He collected himself. This would be best for everyone. "Adeline Sullivan. She came from Crescent City. I think her father was the lightkeeper up at Crescent City. It's called Battery Point. He's dead now, and her mother took over the station."

"Any other information on Miss Sullivan? Birth date, any other particulars you are aware of?"

"She's in her midtwenties, I'd guess. Right now she resides at the Eaton manor."

"What is it you suspect the young lady to be guilty of?"

"Nothing really," John said. "I just want to know more about her."

"Has she committed a crime?"

"Not to my knowledge. Though since her arrival at the manor, Walter Driscoll was attacked, and so was she. Also, someone attempted to kidnap my son this morning."

Everest's hand paused with the pen. "Do you need a bodyguard for the family?"

"I think that's been arranged. How soon do you think you'll have some information for me?"

"I have a man up that way. I'll place a call. I should have some preliminary findings in a few hours. Stop by the office in the afternoon and I'll tell you what I've learned. Will that suit?"

"Perfectly." John rose and shook the man's hand. "Thank you for your discretion."

"That's my middle name. Our business is between us only." Everest walked him to the door.

Back in the sunshine, John walked on toward Henry's offices. The transaction had left him feeling slightly unclean, though the man was pleasant and obviously competent. Pinkerton's reputation was of the highest quality. The franchise employed more investigators and guards than any other agency in the nation—some said they employed more men than the United States Army! With such a network, the agent would be able to dig out any information to be found.

At the Mercy Steamboats office, John ducked inside to ensure Henry had a bodyguard on the scene. Mrs. O'Donnell had the telephone earpiece to the side of her head and waved him past, so he walked down the hall to Henry's office.

A few feet from the office door, he heard a man say, "You won't like the consequences if I don't get my money."

Henry's shout carried loudly to John's ears. "I don't care what you do. This is not my problem. Now, get out of here."

"There are scary things that happen in the world, Eaton. Even children can get hurt."

"What?" Henry's voice rose. "What did you say?"

"You heard me. Consider yourself warned."

Moments later, a seedy-looking man in a rumpled jacket nearly bumped into John. The man's eyes glared from above a nose that appeared to have been broken many times. When he brushed past, John caught a glimpse of a gun under his jacket. He'd seen some shady organized-crime individuals in the city, and his intuition vibrated at the roughness of the man.

John couldn't imagine that his father-in-law would get involved with organized crime. When John poked his head into the office, he found Henry standing at the window and staring out over the bustling street. "Who was that man?" he asked.

Henry turned with a scowl on his face. "Nothing to be concerned about."

"It sounded as though he were trying to extort money from you."

Henry snorted. "It will be a cold day in purgatory when I give money to the likes of him." His expression cleared, and he dropped into his chair. "What brings you to town, son?"

"I wondered if you'd arranged for the Pinkerton agent. I'd thought to do it if you didn't have time."

"I made arrangements as soon as I arrived. The man should be at my estate by now."

John's brow puckered. "Could the fellow who was just here have had anything to do with Edward's attempted kidnapping?"

"I'd wondered about that myself, which was the only reason I spoke with him."

"And what was your conclusion?"

Henry picked up a pipe and chewed on the end of it. "Frankly, I don't know, but I mean to get to the bottom of it." He turned a genial smile on John. "I'm glad you're here. I'm in need of your assistance."

John had learned to be wary of Henry's congeniality. "In what way?"

"The bank is all a muddle. My manager quit without giving notice and left the books in a sorry state. I need someone with organizational skills to get it straightened out. Now that you've been here a few days, I'm hoping you're a bit bored and wouldn't mind helping me out with it. It shouldn't take you more than a few days."

"I manage supplies for the navy. I'm not a banker."

"But you know numbers and how things have to match up. You're an excellent manager. You could whip this into shape in no time. In the meantime, I would be interviewing applicants for the job."

John considered the request. He was intrigued, because working at the bank might give him the opportunity to find out what was behind the attempted extortion he'd just overheard, which might lead to whoever had dared to lay hands on his son.

"Very well," he said. "I'll help you out for a few weeks, but I have no intention of staying here permanently."

"Excellent! Let's head over there now, and I'll explain the job." He held up his hand when John opened his mouth. "I understand it's temporary, but I'm very appreciative of your assistance. Come along."

John followed him across the street and down one block to the bank. He followed Henry past the wooden counter to the hall of offices. Henry pulled out a stack of ledgers, then launched into an explanation of logging deposits and verifying withdrawals that left John's head spinning. He jotted everything down and followed Henry to the vault, where he explained the procedures for locking it up at night. By the time his first training session was completed, it was nearly five.

"Come along, son. I'll give you a ride home."

John had seen nothing that would explain the stranger's demand on his father-in-law, but he meant to find out.

EIGHTEEN

THE FOLLOWING MORNING, Addie worked until ten on Mrs. Eaton's dress. Just before bedtime last night she had requested this afternoon off so she could go see her mother, and she had much to accomplish before noon. The basic outline of the gown hung on a mannequin, waiting to be finished. Cream lace overlaid the lilac silk that Addie had drawn up into an empire waistline. More lace fluttered from the V-neck to frame Mrs. Eaton's face. More lace peeked from a cutout in the side of the gown and from under the hem.

The sophistication matched Mrs. Eaton's style, and the older woman was delighted with it. She'd also asked Addie to create a seaside dress and hat for the yacht race coming up in a few weeks, as well as several merry widow hats and a lingerie hat. It would be challenging to find the time to do all her benefactress wanted and still attend to Edward. She wished she'd never admitted to making her own dresses and hats.

Addie left Gideon in the schoolroom with

Edward, who was copying his letters with a fat pencil. Mrs. Eaton had sent a request for her to come to the salon to discuss the final details on her dress. The telephone rang as Addie passed it in the hall. No one came running, so she picked up the candlestick phone and detached the earpiece. "Eaton Manor," she said into the mouthpiece.

A young woman's voice spoke in her ear. "This is Central. Mr. Eaton's secretary asked me to call and tell him she'd made the arrangements for his trip to Fort Bragg."

"Fort Bragg."

"He goes there twice a year," the friendly voice said. "Though it's a little sooner than usual this fall."

Addie smiled. "You must know everything, working for the switchboard."

"Oh, honey, the things I hear," the girl said.

"I'll tell him," Addie said.

"Are you new there?" the woman asked. "I don't recognize your voice."

"I'm Addie Sullivan, the new governess."

"Oh, so you're Addie. I've heard a lot about you. I overheard Mrs. Eaton tell Countess Bellingham that you make the most divine hats." The girl's voice grew eager.

"I rather like making them," Addie admitted. "From the time I was a little girl, I was making up hats with the bark from trees and ferns."

"I quite adore hats. I'm Katie Russell."

Russell. "Are you related to Inez Russell?" Addie asked, curling her fingers tightly around the phone.

"She's my mother. How do you know her?"

"Someone mentioned her name. She used to be friends with the first Mrs. Eaton."

"That's right. I've heard her talk of Laura." There was a pause. "Oh dear, I have to go. The switchboard is going crazy. I'd like to meet you sometime, Addie."

"Nice to meet you, Katie." The phone clicked off before Addie could say good-bye.

She hung the earpiece back and set the phone on the stand. So Mrs. Eaton had been talking about her. Maybe she could use the contact with Katie to meet Inez Russell.

Carriages and buggies crowded the street, and Addie craned her neck to look to her heart's content. With no one along, she was free to express her wonder at all the people, shops, and excitement. It was a far cry from her former isolated life. Today she could forget that Friday was Henry's birthday ball. She dreaded having to appear.

Her afternoon off stretched in front of her with all the anticipation she used to feel waiting for her father to come from the mainland with a promised Hershey's bar. So many shops to browse through, so many plate-glass windows to gawk at!

She could try to find the Russell house.

Her anticipation died at the thought of walking

up to a stranger's door and asking questions. She'd rather forget her past and enjoy the day, but the nudging desire wouldn't go away. Was it from God? She'd learned to listen to such promptings.

"Fine, God, I'll do it," she muttered. But how? All she knew was they lived on Ferndale Street. She stopped the buggy in the parking lot of the mercantile. Someone here might direct her. Lashing the reins to a hitching post, she walked across the parking lot to the side door as a man exited.

"Excuse me," she said. "Could you direct me to Ferndale Street?"

The man pushed his straw hat to the back of his head. His moon-round face was pleasant, with hazel eyes. "Sure, miss, it's the next crossroad to the south. It only goes right, toward the water. You looking for a particular house?"

"The Russell home?"

He nodded. "It's the last one on the road. Overlooks the sea. Big, gray one."

She thanked him and went back to her buggy. Driving down Ferndale Street, she noticed the houses were large and comfortable but not as lavish as Eaton Manor. The buggy slowed as the horse struggled through the potholes along the macadam road. At the top of the hill, she could see all the way out to the sea and could even catch a glimpse of the Mercy Falls Lighthouse.

Her mother was there by now. A stone lodged in

her midsection at the thought of facing Josephine's disapproving stare again. She was going to have to go see her this afternoon too.

The last house was on the right. A large gray Victorian with white shutters and an L-shaped porch, the home hunkered amid a few straggly shrubs and trees. The salt and wind prevented the manicured look of the Eaton residence. She turned the horse into the dirt lane and sat there a moment trying to summon the courage to go to the door.

How would she announce she'd come to learn about Laura Eaton? What possible excuse could she give for her curiosity? "You'll have to give me the words, Lord," she whispered, clambering down from the buggy.

She smoothed her gloves and squared her shoulders before approaching the beckoning red door. A seagull squawked overhead and swooped low over evergreen huckleberry. Maybe they weren't home. She planted her foot on the steps and marched to the door. There was no bell, so she rapped with the knocker. Moments later she heard the sound of light footsteps.

A young woman about her age opened the door. Dressed in a light-gray skirt and white pin-tucked blouse, she wore a smile that welcomed Addie. Her dark hair was in a fashionable pompadour. Very Gibson Girlish.

One brow lifted. "Hello. May I help you?" Her eyes darted over Addie's shoulder to the buggy.

"I'm Addie Sullivan."

The woman's blue eyes widened along with her smile. "Addie! We spoke on the phone this morning. I'm Katie. Come in." She opened the door wider. "I assume Mrs. Eaton sent you? She could have called, but I'm so glad you came instead."

Were they expecting a message from the Eatons? "Not exactly," she said. Oh, she shouldn't have come.

"Mama will be so pleased you've come by."

Addie stepped onto the wood floor. A staircase in the entry rose to the second story. There was a doorway off the hall on both sides, and one at the back.

"We're just about to have some tea. I do hope you'll join us." Katie led her to the room on Addie's right.

Wasn't Katie going to ask why she had come or how she'd found the house? She hadn't called ahead to find out if this was their at-home day. She followed the young woman into a parlor decorated with a blue velvet settee and chairs arranged around a fireplace. The Eastlake tables were a bit heavy for Addie's taste, considering the delicate chairs. A piano occupied one corner of the room.

The woman on the settee had a throw over her legs. Her smile was as warm as her daughter's. She wore a pale-blue gown, and her hair was up in a French twist.

"Mama, this is Addie Sullivan," Katie said. "The new household member at the Eaton estate."

"I recognized the name the moment you said it," Mrs. Russell said. She put her feet on the floor and patted the space beside her on the settee. "What a delightful surprise."

Addie perched on the cushion. "I know this is quite an imposition," she began.

"Nonsense," Katie said, pouring tea into a cup. "Sugar?"

Addie nodded. "One, please." She accepted the tea after Katie stirred in the cube. "I'm sure you're wondering why I'm here," she said. There was an awkward pause, and Addie searched for a way to ask the questions burning on her tongue. "I was allowed the use of Laura Eaton's desk," she said. "It's so beautiful."

Neither of the other women remarked at her comment, and she knew it was going to be difficult to explain. Mrs. Russell might be an ally. She'd been best friends with Laura. An inner conviction grew that she needed to be honest. There was no other way to explain her appearance here.

"Maybe I should begin at the beginning," she said.

Nineteen

ADDIE TOOK A gulp of tea so hot it scalded her tongue. Her heart hammered loud enough she was sure they had to hear.

Tell them.

She resisted the impulse to pour out her circumstances, but the compassion in Mrs. Russell's eyes held her riveted. The entire story surged to her throat. She set her tea on the table beside her. "I'm not here because Mrs. Eaton sent me. She has no idea how I'm spending my afternoon off."

The two women exchanged glances. "Is something wrong, my dear?" Mrs. Russell asked.

Addie clutched her gloved hands in her lap. "You must set aside all you think you know," she said.

"About what?" Katie peeked at her mother. They both wore puzzled frowns.

"About what happened twenty-three years ago."

Mrs. Russell's brows gathered, and she stared at Addie. "Twenty-three years ago," she said. "My daughter was born. My best friend drowned. It's a time I remember quite vividly."

Surely Laura's best friend wouldn't betray her daughter. Addie so desperately needed a friend, someone she could lean on. She held Mrs. Russell's gaze for a long moment. "I believe I am Julia Eaton."

Mrs. Russell's eyes seemed to swallow up her

face. Her hand wadded up the throw on her lap. "Julia died. Drowned with her mother. How dare you come here and say such a thing?" She searched Addie's face, and her tone lacked conviction.

"I assure you I was shocked as well," Addie said.

Mrs. Russell rubbed her forehead. "Julia. Julia was only two wh-when it happened."

"My father found a baby onshore after a horrendous shipwreck," Addie said. "He believed that baby was Julia Eaton."

"Why would he believe that?"

"Someone paid him to keep the child. Me. And he was curious enough that he subscribed to the San Francisco newspaper to read about any missing persons. I have the article about the boat going down, about the search for Laura and Julia Eaton."

"Is this some kind of plan to blackmail Henry? You should know he's a hard man to cross."

Addie shook her head violently. "I just want the truth, Mrs. Russell. You loved my mother. That's why I'm here. I have nowhere to turn, no one to help me find out what happened."

Mrs. Russell's eyes softened and grew luminous as she studied Addie's face. "You have the look of Laura in some vague way I can't put my finger on. The dimple, the eyes. Your hair color is different, but . . ." She put her hand to her mouth. "What of Laura?" she whispered.

"I don't know."

Mrs. Russell winced. "My poor Laura," she said. "She loved her baby so much."

Addie's eyes burned. "That's what I've heard. I want to know about her."

"Laura was a lovely girl. Just lovely. Full of life and fun. All the men were quite mad over her. She was invited to a party nearly every night."

"What about my father, Mr. Eaton?"

"Henry was smitten the moment he laid eyes on her. I was surprised when Laura responded to his pursuit."

"Why?"

Mrs. Russell took a sip of her tea. "He was a tradesman, and she was from money. But Henry always had big dreams, and he inspired her with his goals and plans."

Addie's pulse leaped, and she leaned forward. "My mother had the money? Not my father? I knew he didn't come from money, but I thought he had amassed a fortune by the time he met her."

"Oh my, no. But Henry knew what he wanted."

"Did he marry her for her money?"

"No, no. He was crazy in love with her. There was never any doubt about that."

Katie picked up her tea. "Where have you been all this time, Addie?"

"On a lighthouse station. North of here. My father was the lightkeeper. My mother took over the job when he died of consumption five years ago."

Katie sipped her tea. "When did you find out that you were really Julia?"

"Not yet two weeks ago. The day before I came here." A lifetime ago. All she thought she knew, the memories, the heritage, was gone. Her future was just as uncertain.

"Does Mr. Eaton know?" Katie asked.

Addie shook her head. "No one knows but Mr. Driscoll. And Lieutenant North."

"Why haven't you told Henry?" Mrs. Russell asked.

Addie bit her lip. "Mr. Driscoll wants to find out who had paid for my upkeep all these years. He thought keeping quiet would be best, until we found out what was going on."

Mrs. Russell stared into space. "Laura came to me the day before she left. She said she'd discovered something terrible. Something she couldn't live with."

"Did she say what it was?"

Mrs. Russell shook her head. "She refused to tell me. She promised to write, but I never heard from her after that." Her voice grew choked, and she pulled a flowered hankie from her sleeve and wiped her eyes. Her lips thinned. "Rumors went around town that she was crazy. That girl was the most sane person I knew. Something dreadful happened. You can count on us, my dear. We will defend you with our last breath. Isn't that so, Katie?"

"Absolutely," Katie said. Her blue eyes glowed.

Why had Addie even questioned the Lord's prompting? He had always guided her. Having friends infused her with new strength.

What a way to end a day off. Addie would rather not have had to face her mother. The foghorn sounded as the sun sank over the ocean, and it would have been a lovely sound to Addie if she'd been sure of her welcome. The glare from the lighthouse washed out over the white foam hitting the rocks. She inhaled the salty air.

Her stomach plunged. She turned and glanced at the lighthouse. Addie waved. What would she call her now? Mama? Josephine? Addie wished she'd never come.

Her mother waved back and navigated the rocky path from the lighthouse to the buggy where they stood. "Girlie, you don't look any the worse for wear."

"I'm not," she said, hugging her mother before she could help herself. Josephine held herself stiffly as always, her arms at her sides.

"Come along," her mother said, stepping away almost before Addie had a chance to inhale the familiar scent of kerosene that clung to her mother's clothing.

Neither she nor her mother spoke until they were settled in the parlor with a plate of cookies and milk. The cookies were fresh, and she knew

Josephine had made them just for her. The cold milk left a creamy taste on her tongue that banished the bitterness of facing a mother who disliked her.

"What have you discovered, Addie?" her mother asked. "Do you know yet who paid for your upkeep?"

"Not yet. Mr. Eaton is a man who demands his own way. He's married to my mother's sister, Clara." She wanted to call back the title "mother" when she saw Josephine wince. Though the woman had hurt her, Addie didn't want to cause any pain. "She enjoys the money and privilege. Lieutenant North was married to her daughter, Katherine. She died in a trolley accident three years ago."

"Does anyone suspect who you are?"

"I told John two days ago. My employer," she added.

Josephine gave her a sharp look. "John? He has given you permission to use his first name?"

She bit her lip. "Not exactly." She rushed on to change the subject. "Did you want to see me for a special reason?"

"You're my daughter. Isn't that enough?"

"You've never really accepted me as your child. That much is finally clear to me."

Josephine's lips tightened. "And I regret that. I was too harsh, girlie. Your father frowned at me from heaven."

"I tried everything to make you love me." Addie's throat closed.

Her mother sniffed. "Love can't be forced. We are too different. You have a tender heart. I fear the Eatons will try to mold you into one of them. Your father would hate that."

"I'll still be his daughter. They can't take out what he put in."

"Power has a way of corrupting, and few people are immune."

She laughed. "Power? That's hardly a situation I'll discover myself in. When Mr. Eaton finds out the truth, he'll be more likely to discharge me."

"You're his flesh and blood, Addie. That means a lot to a man like him."

"Edward is much more likely to be the apple of his grandfather's eye."

"What is your evaluation of Henry Eaton?"

Addie stiffened. What was the point of all this questioning? "He is nothing like Papa. He's loud and flamboyant. Likes all the toys his money can buy. Why, he even has an automobile! The house is filled with things. Expensive paintings and figurines. Silk lampshades and sofas. Rugs that cost the earth."

Josephine gave a disapproving *humph*. "Sounds too grand for the likes of you. Do you feel out of place?"

She considered the question. "Not really. I've been too busy trying to see what I could find out."

"It doesn't appear you discovered much."

"I will, though."

Josephine glanced at the clock, then rose. "Need to wind the light," she said.

"I'll come with you." Addie followed her out the back and to the door leading to the light tower. The metal steps clanged under their feet as they ascended. Josephine checked the kerosene light and filled it, then pulled the chain on the clock-work mechanism that rotated the lens.

"All set for two hours," she said. She squinted in the twilight. "That railing needs to be secured better. It's about to fall off."

Addie studied Josephine's face. "Why did you really ask me to come?"

Josephine pressed her lips together. "Someone broke in before I left Battery Point. Whoever it was riffled through Roy's desk. I fear it had something to do with you."

Addie raised her hand to her throat. "Was anything taken?"

Josephine shook her head. "Not money. I think some of the things Roy had saved about your situation are missing, but I'm not sure."

"They took no valuables?"

Josephine laughed. "What was there to take? I have no valuables, girlie."

"Your wedding ring and Papa's watch."

"They were in the lap drawer. The intruder left those."

The wind picked up as the sun sank in the west. Addie's dress billowed as they started back to the front of the house. "So it didn't appear to be a normal break-in," Addie pressed.

Josephine gripped her arm. "I admit I'm frightened."

"You weren't harmed?"

"I wasn't home. That's why I decided to take this station. It's closer to town and has a few more neighbors."

Addie had never known Josephine to show fear, not even in the face of a howling storm. She prayed for Josephine's safety as they walked through wisps of fog swirling about their feet.

TWENTY

BY THE TIME Addie returned to Eaton Manor, it was time for Edward's evening meal, but he wasn't in his room. Addie checked the playroom, then the bathroom. No small boy. After yesterday's scare, he wouldn't be outside. The servants now guarded the doors. Her fingers trailed along the smooth redwood of the banister on her way to the first floor. She stopped his nurse, who was carrying a basket of Edward's laundry toward the back kitchen, and asked if she'd seen Edward. The nurse told her he was in his grandfather's study.

Mr. Eaton was in the salon, having his evening claret. He would not take kindly to his grandson's intrusion. Addie went past the drawing room to the third door on the left. Mr. Eaton's study. Peeking past the open paneled door, she saw Edward seated behind the polished desk. "Edward, what are you doing in here?" she asked, approaching.

"Looking for Gideon," the boy said. "I couldn't find him anywhere." He stood and clapped his hands, and Gideon padded to him.

She held out her hand. "Come, dear, before your granddad finds you in here. I suspect he wouldn't be pleased."

A picture on a shelf of the bookcase caught her eye, one she hadn't seen last time she was in here. She picked it up. A young woman in a white dress sat on the porch steps with a small girl in her lap. Addie caught her breath and stared into the child's face. The curly hair, the wide eyes, even the dimple in the right cheek told her she was looking at herself. She saw the same dimple on the woman's face, but her hair appeared lighter and straighter, her face more rounded.

Her mother. The certainty grew along with the lump in her throat.

A locket around the woman's neck caught her attention, and Addie's fingers outlined the one nestled inside her dress. She tugged it out, and the heat of her skin warmed it in her hand. Every flourish, every detail, was as familiar to her as the lines in her palm.

Gideon whined, then began to bark. She turned

from the desk in time to see the dog take hold of the waist of Edward's pants and tug him to the ground. "Edward, are you all right?"

The dog licked Edward's face, and the boy giggled. When he started to get up, Gideon nudged him, then put his paws on the lad's chest. Edward lay down, and his smile faded.

"I don't feel good," he mumbled.

She dropped to her knees beside him. "Edward?" His hand grabbed at her as his eyes rolled back in his head.

"Help! Somebody help!" she shouted. With the boy cradled in her lap, she breathed a quick prayer. Was this another episode of epilepsy or something else?

Footsteps pounded in the hall. Mr. Eaton careened through the door with his hair tousled. "What is it?" His gaze went to his grandson. "He's having a fit!" He fell to his knees and pulled the boy off her lap to lie flat on the floor.

As Mr. Eaton slid Edward away, Addie felt a pain in her neck and realized the child had her locket clutched in his hand. The chain gave way, and the pain subsided, but the necklace dangled from Edward's clenched fingers.

"There, my boy," Mr. Eaton said, smoothing the hair back from his grandson's forehead. "Wake up, Edward."

The child's eyelids fluttered, but he didn't awaken. His hand flailed, and the gold chain hit

Mr. Eaton in the cheek. Addie gasped and tried to grab it, but the man's fingers pried it from the lad's fist first.

Mr. Eaton stilled as he examined the locket. "Where did he get this?" he demanded.

Addie put her hands to her throat, where the skin burned. She couldn't force a word past her dry lips. Waves of heat rose in her chest.

"It's yours?"

"It was my mother's," she said.

His fingers clenched around the locket. "Your mother's," he echoed. "Who are you?"

"Addie Sullivan."

He pried open the locket to reveal the picture inside. "This is Vera's picture in your locket." His voice was hoarse.

His eyes widened, and his gaze went back to her face. "Where did you come from?"

Should she tell him everything she knew? She eyed his tight mouth. He might throw her out. "The man I know as my father was a lightkeeper. I grew up at Battery Point." She caught herself before she revealed Mr. Driscoll's involvement. "My mother recently revealed that my father found me after a shipwreck."

Mr. Eaton gasped and reared back. "Laura," he whispered. "My dear Laura." Moisture filled his eyes.

His obvious emotion brought tears to her eyes. Everything she'd heard was true. He'd loved her mother very much, but what about her? "That necklace was around my neck."

"So you're . . . Julia?"

She swallowed past the tight muscles in her throat and searched his expression for a hint of joy. "I suspect that is so."

Sternness replaced the longing in his eyes. "Is this a scheme to take my money?" he asked. "How did you get this locket? The truth, now!"

"I told you everything I know, sir," she whispered. "My mother swears it is so. I myself have no memory of that night, though I have a dreadful fear of storms."

"It might be true," he said. He glanced at the still-sleeping Edward, then stumbled to his feet. "Your father. I must speak with him."

"He died of consumption five years ago. My mother took over for him, but she transferred to Mercy Point Lighthouse this week. Her name is Josephine Sullivan." She touched Edward's warm cheek. "What of Edward?"

"He will awaken soon. I'll send his grandmother to him. I want you to come with me."

"Yes, sir," she said. "Might I have my locket back?"

His features hardened, then he dropped the necklace into her outstretched palm.

Did his passion for her mother extend to her? She prayed it was so. Her pulse galloped at the thought that she might finally be welcomed into the bosom of the family she longed for.

• • •

The automobile rattled over the potholes in the dirt road that led to the lighthouse. Addie held on to her hat when the bottom of the machine dipped and swayed. Riding in this thing wasn't as much fun as she'd expected. She felt bounced like a badminton birdie. The car tore along the street at such a fast clip that she'd been hard pressed to keep the wind from ripping her clothes. She suspected they were traveling more than twenty miles an hour.

She sneaked a peek at Mr. Eaton. His jaw was grim, and both hands gripped the steering wheel. She caught him stealing glimpses of her from the corner of his eye. Perhaps he suspected she was an imposter.

He cleared his throat. "You have th-the look of Laura," he said.

"So Mr. Driscoll said."

He lapsed into silence again. The automobile lurched around a corner, then down a hill before stopping at the footpath to the lighthouse. He clambered from the automobile and extended his hand to help her down. She prayed she wasn't reading too much into the way he held on to her fingers a few moments longer than was necessary.

"This way," she said. She led the way up the hill past purple wildflowers blooming on the slopes. The waves crashed against the shore, and she drew a deep breath of salty air. In an instant, the tension in her shoulders eased, and her erratic breathing evened out. The rocky path led to the house, and she opened the door.

"Josephine?" she called.

Mr. Eaton turned to stare at her, and she realized how odd this was. She'd just told him about her parents, yet she called her mother by her Christian name. Turning from his questioning eyes, she led him across the painted board floors to the parlor. "Josephine?" she called again.

The stillness confused her. After rising at three in the afternoon, her mother was usually bustling around, polishing the lenses and preparing for another long night of tending to the light. The parlor was empty. So was the kitchen. She hurried up the steps and checked the bedrooms. No sign of her mother.

After returning downstairs, she stepped through the kitchen to the back door. Mr. Eaton followed her onto the stoop. Sea spray misted her face. The tide was rolling in, leaving flotsam on the rocks as the waves ran back to the depths, gleaming in the moonlight. She cupped her lips and shouted for her mother. No voice replied except for the squawk of two seagulls soaring in the blue sky.

"Perhaps she went to town," Mr. Eaton suggested.

She shook her head. "Not at this hour."

"Could she be down at the water? Or in the tower checking something?"

She peered toward the light tower attached to the back of the home. "It would be unusual for her to be there now, but not impossible. I shall check. Would you like to come with me or stay here?"

"I'll escort you."

The tower would likely be accessed from upstairs. She climbed the stairs and found the access door at the end of the hall. "Josephine!" she called up the steps. Her words echoed against the round walls. "I don't think she's here."

"Shall we ascend to make sure?"

"She would have heard me." Addie studied the open network of the iron staircase but could see nothing. Mr. Eaton put his foot on the first step, then glanced at her, as if seeking permission. She nodded and followed him up the circular stairway. The metal clanged as their shoes struck the treads. The noise reminded her of a mourning bell.

The air was close and stale. As they neared the top, the scent of kerosene grew stronger, but it was carried on the wind of some fresh air. Her steps quickened, and she lifted her skirts to prevent tripping. She came up against Mr. Eaton's broad back. His arm came out and prevented her from stepping onto the platform. "What is it?" she asked.

"You stay here a moment, Miss Sullivan." He planted his other foot onto the metal floor, then disappeared from her sight.

In spite of his admonishment, she followed him. At first his bulk blocked the view of the floor where he knelt. Then he stood, and her gaze fell on the still figure there.

Josephine lay face forward. The back of her head didn't look right. Addie put her hand to her mouth when she realized that blood matted Josephine's hair. A scream tried to escape from her mouth but lodged somewhere below her Adam's apple.

"Mama?" she finally managed to whisper. She moved closer.

Mr. Eaton blocked her from reaching her mother. "I'm most sorry, Miss Eaton, but I fear she's dead."

A wave of dizziness assaulted her. "Dead? You must be wrong. Let me tend to her. I can help her."

She evaded Mr. Eaton's hands and knelt beside Josephine. When Addie touched her, her skin was cold, so cold.

It was only then that the scream managed to rip free from her throat.

TWENTY-ONE

ADDIE SAT ON the sofa with her hands clasped together. So much needed to be done. Josephine's body would need to be prepared and a casket found. The lighthouse would need to be cleaned and the parlor readied for the funeral.

Who would come? Sadly, few people knew her mother, as she was new to the area. Perhaps she should arrange a quiet burial. Her fingers tightened. Money. It would take money to bury Josephine. She supposed she had money in a bank somewhere, but the thought of digging through the Sullivans' personal affairs made her shudder. Still, it had to be done.

A cup of tea might fortify her. In the kitchen, she put loose tea in a tea infuser, then dropped it into a cup and poured hot water from the teakettle sitting on the woodstove. While it steeped, she stepped to the back door and peered out onto the lawn, where the constable stood talking to Mr. Eaton.

Mr. Eaton had taken his automobile to the neighbors for help. They'd called the constable. Addie's mind didn't want to examine why a constable had been necessary, but she forced herself to consider the circumstances.

Murder. Josephine had been murdered. Someone had hit her on the back of the head. A sob escaped her lips. Through the window she saw Mr. Eaton follow the constable toward the back door. She opened it as they neared.

Mr. Eaton's expression was grim as he shut the door behind the constable. "Ah, tea. So thoughtful of you, my dear. Three sugars, please."

She lifted the infuser from the cup and added sugar, then handed the tea to him. Her own desire for a cup of tea had vanished. "Do you know who did this?" she asked the constable.

The man removed his hands from his pockets and shook his head. His round spectacles made him look like President Teddy Roosevelt. "We will investigate, but I have little hope. The lighthouse has no near neighbors. Did your mother have any enemies?"

So he suspected murder. She forced down her nausea. "Not that I know of. She just moved here."

He glanced around. "Is there anything missing?"

"I haven't looked." She rubbed her head. "I've not been thinking."

"Would you accompany me as I look around?"

"Of course." She sent a plea toward Mr. Eaton, who was sipping his tea.

"I shall assist as well." He drained his cup, then set it on the table. "Where did your . . . she keep her money?"

Mr. Eaton didn't want to call Josephine her mother. In other circumstances, it might have been funny. "The study is across the hall from the sitting room. I'll show you."

The house seemed so empty. Their footsteps bounced off the walls and floors in an eerie tattoo. She pushed open the door to the study and gasped. Papers lay strewn on the floor, and drawers hung open. She picked up her mother's favorite globe, chipped and broken, and held it to her chest. Words escaped her.

The constable took spectacles from his pocket and placed them on his nose. "It appears the perpetrator was looking for something." He picked up a sheaf of papers and began to sift through them.

Addie's head swam, and she rounded the desk to drop into the chair. The left drawer hung open. Her father's money box still lay inside. She lifted it out and turned the key. Inside, she found stacks of money and coins.

"The murderer wasn't after money," she said, holding the box out to the constable. "When I was here this afternoon, Josephine said this had been hidden, but it's in plain view now."

"It's all there?"

"I don't know how much she had, but there's over a hundred dollars here."

Another officer poked his head in the doorway. "Sir, the coroner is here."

The constable made notes. "I'd be obliged if you would make a note of anything you find missing. I need to speak to the coroner." He exited the room behind the officer.

Mr. Eaton lifted a paper from the floor and scanned it. "Is there anything here to validate your claim as my offspring?"

Could he not bring himself to say *daughter?* "Josephine showed me some newspaper clippings. They were here in the lap drawer." She yanked it out and riffled through the contents.

He moved to stand at her right arm. "Let me see."

She sorted one more time, then leaned back. "They're not here."

He sat heavily in the chair. "Then there is no proof of your claim."

She clutched the locket in her pocket. "There is this," she said.

He fixed a stare on her. "You wouldn't be the first pretty face to try to hoodwink me."

Heat ran up her neck, but she refused to let her gaze drop. "Sir, I know nothing beyond what was told to me."

"Which was?"

"That Roy Sullivan found me on the beach."

"What else?" he prodded.

"He was paid to care for me."

She heard Mr. Eaton's quick inhalation, and her pulse ratcheted up. Of course. The person who had killed Josephine had paid for her upkeep. It made perfect sense. The culprit feared being exposed and having to face her father's wrath. "The money is still here, but the newspaper article is gone." Where else might her mother have hidden proof of their story?

She leaned forward. "This desk has a secret drawer."

Once, her father had shown her how to find the spot, and when she was a child, she used to hide under this desk and press the access tab for fun. She'd never looked inside. Kneeling under the desk, she ran her fingers over the wood until she found the button. When she pressed it, the drawer sprang open. She lifted out the tray inside, then scrambled to her feet and laid it on the desk.

Mr. Eaton hovered over her shoulder as she sorted through the contents. On the blotter she laid out a bank book, some bills, an envelope of photos, and a copy of a birth certificate inscribed with the name Julia Eaton. The birth date was Addie's own.

John glanced at his timepiece, then returned it to its home. "You have no idea where they went?"

Clara shook her head. "They rushed out and left a message with Molly that they'd return as soon as they could. It's been hours."

John put his hands in his pockets. He could go through some files in Henry's office while he waited. Some of the numbers at the bank weren't adding up, and he needed to talk to Henry about them.

The front door slammed, and Henry's voice called, "Clara, come here."

Clara started to get up, but John shook his head. "I'll help him." He stepped into the hall and found Henry holding Addie by the arm. She swayed where she stood, and even her lips were pale.

"What's happened?" John asked. "Has there been an accident?"

Henry hesitated. "Murder," he said. "Miss Sullivan's mother was murdered at the lighthouse today."

The young woman's eyes welled with tears. John stepped to her side. "I'm sorry, Addie," he said. "Is there anything I can do?"

Her reddened eyes closed, then she shook her head. "The police are investigating."

"Where is Clara?" Henry asked.

"In the parlor."

"Come with me. You all should hear this at once." Henry led Addie into the parlor, where he seated her in a chair.

"Henry, where have you been?" Clara demanded in an indignant voice.

Henry seated himself beside her and patted her hand without glancing at her. "It has been a most extraordinary day," he said. "In many ways."

A faraway expression dimmed John's father-in-law's eyes, and he kept glancing at Addie.

"A most extraordinary thing," Henry murmured. "It appears Miss Sullivan is my daughter."

John tensed as Clara shrieked and fainted onto the sofa. He sprang to her assistance. The maid rushed in with rose water, and he dabbed Clara's handkerchief in it and ran it over her face. "Clara." He patted her cheeks.

"She'll be fine," Henry said. "You don't seem surprised, John. Were you aware of this situation?"

John rose and propped Clara's head on a throw pillow and lifted her feet to the sofa. "I was. Miss Sullivan confided in me a few days ago."

Henry glowered. "So I'm the last to know?"

"No, sir," Addie said quickly. "Mr. Driscoll knows because he found me, but I've told only Lieutenant North."

"Walter knows and said nothing? Why did neither of you tell me?"

Her eyes flashed an appeal toward John, and he sprang to her defense. "Miss Sullivan wanted more proof. She knew you would demand something more than a locket."

"She's quite right too. And we found more."

He withdrew something from his inner jacket pocket and plunked it down on the coffee table.

Three sets of eyes pinned Addie to her chair. She tried to decipher the emotion she saw in John's eyes before deciding it was compassion. She longed to clasp his hand and draw strength from him for the coming ordeal.

Mrs. Eaton had been brought around. With her complexion pale and a light sheen of perspiration on her forehead, she lay back against the cushions, uttering an occasional moan and an "oh dear."

"Buck up, Clara," Henry said. "This is quite an unusual situation, and I shall need your full attention."

She brought her lace hankie to her nose. "What nonsense is this, Henry?"

Mr. Eaton removed his jacket and unbuttoned his vest. He filled his pipe and lit it. Drawing in two quick puffs, he sighed and turned back toward his wife. "Little Julia didn't die in the shipwreck." He gestured toward Addie. "There she sits."

Addie wanted to be anywhere but here. She was

aware how it appeared—as though she'd sneaked into the household under false pretenses in order to gain something from them. All she wanted was a family.

"Is this what you're claiming, Addie?" Mrs. Eaton asked. "That you're Julia Eaton?"

"I think Mr. Driscoll should be here," Addie said. "He might be able to explain it better than I." Addie heard footsteps, then Mr. Driscoll stepped into the room.

"What's going on?" he asked.

Mr. Eaton puffed furiously on his pipe. "Addie here tells me that you brought her into the house, knowing she was my daughter. Would you care to explain yourself?"

Mr. Driscoll's gaze moved from person to person. "Someone paid the lightkeeper to care for Addie. To keep her from this house."

Mrs. Eaton gasped. "Paid to keep her away? What could be the reason?"

Mr. Driscoll shrugged. "That is what I wanted to find out. I kept her true identity hidden because I feared if I brought her here, her life might be in danger."

"Her life?" Mrs. Eaton scoffed. "No one would harm her."

"Walter has a valid point," Mr. Eaton said. "After all, someone attacked her. And now someone has killed her adopted mother."

Addie stood and clutched her hands together.

"What if the attack on me in the forest was deliberate and had nothing to do with Mr. Driscoll's attack?"

"We don't yet know what happened to your mother," Mr. Eaton said. "Sit down, child. You're overwrought."

Addie had seen no real sign of joy from him. No warm hug. No tears of relief. He'd simply announced her existence to the family as if she were trying to shock them. She supposed it would take a while for the truth to sink in. The last time he'd seen her, she had been a child of two. How could she expect him to entertain warm thoughts of her when for all these years he thought she was dead? She glanced at John and found him studying her with troubled eyes. Did he harbor new questions about her motives, or would he trust that she wanted nothing more than to know and love her family?

Mrs. Eaton clenched her small fist. "So you slipped into the house to spy on everyone here?"

"No!" she said. "I mean, I want to know who I am. I wanted to learn about my mother. I had no idea I wasn't Addie Sullivan until Mr. Driscoll showed up."

John focused on Mr. Driscoll. "How did you come to find Miss Sullivan?"

Mr. Driscoll gestured to Addie. "Show them the locket."

Her icy fingers found the locket in the pocket of her dress, and she held it out.

"It's just a locket," Mrs. Eaton said.

"It was Laura's," Mr. Driscoll said. "I gave it to her myself." He took the necklace from Addie's fingers. "Look. Here is her mother's picture." He opened it and showed it to Mrs. Eaton.

Mrs. Eaton stared at it. "It is Vera," she whispered. Her hands shook when she handed it back.

"Exactly," Mr. Eaton said.

"How do we know this locket didn't wash up on shore? Maybe she found it and thought it would be a suitable way to insinuate herself into the family," Mrs. Eaton said.

"How could she have known of Vera's identity or her connection to us?" Walter asked. "Also, I discovered more proof today, but let me recap how I found Adeline. A friend showed me her photographs taken on her vacation along the north shore. She was so proud of them. I indulged her and flipped through them. This picture caught my attention." He handed a picture to Mr. Eaton.

The photograph shook in Mr. Eaton's hand. "She looks very much like Laura in this."

"The lighting favors that impression. But the way she stood, the curve of her cheek. They were enough to draw me to investigate. When I met Adeline, I saw the locket and was certain."

Addie saw the picture over her father's shoulder. She'd only heard about it until now. Mr. Driscoll must have been busy gathering proof. "What did you find today?" she asked.

Mr. Driscoll reached into his pocket. "Here are two pictures of Addie. One at age three and one at eight. Compare it to the picture of Julia at two. The one in the newspaper clipping."

Addie's mouth gaped. She hadn't been aware he had them. Josephine must have supplied them to him.

John reached for the photos. His brows gathered as he studied them. "There's no doubt it's the same child," he said, passing the photos to Mrs. Eaton.

She gave them a cursory glance and handed them to her husband. "What is it you want, Miss Sullivan?"

The older woman's stiff return to a formal mode of address signaled her displeasure, and Addie clasped her hands together once more. Any hope she had for a warm reception into the bosom of her family evaporated like the morning fog.

"I'd prayed for a warm welcome," Addie managed to say past the boulder in her throat.

Mrs. Eaton dabbed at her eyes. "Of course, if we were sure you really are Julia, it would be different. I fear I don't quite believe you yet."

Mr. Eaton glowered. "How can you argue with these pictures, Clara?" He turned toward Addie with a smile. "I don't quite know what to say, my dear. But I'm very glad you're home."

When he enveloped Addie in a hug, she hardly

knew how to react. She inhaled the smoky scent of his pipe tobacco and the spicy hair tonic clinging to him, then put her arms around him and hugged him back. The awkwardness grew until he released her and stepped back.

"Might I see the pictures?" she asked. When he handed them over, she stared with fascination at her younger self. Any lingering doubt she might have had vanished when she saw her three-year-old self compared to two-year-old Julia. In the older picture, she stood in the front of the lighthouse with Roy. Her gaze lingered on the father of her childhood.

Mr. Eaton held out his hand for the pictures when she was done. "We must celebrate tonight," he said. "A night on the town! I'm taking you all to dinner."

"It's been an upsetting day," Addie said. "I really am not up to it." Though Josephine hadn't really loved her, Addie still mourned.

"We'll come home early," Mr. Eaton said. "We'll dine in a private room."

She couldn't bear the thought of more scrutiny, more questions. Her head throbbed, and she had never been so weary. "Very well," she said. She smoothed her plain gray skirt. "What should I wear?" she asked.

Mrs. Eaton rose. "Come with me. I shall find you something suitable. We can't have my niece not in the very top of fashion."

"Not black," her father called after them. "This is a celebration."

It wasn't a celebration for her. It was acceptance of a sort. Though not the homecoming she'd hoped for.

TWENTY-TWO

GASLIGHTS GLITTERED OVER sparkling crystal and fine china in the private dining room at the Colony Bay Restaurant. Through the large plate-glass windows, John watched the water on the bay reflect the lights along the boardwalk. He couldn't get his mind around the fact that the beautiful young woman beside him was his wife's half sister.

Addie took a sip from her water glass. The tension radiated from her shoulders and showed in the tight press of her lips. She hadn't smiled since they'd been seated. She was a true Eaton tonight. Her hair was piled onto her head, and a tiny beret perched on her curls. The emerald gown was lavish with lace and glitter.

Several men came up to talk to Henry. "Lord Carrington, please join us," Henry said.

John wanted to roll his eyes. He watched the English lord bow over Addie's hand. The man's interest was palpable. John couldn't gauge how Addie felt. When he couldn't take any more, he rose and held out his hand to Addie. "Would you care for an after-dinner stroll along the waterfront, Addie?"

She sent a relieved smile his way, then rose and put her gloved hand on his proffered arm. "We'll meet you at the carriage later," he told Henry.

He led Addie out past the soft murmur of laughter and voices in the main salon, to the doors, and onto the waterfront. The soft waves lapped at the shore but failed to drain away the anger that had built in him through the evening. There was no reason for it. She'd confessed to him before the news came out, but watching her step into the bosom of the Eaton family sickened him. And it was all about how they'd change her. He knew what was in store for her and wished he could abort it.

He stopped under a gaslight. "It's about to begin, Addie. They'll try to make you just like Katherine. She wanted the biggest house, the most glamorous clothes, the most expensive buggy."

"Money means nothing to me, but family means everything. I never knew my sister, so her behavior has nothing to do with me."

In the wash of golden light, he studied the curve of her cheek, the shape of her eyes. "Now that I know, I'm astounded I didn't see the resemblance. You're an Eaton through and through."

She winced. "You say that as though it's a curse. You're part of the family as well. As is your son."

He touched her cheek, so soft under his fingers.

"A fact I would be swift to change if I could. You're too good for them." He dropped his hand and began to walk again. He steered her toward the pier. "How will all your talk of God and praying fit in with this family whose god is possessions?"

Her gloved fingers tightened on his arm. "God is the most important thing in my life."

"I expect that to change very quickly. Henry will have plans for you. You'll be expected to live up to the Eaton name."

"I'll always be Addie Sullivan," she said. "Nothing will change that. Can't you understand my desire to know my roots?"

"They'll make it more than that, Addie. Or should I say Julia?"

She shook her head. "I don't answer to that name."

She had no idea how her life was about to change. He clasped her hand tighter. "Henry will be quick to call you Julia."

He stopped at the edge of the pier. Lanterns glowed upon the yachts out for an evening sail. The slap of the waves against the boards under their feet should have been peaceful but only contrasted with the storm of emotion he somehow kept in check. Her perfume mingled with the scent of brine. Somehow he'd begun to care about her. That was the real reason for the emotion churning his gut. Things would change now. Henry would want her to marry money, a title. John could see it coming.

She was close, so close. Her eyes widened and grew luminous in the light. He saw her hitch in a breath. Her gaze dropped to his mouth, and he knew she felt the same attraction he did.

He took her shoulders and pulled her to him. Her palms lay against his vest. He bent his head. Her lips were soft and tasted of the cinnamon apples she'd had for dessert. Her hands stole around his neck, and he drank in the sweet taste of her, the way her softness molded against him. Taking his time, he pulled her closer and deepened the passion sparking between them. Her glove moved up and cupped his face, and her breath stirred his skin.

He broke the embrace and stepped away. "We should go back."

Her kiss was untrained, and he knew she was as innocent of men as she seemed. This might have been her first kiss. And he found himself wishing he could do it all over again.

The household slept. Though Addie was exhausted, she kept replaying the kiss she'd shared with John earlier in the evening. She touched her lips and swung her legs out of bed.

Her mother's desk might distract her. She made her way quietly to the schoolroom. The white paint glowed in the shaft of moonlight slanting through the window. The thought of what was in the drawer hadn't been far from her mind all evening. It seemed even more important tonight, having lost the mother who had raised her. She needed a knife or a letter opener to get it open. She slipped into the hallway. It was pitch black, and she had to feel her way down the stairs. She found a letter opener in her father's desk drawer, then returned to the schoolroom.

She turned the wick of the gaslight higher when she entered. The light chased the shadows from the room. She sat in front of the writing desk, then fit the edge of the letter opener into the crack of the hidden drawer. Patiently, she pried at the panel until it gave a bit; then she used her fingers and managed to pop it open the rest of the way.

She reached into the cavity and felt around the space. Paper crackled under her fingers, and she released it from the tape holding it in place. A simple letter in an envelope. That's all. Why would this letter be important enough to hide away? She replaced the panel, then carried the letter over to the light. The envelope was addressed in her mother's familiar looping handwriting.

To Whom It May Concern.

She stared at the words. Was this her mother's last will and testament? Addie hesitated, not knowing whether she had the right to read it. Maybe she should give it to Mr. Eaton. Or Mr. Driscoll. She flipped it over. The flap was loose on the back. Either it had come loose with the passage of time or her mother had never sealed it. She lifted the flap. The letter was right there.

She couldn't resist the temptation. Her goal here was to find out who had paid for her to be kept from her family. This could be a vital clue. She slid out the letter and unfolded it. Her mother's legible writing filled the page.

To Whom It May Concern,

If you are reading this, then I am dead. Or worse. I fear leaving all the evidence in one spot, so I've left it in three places. Sunshine, dust, and pigeons. If you find this, tell no one in this house. Trust no one. Remember me.

Laura Eaton

What could it mean? Addie studied the words. Sunshine. The solarium, perhaps? She glanced at the clock on the fireplace mantel. Nearly midnight. No one would be up and about. Even John shouldn't be prowling around now. She could slip downstairs and search the solarium. It was on the backside of the manor, and she should be able to turn on the lights without alerting anyone to her presence.

She stuffed the letter back into the envelope, then put it in the pocket of her dressing gown. The door creaked when she opened it, and she froze and listened for any movement or noise from the hall. Nothing but silence. She moved to Edward's room and found him peacefully sleeping. He wouldn't miss her dog for a few minutes. Gideon would alert her to the presence of anyone else, though when she heard his nails click on the wood floor, she regretted her decision.

Downstairs, all was silent except for the ticking of the great clock in the entry. She felt her way along the dark hall, past the library and the music room. The door to the solarium stood open, and she stepped inside and turned on the gaslight. The illumination eased the prickles along her back, though the great glass windows reflected the light back at her so that she couldn't see out into the yard. Anyone might be out there watching.

She told Gideon to lie down, then surveyed the space. Where might someone have hidden something that would ensure its invisibility through decades of cleanings and new arrangements? The rattan furniture had cotton cushions that would have been beaten and even replaced in the twenty-three years since Laura ran from here. A couple of tables added style to the furniture. Pots of plants and plant stands lined the windows. There were even three full-grown potted palm trees. Anything hidden in the plants would have rotted.

She turned her gaze to the table and chairs. In the Eastlake style, their ostentatious ornamentation could maybe house a hiding place. She pulled out a chair and examined it. The cushions matched the settee and were removable. She lifted up the cushion to reveal the smooth seat. Nothing there. When she turned the chair upside down, she checked the legs and the underside of the seat but found no obvious hiding place. She examined each of the chairs in turn. Nothing. The table held no surprises either.

She should just go back to bed. Rubbing her eyes, she turned to go back to her room. She noticed a music box in the corner. The mahogany case was smooth and unscratched as though it was seldom used. She lifted the lid and it began to tinkle out the tune to the "Wedding March." She closed the lid and lifted the box from the table. Carrying it to the settee, she laid it on its top and examined the underside. There was a tiny cover over something. The clockworks that turned it?

Carefully prying the cover off with a fingernail, she removed it. At first all she saw was gears and wheels. She picked up the box and held it under the light, tipping it this way and that. The light revealed the corner of a piece of paper. She wiggled her fingers into the opening and managed to snag the paper between her index and middle fingers.

The tiny scrap was rolled up tightly. She unwrapped it to reveal two handwritten words.

Insane asylum.

What on earth? What did that have to do with her mother running away?

John couldn't sleep. He kept remembering how soft Addie's lips were, the scent of her breath. He was coming to love her in an intense way he never expected, and he doubted Henry would allow them to marry. With Addie's deep desire for a family, he feared she wouldn't stand up to her father's tyranny either. If she even saw it as tyranny.

He sat on the edge of the bed and noticed a glow through the window. John's room was directly over the conservatory, and there should be no light out there at this hour. He peered out the window and realized the illumination spilled from the house. Someone was in the conservatory.

He put on his robe and slippers, then snatched his pistol from the shelf at the top of his closet before going in search of the meaning of the light. When he reached the conservatory, he found it empty and unlit. But the faint odor of the gaslight still hung in the air, and the globe was warm.

Maybe a thief was on his way out of the house with his booty. John moved quickly toward the back door and found it locked. On his way to check the front door, he noticed a ribbon of light spilling from under the library door.

He brought his gun up and flung open the door. When he saw Addie whirl to face him, he dropped the weapon back to his side. A pile of books lay on the floor at her feet. She'd taken at least fifty from the bookshelves.

He advanced into the room. "Addie, is something wrong?"

She put the book in her hand onto the top of the stack. "You frightened me."

"I'm sorry. I thought someone had broken in. What are you doing down here so late?"

He watched her as the color came and went in her cheeks, and she put one bare foot atop the other. John crossed the three steps separating them to take her in his arms. She nestled against him, her head against a heart that felt as though it would leap from his chest. Her tiny feet stood on top of his slippers, and he bent his head and kissed her again. "I'm glad I came to investigate the light," he murmured against her warm lips.

She returned his kiss, then pulled away. "There's something I must tell you, John." She colored. "I'm sorry. You haven't given me leave to use your Christian name."

"I think the first time I kissed you gave you permission for anything," he said, resisting the urge to pull her back into his arms. He would never get enough of the sweetness of her lips.

Her smile warmed the room more than the gaslight. "I found something, John. In Laura's desk." She pulled a paper out of the pocket of her dressing gown.

He took it and read it. "Your mother wrote this. 'Sunshine, dust, and pigeons.' What does that mean?"

"I found the sunshine clue in the conservatory. It was in the music box." She reached into her pocket again and pulled out a tiny scrap of paper.

He read the two words. " 'Insane asylum'? What could that mean?"

"I don't know. My mother said to tell no one in this house. She obviously feared for her life. I have to know what happened to her."

He embraced her again. "Darling Addie, that was a long time ago. What difference does it make now?"

She lifted anxious eyes to him. "It's not in the past, John. Someone killed the woman who raised me. Someone paid to keep me away from here for twenty-three years."

He pulled her against his chest again. "I won't let anyone hurt you, Addie. I'll help you find out who is behind this."

"I knew you would. That's why I told you," she said against his chest. She pulled back to stare into this face. "How did my father meet Laura and then Clara?"

"He was helping his father in the blacksmith shop and met Laura's father, the senior Mr. Driscoll, who took a shine to him. Mr. Driscoll hired Henry to work at the estate, and he met Clara there. He saw Laura from a distance and was smitten. He arranged for one of her friends to vouch for him."

"Did you meet Laura's father?"

He shook his head. "He died shortly after Henry married Laura."

"What about Laura's mother?"

"She died of childbed fever after Laura was born." He dropped his hands from her shoulders. "Why all these questions, Addie? And why are you poking through these books?"

"I came in here thinking the dust clue might be in the books."

"A good guess." He released her with reluctance, then stepped over to pick up a book. "How far did you get?"

She joined him in front of the bookshelves. "Through all of them. I found nothing."

"We'd better put these back and get to bed. Tomorrow we'll figure out where to look next. We're a team."

"A team," she echoed with a smile breaking out.

But maybe only until Henry got wind of their romance.

TWENTY-THREE

ADDIE CLASPED JOHN'S hand as he escorted her toward her room. She didn't know how to cope with how John made her feel, as though her heart would gallop right out of her chest. She noticed things about him too . . . like how his hair curled at the nape of his neck, and the clean masculine scent of his skin. She wanted to kiss him again.

He stopped outside her closed bedroom door, then reached up and caught a curl around his finger. "He'll try to stop us, Addie."

"Us?" she managed to whisper.

"You're not one to play games, and neither am I. We can't deny we have feelings for each other."

"My father will have to listen to what I want," she said.

He stepped closer. "Has his response been what you expected so far? His goal in life was to marry Katherine to royalty. He nearly had apoplexy when she married me."

"He's rich. What does a title matter?"

"Henry is nouveau riche. He wants the old name to go with it. He'll try to sell you to the highest bidder."

She shifted. Her father couldn't possibly be as bad as John said. "I won't be sold." She took a step back. "I'd hoped for a warmer welcome from him and Mrs. Eaton, though. Has she always been jealous?"

He continued to wind the curl around his finger. "Clara has had a full life with Henry. They raised a child together. You're an unexpected wrinkle from the past, disrupting things. I heard Katherine mention a few times that her mother always felt Henry loved Laura best."

"Why would she think that?"

"Well, he's refused to take down that portrait in the bedroom they used to share. Walter has it now."

"What would you do if you remarried?" she asked. "Would you remove traces of Katherine?"

His bemused smile faded, and he dropped his hand. "I have Edward to think of. He would need reminders of his mother. And that she . . . loved him."

Why had he hesitated? Of course she loved her son. "You said his condition embarrassed her, but I'm sure she adored him."

He pressed his lips together. "What society thought was most important to Katherine."

"Does Edward remember her?"

"He sometimes mentions her. I think he remembers her good-night kisses. That's about the only time he saw her."

Addie tried not to show her horror. How could a mother not care for her child, especially a wounded one like Edward? She resolved to show him even more love and compassion. But firmness too. The lad needed structure and discipline.

John was so close she could feel his body heat radiating across the few inches between them. "I'm sorry if I seem too curious."

The tenderness returned to his eyes. "You can ask me anything, darling. I have no secrets from you."

He brushed his lips across hers, then stepped back before she had time to respond. "Sweet dreams."

"Good night," she murmured, watching him

retreat to his bedroom. When his door shut, she stepped into her room with a smile lingering on her face.

She took a step back when she saw her uncle sitting in the chair by the window. "Mr. Driscoll, what are you doing here?"

He rose. "I think you should start calling me Uncle now, don't you, Adeline?" He smiled.

"Yes, sir. But what are you doing?"

"Waiting on you. I want to know what you were doing in the library."

"Looking for evidence my mother hid."

"Evidence of what?" he asked, his smile fading.

The note had said to tell no one, and though she trusted her uncle, she resolved to honor her mother's request. "About why she left when she did."

"I assumed it was for a trip."

Addie shook her head. "No. She discovered some kind of devastating news. Something she couldn't handle."

"What does that have to do with who paid for your upkeep, Addie? That's our real question."

"I only care about finding more about my mother," she said, choking out the words. "I want to know what happened to make her take that trip."

Mr. Driscoll turned a kind glance on her. "She's dead, my dear. No matter what you find out about her, you can't bring her back."

Her eyes burned, and her throat closed more

tightly. "I have this vague memory of my mother singing." She hummed the song. "Something about hush-a-by baby. I remember her eyes. Green with thick lashes. Her voice was so sweet, and her hands were soft."

His eyes grew moist. "She sang that all the time. Laura was an excellent mother."

"So you must understand why I want to know about her."

He put his hand on Addie's shoulder. "All you need to know is that she loved you. What else matters?"

"Did she know God? I want to know what things were important to her. I come from her, and I want to make her proud."

His hand dropped away. "It's a useless pursuit, child. Help me find out who paid for your care, and we might discover who attacked us. And who killed Mrs. Sullivan."

"Where did you get the pictures you brought today?"

"The attorney. Though he still won't tell me who has retained him, he found the pictures in a file at his home. They were the proof we needed to tell your father, so the timing was perfect."

"Do you think my father was glad to find me? He showed so little emotion."

"He was crazy about you when you were a child. I think he was overjoyed. I can't say the same for Clara."

Addie's smile faded. She liked her aunt. "I'd hoped she'd embrace me like a daughter, since Katherine is gone."

"You're a tie to Laura, and she couldn't abide her sister."

She twisted the tie on her dressing gown. "Why not?"

"Clara met Henry first. He courted her before he met Laura, but one look at the older sister, and he never noticed Clara again."

"He married her, though!"

"I think that was Clara's doing. Henry was lost, aimless when he couldn't find Laura's body. He neglected his work, didn't shave for days."

"Poor man." So much love. She had only to stir the embers and he would love her like that.

"Clara came in and ordered him to bathe and get ready to take her to dinner. To my surprise, Henry obeyed her. She dragged him out of his depression by the sheer force of her will."

"She doesn't seem the dragon sort."

He laughed. "I love my sister, but she can be a bulldog when she wants something. And she wanted Henry. I think she was determined he wouldn't escape a second time."

"She must have really loved him to do that."

"*Obsession* would be a better word. She never went out with another man, not even when Henry married Laura."

The more she was around John, the more she understood obsession. "They seem happy."

"Clara is. Henry changed after Laura died. He was always laughing, joking around. After her death, he became all business and built the town with his money and power."

What must it be like to be loved the way Henry loved her mother? Addie imagined a life spent with John at her side. Pure bliss.

"Get that look off your face, Niece," Mr. Driscoll said. "I warned you about John. He's not for you."

"Why not? I care about him. I believe he cares about me."

"For one thing, Clara would never allow it. She plans to marry him off to money and a title."

"I can't imagine why Clara would care. He's not her son."

"He's her grandson's father. That says it all."

"You said he was a philanderer. That's untrue."

"I wanted to warn you off. If you think he'll escape the future mapped out for him, you're deceiving yourself. And your father will begin to play his queen on the chessboard of life. He won't let you deny him that pleasure."

"I think I'll wait and see what the Lord has planned for us," she said.

He snorted. "Your future is what your family makes of it. Nothing divine in that calculation."

She followed him toward the door. He was so wrong. God moved them about at his will. If her

Maker intended her to marry John, it would happen. If that wasn't his plan, she'd have to find a way to accept it.

After he left the bank the next day, John found Clara reclining on the davenport with a damp cloth to her face. "Headache?" he asked.

"It's quite abominable."

"I'm sorry. Is there anything I can do for you?"

"Shut the curtains, if you would. The light is stabbing my eyes."

"Of course." He pulled the heavy drapes across the windows. "I'm going to town with Addie and Edward."

She pulled the cloth away and winced. "Whatever for, John?"

"I'm going to take Miss Sullivan to see the constable, and I thought I'd take Edward to visit my parents. They were away on vacation and returned yesterday. They'll expect to see us as soon as possible."

"Please get used to calling her Julia, dear boy. Henry will insist on it." She peered at him through puffy eyes. "You're not . . . interested in her, are you? That will never do, you know. Henry has plans for her already."

John's elation at the thought of a few hours with Addie and his son vanished. "What kind of plans?"

"Lord Carrington," she said. She put the cloth back

on her head. "Leave me be, John. I can't talk now."

Carrington. A man much too old for sweet Addie. But she would be influenced by her father's desires. When he reached the yard, he found Edward with Addie and her dog under a redwood tree. She was lying on her back with her slippers resting on the trunk. Edward's head was on her stomach, and the dog lay with its head on its paws. Her hair hung from its pins, and his eyes traced the silken strands looped on the grass.

"My nymph," he said.

She jerked to an upright position and began tucking her hair back into its proper position. Though she sprang to her feet, bits of mud and grass clung to her skirt as a reminder of the unladylike position in which he'd found her. His smile broadened.

Edward sat with his knees clasped, and John beckoned to him. He got slowly to his feet. "Are you ready for our visit to Grandma?"

Edward scuffed his feet in the grass and grimaced. "Do I have to go, Papa?"

He steeled his voice. "Yes. Grandma would be very disappointed if I didn't bring you."

"Her house stinks."

John winced. "That's very rude, Edward. Get in the buggy." He turned his smile on Addie. "Can you bear to spend the day in my company?"

Her dimple came. "I think I can endure the suffering."

He took her hand. "I'll take you to lunch to ease the pain."

Her eyes smiled. "What about Gideon?"

"We couldn't leave our guard dog behind." He clasped his hands around her tiny waist and assisted her into the seat. The honeysuckle fragrance drifted from her skin. He lifted Edward up beside her, then whistled for the dog to leap into the back of the buckboard. John sprang onto the front seat beside them and took the reins.

The buggy clattered down the cobblestone drive to the street. He reined in the horse, then pulled onto the thoroughfare. Weekdays were normally busy in Mercy Falls, and this Thursday was no exception. Buggies and automobiles jostled for position on the narrow streets. John and Addie passed street vendors hawking food.

He reined in the horse in front of the brick police station. "Why don't you wait here and I'll see what I can discover. I'm used to dealing with officials."

The animation had drained from her face. "Thank you."

He went inside and found the officer in charge of Josephine's murder investigation. There was little the man could tell John, and he said they wouldn't be able to release the body for a few more days. John strode back to the buggy and climbed to his seat. "He'll call when we are able to pick up the body," he said. "You'll have a few more days to make arrangements."

"I still can't believe it," she said. "It seems so pointless. She knew nothing."

"You're convinced her death is related to your identity?"

"Are you not?"

Was he? He picked up the reins. "I think it's likely," he admitted. "I'm sorry you're having to deal with this."

"God is in control," she said. "I rest in that."

He glanced at her from the corner of his eye. "What was it like growing up in a lighthouse?"

"I loved it. Helping my father maintain the light, working around the property. When a ship-wreck happened, he would be called upon to rescue the survivors. There often weren't any, though, and that was hard to endure."

He winced at the woeful tone in her voice.

Her gaze wandered to Edward, who leaned against her with his eyes closed. "I've been meaning to ask you about Edward. How long has he had—this condition?"

"Since he was about two."

She pleated her skirt with her fingers. "What is the cause? I know little about it."

"No one knows. It's thought to do with impulses in the brain, but they are uncontrollable."

"Has his condition stayed stable? Does he normally have as many episodes as he's endured since my arrival?"

He slapped the reins. "It's worsened a bit this

year." The truth of that was like having an injury probed with a knife.

"I'll try to find an herb that will help. I shall research it." Her voice held determination.

He smiled. "My little healer. You try to fix everyone. Can you fix my heart?"

"Has someone harmed it?"

"I fear it's been irretrievably ensnared by you."

Her smile widened, and she placed her small gloved hand on his forearm. "That's a perfect state for it. I shall endeavor to keep it that way."

"And what of the state of your own heart?"

She sobered. "I fear it is as entangled as yours."

"I pray it stays that way, no matter what your father plans."

"I'm sure he has more important things to worry about than the state of my heart."

"There is nothing more important than that." The buggy entered the city limits, and he slowed the horse. "Have you had any more thoughts as to the meaning of your mother's cryptic note?"

She withdrew her hand from his arm and adjusted her glove. "I did. *Dust* could be the attic."

"And pigeons?"

She shook her head. "That clue has stumped me."

"Perhaps the labyrinth in the garden. The pigeons love the birdbath in the middle of it."

She clapped her hands together. "The very thing! I've been meaning to explore that labyrinth and haven't had the time."

"We'll explore it together if you promise me a kiss when we get to the middle."

Color stained her cheeks. "A lady never promises any such thing."

"I might have to steal one, then."

She opened her fan and waved it, but he could see the heat spreading up her face and grinned. Had he and Katherine ever indulged in romantic banter? He couldn't remember anything like this.

TWENTY-FOUR

EDWARD BEGAN TO stir on Addie's shoulder. He lifted his head, then flopped it down with a contented smile on his face. She glanced at John from the corner of her eye. She'd noticed how the child relished his time with his father, and seeing it, Addie ached for the same relationship with her real father. Things would change soon. Her new papa would love her unconditionally, just like God.

The springs on the buggy squeaked as John shifted in the seat. Wide awake now, Edward squirmed from her lap to sit between her and John.

"We're almost to Grandma's," John told Edward.

The boy's high spirits subsided, and he leaned back against the buggy seat. Addie knew better than to ask questions about the situation with John's parents. Edward had said the house was smelly. Did John come from folks like the ones in the tenement? He seemed much too lofty to have

239

grown up in a place like that. His military bearing seemed innate.

The buggy rolled past a sea of women in the street. "What's happening?" she asked. She craned her neck to take in the banners, which said Votes for Women and Equal Rights. "Oh, it's a suffrage march. I wonder if Sally is here?"

"Sally?"

"One of the chambermaids. She invited me to come to a meeting." She saw men in the parade as well.

"I've been to a few."

"You're in favor of voting rights for women?"

"Certainly," he said, tossing her a smile. "No one can tell me you are incapable of knowing your own mind or comprehending the issues."

She smiled back at him. "My father always said too many people are afraid to speak the truth."

"He was right." The buggy stopped in front of a butcher shop in a block of town lined with aging storefronts and cracked sidewalks. John seemed distant as he got out of the buggy and lifted his son to the street. His big hands circled Addie's waist, and she was close enough to see the gray rim around his dark eyes. She followed him into the shop where two women turned at the tinkle of the bell on the door.

Addie glanced around. Meat hung from hooks around the perimeter of the small room entirely constructed in wood, even to the slatted ceiling.

More meat lay on the counter. Hams hung in the windows. The man behind the counter wore a voluminous apron that used to be white over his vest and tie. The streaks of red made her stirring hunger vanish.

"Why, it's little Johnny," an older, plump woman declared as she waited in line. "I haven't seen you in years, Johnny."

"Hello, Mrs. Gleeson," John said. An easy smile lifted his lips.

"We're so proud of you, Johnny. On a submarine! My, what an exciting life. Are you home for good?"

"No, ma'am, I'm just on leave." He pulled Addie to his side. "This is, um, Julia Eaton, Mr. Eaton's daughter."

The woman stopped short, and consternation squinted her eyes. "I beg your pardon?"

Addie extended her hand. "I realize it's confusing, Mrs. Gleeson. I'm pleased to make your acquaintance. My father thought I'd drowned some years back, but as you can see, I'm quite well."

The woman's mouth gaped. "Oh my stars." Mrs. Gleeson took Addie's hand as the customer in front of her took her packages and exited the store. Mrs. Gleeson made an obvious struggle to recover her aplomb. "Is that your boy?"

From the way she eyed Addie, the story would be all over town by lunchtime. Addie stepped back and dropped her hand to her side. Would her father be upset? But no, he'd been introducing her last night as his daughter.

John put his hand on his son's head and pulled him away from Addie's skirt. "This is Edward."

"What a fine lad. He's the spitting image of you. Your mother and father must be so proud. Isn't that so, Leo?" she called to the butcher, who stood watching them with a cleaver in his hand.

"That's right, Evelyn," the man said.

Addie studied him and realized he was John's father. They shared the same ears, finely formed and close to the head. She sent a tentative smile his way, but he remained focused on his son.

Mrs. Gleeson turned back to the counter. "I'll have two pounds of that pork loin you mentioned, Leo. Then I'll let you visit with your boy."

Addie waited for John to address his father, and when he merely moved to a corner of the room and waited, she shuffled out of the way of the door and studied the meat in the display case. Flies buzzed above it, but the glass kept them out. Fresh steaks, ground beef, and lamb lined the trays inside. The air was heavy with the smell of meat, and she understood Edward's reference to the odor in the place, though it wasn't offensive to her.

Mrs. Gleeson took her purchases wrapped in white butcher paper, then placed a final pat on Edward's head. "Don't be a stranger, Johnny," she admonished. The bell tinkled over the door, and she was gone.

"Lock the door there, Johnny, there's a good boy," his father said. He transferred the meat to an ice chest while his son complied with his request, then beckoned to them. "Your ma is upstairs. She'll be glad to see you. Supper should be on the table shortly."

"We can't stay for supper, Pa. I was in the neighborhood and thought I'd stop by and bring Edward over to say hello."

"It's your loss, boy. Your ma is making beef stew, your favorite." Mr. North wiped his hands on the bloody apron that swathed his generous chest and stomach, then whipped it off and rolled it into a ball.

"Edward might have a taste. I don't believe he's ever had beef stew." John took his son's hand and glanced at Addie as if to say, *Come along.*

She was eager to meet the people who had raised this man she was coming to love.

John had walked these narrow back steps a thousand times. His mother made sure they were spotless, and the aroma of beef stew wafted down the hall. Edward's feet dragged, and John tugged on the boy's hand. "Come along, Edward. I bet your grandma has cookies. There are always cookies in the jar."

His son's expression lifted. "Oatmeal?" he asked.

"Probably. And with raisins." He led the way

through the parlor to the doorway into the kitchen, then paused and listened to his mother sing the words to "Shoo, Fly, Don't Bother Me!" The tune brought his childhood rushing back.

His mother turned from where she stood at the stove, and her ready smile came. "Johnny!" Her smile widened when she saw the boy. "And Eddie. Come give your granny a kiss."

"My name is Edward," the child said, but he tugged his hand from John's and went to give his grandmother a kiss.

John's heart swelled at the sight of his mother clasping his son to her bosom. He joined them and dropped a kiss on the top of her head. "Hi, Ma."

She released Edward, who dashed to the cookie jar sitting on top of the icebox. "Can I have a cookie, Grandma?"

"I just baked them. Help yourself. I'd rather you call me Granny, sweetheart." Her bright blue eyes etched with lines caught sight of Addie. "And who is this, Johnny? Your girl?"

Heat encased his neck. "This is Miss Addie Sullivan, Ma. She's been teaching Edward his numbers." He hesitated, uncertain how to explain her real identity.

His mother's eyes sharpened. "This is the long-lost Eaton daughter? Julia Eaton?"

The news must have traveled already. "That's right." He turned to Addie. "Addie, this is my mother, Mrs. Ursula North." He watched his son open the cookie jar. "Just one for now, Edward."

Addie pulled her hands from behind her back and came forward to take his mother's outstretched hand. "Pleased to meet you, Mrs. North."

"What a pretty little thing you are," his mother said. "We need to fatten you up some though. Would you like a cookie?"

"I'd love one, thank you." Addie dug a cookie out of the jar, her eyes roving the dining room. "You have a lovely home."

John took another look at the room he rarely noticed anymore. His grandfather had made the maple table in the middle of the room. A red and white tablecloth hid the initials he'd carved into the top when he was five, and matching fabric covered the fronts of the base cabinets along one wall. The rose wallpaper was starting to fade, and the linoleum counter as well. But everything was spotless, including the rug on the painted wood floors under the table. The old pie safe was packed with dishes and pots. He noted the new wood cookstove.

His mother smiled. "Thank you, my dear. I've been telling Johnny's father that I want to redecorate. He hasn't agreed yet, but I'm wearing him down. Where's your father, Johnny?"

"He came up ahead of us. I think he's cleaning up."

"Good. I'm about to put supper on the table. Oh, and Mrs. Eaton called. She'd like you to stop by the mercantile and pick up an order for her. Something about hats."

"It's a good thing Addie is with me, then." John heard footsteps in the hall and tensed. "Here he comes now."

His father joined them in the kitchen. "Supper about ready, Ma? I'm starving."

"Sit down, Pa. John, you and Miss Sullivan sit down. Eddie, come help your granny get the food." She took the boy by the hand. "I've got apple pie afterward."

John didn't know how to get out of the meal without hurting his mother, so he did as he was told and pulled out a chair for Addie. Her green eyes were wide, and he knew she wondered why they were here. He had the same thought as his father took the head of the table. His dad would be needling him before an hour was up.

His mother set steaming bowls of beef stew and dumplings in front of both of them. Edward carried the freshly baked bread to the table. John's father lifted the boy to his lap once Edward completed his task.

"You're a fine boy, Eddie. You should have your papa bring you over for the day, and I'll show you how to carve up a chicken. That's the first thing you need to know if you're going to be a butcher like Grandpa."

Edward stared into his grandfather's face. "I'm going to be in the navy like Papa and go on the submarines. It smells funny here, Granddad. I don't like the butcher shop."

John's gut clenched, and he rushed to intervene before his father exploded. "Great stew, Ma. The dumplings are perfect."

"Thank you, son." His mother slid into her seat at the other end of the table. "Pa, let's not have any arguments at the supper table."

Her plea had no effect. John's father's brows lowered. "Always gone, never home with your family. Parenting is more than begetting a child, Johnny. You need a trade that takes you home to your wife and kids every night."

John set Edward down. "Go eat your stew."

John took a bite but barely tasted it. He heard Addie put down her spoon.

His mother's smile had faded, too, and her face bore signs of strain. "Leo, please," she said.

His father said nothing and began to eat his stew. The air thickened, and it was all John could do to continue to lift his spoon to his lips.

His father eyed Addie. "You're teaching the boy?" he asked.

She put down her bread. "Yes, sir. Just the basics, like his numbers and letters."

"He learning them all right? I mean, his—" He broke off and glanced at his son.

"Edward is a smart lad," John said, louder than he'd intended. "He's picking it up quickly."

"I've got a dog now, Granddad," Edward said.

247

"His name is Gideon, and he lets me know when I'm going to fall."

The older man's brows rose. "Is that right?"

"Well, I'm sharing the dog," Edward said. "He belongs to Teacher too."

"What's this about, Johnny?" his dad asked.

"Ever since Miss Eaton arrived, he's been fixated on her dog. He thinks the dog warns him before an . . . episode," John said.

"That so?" His father turned curious eyes on Addie.

"I've seen it. Gideon does seem to sense when Edward might be having a problem," Addie said.

"Don't that beat all," his father murmured. "What about school?"

"He's not ready yet," John said.

"It's a mistake to coddle the boy," his father said. "If people are going to make fun, he needs to learn it and toughen up."

John gritted his teeth to keep back the retort. He took the last bite of his stew. "Great supper, Ma. We'd better go."

"I want my apple pie," Edward protested.

"Maybe next time." He grabbed his son's hand and escaped the censure.

TWENTY-FIVE

JOHN TURNED THE horse into a lot by the mercantile. "Here we are. It's nearly closing time." He alighted and held out his hand to help her down. His broad shoulders and bowler towered over her when he set her onto the street. She took his arm, and they entered the side door of Oscar's Mercantile. John removed his hat and tucked it under his arm. The scent of cinnamon, coffee, candles, and leather tickled her nose as soon as they were inside. A counter of fabric bolts caught her eye first, and she stopped to examine them. The quality ranged from common gingham to nicer satins and wools. She picked up a thimble painted with a rose and exclaimed over it, but John's interest had been caught by a display of saddles along the opposite wall.

A middle-aged woman approached John. Her skirts rustled, and the harsh black dress she wore did nothing for her pale skin. Her yellowish-white hair had been arranged in a thin pompadour that exposed her scalp in places.

"Lieutenant North, I assume you're here to pick up Mrs. Eaton's order?" she asked in a gravelly voice.

"I am," he said. He nodded toward Addie. "This is Miss Julia Eaton. Miss Eaton, this is Mrs. Silvers."

"Oh my," the woman said, her eyes widening. "Mr. Eaton's long-lost daughter! The news of your return has spread through town. What a wonderful surprise for your father."

Addie smiled. "A wonderful surprise for me as well, Mrs. Silvers. I've longed for an extended family all my life."

"And Mrs. Eaton raved about your dressmaking ability before your identity was known," Mrs. Silvers said, taking Addie's hand. "I'm very pleased to meet you."

Addie extricated her palm from the woman's overenthusiastic pumping. "I'm sure whatever she said was an exaggeration of my poor skills."

Mrs. Silvers's gaze roamed Addie's gown and hat. "If you created what you're wearing, I must say Mrs. Eaton didn't praise you enough."

Was this how everyone would react to her now that she was known to be an Eaton? "Thank you, Mrs. Silvers."

The older woman turned. "I expect you want to see the items. Come this way."

She led them from the dry-goods department past rows of jams and jellies until she reached the wooden counter. "Here we go." She lifted a box from the back counter and placed it by the ornate cash register.

Addie peeked inside and nearly gasped. "Are those egret feathers?" She saw a flash of red. "And is that a cardinal?"

Mrs. Silvers beamed. "Yes indeed. Aren't they lovely?"

Addie put her hand to her mouth. "I'm sorry, but I don't use bird feathers on my hats. Especially not egrets and certainly not stuffed cardinals."

She couldn't look away from the poor dead cardinal until John took her shoulders and pulled her away from the counter. Her eyes burned, and she gulped. "I'm so sorry for your trouble, Mrs. Silvers, but I could not bear to touch them."

Mrs. Silvers drew herself upright. Her lips were pressed in a tight line. She lifted the box and put it on the back counter. "I went to great trouble to meet Mrs. Eaton's specifications."

"I'm sorry," Addie said again. "I'll be sure to tell Mrs. Eaton the reason we return empty-handed."

She wanted to rush from the store so she didn't have to look at the box, but if this was what Mrs. Eaton had referred to when she said she'd ordered the final trim, an alternative must be found. Addie searched the shop, sighing in relief when she spied a fitting substitute. "The velvet rosettes are beautiful. I'll take three of them. And some of that tulle."

Neither would come close to what the woman had spent for the bird and feathers. John stood with his hands behind his back, obviously clueless to what had just happened.

"No matter. I shall be able to sell the feathers to other, less sensitive, women," Mrs. Silvers managed an ingratiating smile. "Is there anything else?"

Addie shook her head, miserably aware her aunt would be unhappy. John took the bag, and she followed him outside. With the purchases stowed in the back, he helped her board the buggy.

"What was the problem?" he asked as the horse pulled them onto the street.

Addie shuddered. "I never use birds on my hats. Have you read about the bird hunts? They trap the birds, kill them, then pluck out the feathers and discard the carcass. They're slaughtered merely to adorn a vain woman's hat."

"Some women often don't care who is hurt as long as they have what they want," he said, a slight smile lifting his lips. "I fear Mrs. Silvers will never get over the affront."

Heat swept up her chest to her neck. "I'm sure it's my fault. I've grown up among seagulls and fish. They'd done little to teach me proper manners."

He laughed, a short bark full of genuine delight. "I like never knowing what you're going to say next." He slapped the reins on the horse's rump. "You realize you won't be allowed to teach Edward when Henry has a chance to think about it. I'll have to find another tutor to go with me to San Francisco."

She smoothed the glove on her hand. "I'd wondered about that. I could ask to continue, but he might say no."

"He'll certainly say no to allowing you to accompany me to the city."

"I want to get to know my family better," she admitted. "But I find I want to know you better even more than that."

The buggy exited town and entered the shadow of the redwoods. "We must see what we can do about that," he said.

The painted columns of the manor glistened in the sunshine, but the view of the massive structure made Addie shudder. She had to go in and tell Mrs. Eaton she had refused the bird and feathers the woman wanted on her hat and gown.

"Are you cold?" John asked, stopping the carriage. He stepped down and held up his hand to help her.

"Not at all." She accepted his assistance. "I'm dreading telling Mrs. Eaton about the feathers."

He set her on the ground, but his hands stayed on her waist. "I assumed you'd already prayed about it."

"I did. She might not be paying attention to God." She smiled to show him she was joking. "I enjoyed the jaunt very much."

He glanced at the house, then stepped back with obvious reluctance. "Not half as much as I did." He handed her the purchases. "We could search the attic later. Or the labyrinth."

More hours spent in his company. "It won't be

dark for several hours yet. Let's examine the labyrinth."

"I think we'd better face Clara first."

She walked toward the towering porch columns, whispering another prayer that Clara would accept her decision. She sensed John staring at her. Taking courage from his concern, she carried her box of tulle and flowers inside.

The grandfather clock in the grand hall struck six. At this time of day, Clara would likely be in her study poring over menus for tomorrow. Addie navigated the labyrinth of halls to the room. The door to the study was shut. She took a deep breath and rapped on it.

"Come in," Clara called.

Addie twisted the brass knob and pushed open the door. Clara looked up from where she sat at her rosewood desk. She wore a white serge dress with blue silk piping. "Ah, Julia, you have the things I ordered? Let me see!"

Addie stepped nearer. Her tongue refused to form the words she needed, so she let Clara take the box and withdraw the items from inside.

Clara frowned and looked up at Addie. "Where are the feathers? And the bird? I ordered a cardinal. The bright splash of color will be most becoming with my skin tone."

Addie wet her lips. "I'm sorry, Mrs. Eaton. I should have mentioned it sooner. I know bird feathers and stuffed birds are quite the fashion, but I can't in good conscience use them on my creations."

Clara's delicate brows rose. "What nonsense is this? Those egret feathers cost the earth! And I ordered the size of the bird most specifically."

"The mercantile had them in, and I saw them," Addie said. "But the willful destruction of birds for vanity's sake is something I can't endure. I bought these other things instead."

Clara stamped her foot. "I don't want other things!" She tossed the tulle and ribbon flowers back into the box. "I'll be a laughingstock to go out in plain tulle."

"I keep up on all the styles. The simpler things are all the rage in Paris. If you allow me to follow my vision, you'll be on the cutting edge of fashion."

The red in Clara's face began to soften to pink. "Simpler things? What do you have in mind?"

"Fashionable women in Paris are beginning to wear turbans for night. I mentioned that to you earlier. And the day hats are larger, to frame the face. I have so many ideas." She prayed silently for Clara to listen.

"Turbans? Truly?" Clara appraised the purchased items again. "Out of tulle?"

"No, no, the tulle is for the day hat I have in mind for you. The turban will be in velvet. It's quite unusual. No one else in California will have one like it."

Clara's blue eyes widened, and a glimmer of avarice shimmered in her eyes. "I am most intrigued, Julia. Do you have a sketch?"

Addie's sigh eased from her lips. God had answered her prayer. "I'd like you to trust me and let me make it for you. It looks so much lovelier on than in a sketch. The color will be most attractive with your eyes and fair skin."

"Will it be done in time for the ball?"

"Yes, ma'am. It's nearly done already. I just need to add final touches."

Clara drew on her gloves. "Very well. Carry on with your vision, Julia."

"Thank you, Mrs. Eaton. I won't let you down."

"I trust that is the truth, my dear. I hope you realize how important this ball is to me. And to Henry. His associates from San Francisco will be here and even one of his clients from New York. I'm counting on you to make sure that if anyone's toilette is discussed with awe, it is mine." She touched her closed fan to Addie's cheek. "And per-haps you should begin to call me Mother and Henry Father. Our friends will expect it."

"Yes, Mother," Addie said, the word rolling awkwardly off her tongue.

Clara started for the door, then turned. "Oh, and Julia, one more thing. Have you anything suitable to wear yourself?"

Addie had been expecting this. Her father would want her to meet the people of his social circle.

"I'm afraid not, Mother. And I have no time to make a ball gown."

"I have too many to count. We're close to the same size. Have Molly show you my closet."

"This is a masked ball, isn't it? May I purchase a mask in town?"

"I have at least ten. You may take your pick." Mrs. Eaton swept out of the room.

Shaking, Addie sank onto the settee. While the thought of attending a ball was intoxicating, she dreaded fending off Carrington. John's chocolate eyes came to mind. Dancing in his arms would be worth dealing with Carrington.

TWENTY-SIX

HENRY STOPPED ADDIE as she headed toward the labyrinth in the garden just before dusk. "Your mother informed me that you needed a dress. There is no need to wear one of her cast-offs. I want you to be the talk of the state after the ball. Buy whatever you like, my dear."

"Thank you, Father." She managed the proper address, though it was still difficult to think of him as her real father. "I don't think there is much time to find one."

"If you'd like to go to the city, I'll be happy to take you." He wagged a finger at her. "Remember, there will be royalty at the ball. Men who might be interested in an alliance with the Eaton name."

"When I marry, I wish the man to love me for myself, not for your money."

He snorted. "Such romanticism, my dear. Infatuation never lasts. Only a solid alliance. Don't you worry your pretty head about it. I'll ensure you make a strategic match."

That's what she feared the most. She managed a smile, then escaped through the kitchen to the garden. Birds chattered from the manicured trees surrounding the garden. The wind tugged strands of Addie's hair loose from the ribbon that caught it at the back of her neck. The heavy scent of roses wafted on the wind, and she inhaled it with appreciation. She missed her dog, who now spent more and more time at Edward's side. It hurt her every time she had to order him not to accompany her, but the boy needed Gideon's help.

A twig snapped, and she turned to see John approaching. He'd removed his jacket and tie and rolled up the sleeves on his white shirt. His head was bare, and he wore an eager smile. Her mind flashed to his promise to steal a kiss. "Have you been through the labyrinth many times?" she asked.

He offered his arm. "Only once or twice."

"Have you any idea where to search?"

"A few thoughts." They stepped through the opening of the six-foot clipped shrubs. Flagstones paved the wide path, which meandered past banks of flowers and rock gardens.

"I love this," Addie said. "I could stay here forever." She paused at a statue of a horse. "Should we examine everything that might hold a hidden compartment?"

"That particular statue was installed only three years ago, so I believe we can forgo a study of it."

With her hand on his arm, they strolled deeper into the labyrinth. "I hope you know how to get out," she said.

"I have a good sense of direction, but I wouldn't mind being stuck in here with you for a few days."

She lifted a brow. "You might change your mind when I grow grouchy from hunger."

"Oh you're that kind of lady, eh? One who demands food?"

"Especially sweets."

"I admit I noticed how you prefer the trifles."

"Don't talk about it or I might have to go back for food."

He led her into a circular area twelve feet across. Benches and iron chairs rimmed the grass. In the center stood a fountain with a stone hummingbird rising ten feet in the air. Water gurgled from the bowl to spill over colorful rocks in a lovely pool. Speechless, she stood and drank in the scene.

"I know what you're thinking," John said. "You're wishing you didn't have your shoes on. I don't mind if you want to go wading."

Addie turned an impish smile his way. "I fear my father would highly disapprove of my tendency to shed my shoes at a moment's notice."

He grinned. "It's one of the things that endears me to you."

She removed her hand from his arm and stepped nearer the fountain. "Was this here during my mother's lifetime?"

"It was installed when the labyrinth was built in 1860. So we should examine it closely."

She glanced at her feet, then back at the statue. "The only way to go over every inch is to wade into the pool."

Amusement lit his eyes. "I shall allow you the honor, since I know you want to do it so badly."

"I think you'll need to join me. It's much too tall for me to reach to the top of the hummingbird."

"Oh, the sacrifices I make for you." He settled on the bench and yanked off his shoes.

Smiling, she sat on the grass and reached under her skirt to remove her shoes and stockings. The moist grass cooled her feet when she stood. Her dress would get damp, but she didn't mind. She tried to hold the hem above the pool and waded toward the fountain. The water splashed onto her skirt, and when she reached the fountain, she gave up the struggle to stay dry, as she needed both hands to examine the statue.

John joined her, and they poked fingers into every crevice and ran palms over every surface. Nothing. She tried to hide her disappointment as he helped her from the pool of cold water. "Now what?" she asked after they'd donned their shoes again.

He was staring at the rocks. They'd been stacked and mortared as a support for the hummingbird. He walked around to the back, and she followed. "What is it?"

"Just checking for loose mortar. Ah, let's check this." He dug his fingers into the cracked mortar of a rock and wiggled it loose. The cavity was empty.

"If she'd hidden it in a loose rock, wouldn't it have been repaired by now?"

He nodded. "Quite possibly." He gazed around the circular parklike area.

"Where does that path lead?" she asked, indicating a trail leading out of the center.

"Out of the labyrinth eventually. A labyrinth isn't the same as a maze. There are no dead ends. It's a place for reflection and prayer. A few feet along that path, there used to be a small altar and prayer bench."

"Oh, I want to see!"

He clasped her hand in his. "This way."

Her fingers curled around his hand, and she was glad she'd neglected to draw on her gloves. The warmth of his skin connected them in a new way. She nearly asked him why he hadn't stolen his kiss. They reached a small brick archway. Stepping through it, she saw a matching bench and altar surrounded by flowers. Pigeons roosted atop it.

"It's so lovely," she said. A warm breeze enveloped her when she approached the bench. The back arched to match the altar. She sat and breathed in the fragrance of the flowers. "I must come here often."

He sat beside her, and silence descended. She heard only the chirping of birds as they searched for a good hiding place. Her gaze fell on a sundial. "What about that?"

"Maybe."

They approached the sundial. It stood on a stone column embellished with carved rosettes. She ran her fingers over the stone in search of any part that moved.

"Here!" John twisted on a rosette, and the ornamentation dropped into his hand. He reached inside and withdrew a piece of paper. "Our pigeon clue!"

Her fingers trembled when she took the paper he passed to her and unfolded it. "It reads, 'Father murdered,' " she whispered.

Friday morning, the cranky motor on John's 1906 Harley-Davidson didn't want to start, and he had to fight with it before drawing out the familiar *putt-putt* of the engine. He rode it to Mercy Falls. As he reached the center of town, he realized a line had collected outside the bank. Frowning, he parked the motorcycle by the front door. He climbed off and strode toward the door.

"There he is!" Mrs. Paschal cried. She rushed toward him with her hands outstretched. "Lieutenant North, I want my money."

"What's going on here?" John asked. The line stretched down the block and around the corner.

"It's my money, and you have to give it to me," the woman said, clutching at his coat sleeve.

"Of course you can have your money, Mrs. Paschal," he said soothingly. "The bank will open in forty-five minutes. I have to run an errand and I'll be right back. The tellers will be along in a few minutes."

"I want my money now!" she shrieked, grasping at him.

He evaded her hands and rushed back to his Harley. He leaped into the seat and gunned the engine, then turned back the way he'd come. He realized he was sweating, and he wiped his forehead. "I think there's a run going on at the bank," he said out loud, though there was no one to hear. "A real run."

He turned the Harley into the Eaton Manor driveway. When he stopped the motorcycle outside the house, the door opened, and Henry rushed from the manor.

He reached John's Harley. "John, where have you been? There's a run developing at the bank."

"I saw. I just came from there. Do you know what's caused this?"

Henry scowled. "The Knickerbocker Trust Company just failed. I got a telegram about it early this morning."

John winced. "We should be all right. We've got

plenty of reserves." He noticed Henry wasn't meeting his gaze. "We do have plenty of reserves, Henry. No need to worry."

Addie came through the front door with her dog by her side. She knelt and rubbed Gideon's head, but her gaze lingered on John. He could feel the waves of empathy rolling from her, and it gave him strength.

Henry leaned against the doorjamb. "I loaned ten million dollars to Knickerbocker just yesterday." His voice trembled.

A loan of that magnitude! John struggled to stay calm. "Without telling me? No wonder numbers weren't adding up." He struggled to maintain his temper.

"I was going to tell you. It was a temporary loan, and I expected to recoup it with 10 percent interest."

John did calculations in his head. "That leaves us with only 5 percent reserve. We might be in trouble."

"I'm aware of that," Henry snapped. "Get over to the bank and calm them down. Tell them you'll give them part of their money today and the rest later."

"That's hardly accurate. You did this, Henry."

Henry jabbed a finger in John's chest. "It's your job to make sure we're not bankrupt by the time this day is over."

"No. It's your problem, not mine. I was only

helping you out, and you know it. Besides, you won't be bankrupt. There are the other businesses. The boats, the dairies." But the bank's failure would be catastrophic to the people who had entrusted Henry with their money.

He realized Henry hadn't answered him. "The other businesses are in no danger, right?" John asked.

Henry had gone white. "They're mortgaged, son. To the hilt. If the bank fails, I fail."

John couldn't breathe. The scale of this was too huge to take in. "I see." He straightened his shoulders. Addie's future was at stake. Edward's too. "I'd better see what I can do at the bank."

Henry clutched at his arm. "This doesn't affect only me, you know. It's you and Edward." He squinted into John's face. "Julia too."

"Is this why you asked me to help out? So I could take the blame if your risk failed?"

Henry's face reddened. "Of course not. You're family. I'd hoped your oversight would see us through. Obviously I was wrong."

John's fists clenched. Henry had set him up. "You didn't even consult me about the loan to Knickerbocker. I would have advised against it."

"Precisely why I didn't mention it. If this gamble paid off, I would have been able to reestablish myself."

"Instead you've brought your family to the edge of ruin."

And Henry would be out on the street. John had seen that crowd at the bank. There would be no talking to them. "I'd better get to the bank," he said.

Twenty-seven

PEOPLE SHOUTED AND shoved one another in the bank lobby. John fought his way through the crush, then slipped into the back rooms, where two of Henry's tellers cowered in the corner.

Paul Lingel swiped a lock of hair back into place over his bald spot. "What are we going to do?" he asked in a quavering voice.

John fixed a stare on both tellers. "We're going to do business as usual. I shall go out there and try to restore order and confidence. I want both of you to be smiling and confident."

Paul straightened his tie and knocked mud from his black pants. "Yes, sir."

John took a deep breath, then strode out to the oaken counter. "Good morning!" he called, stretching his mouth into a smile. "You're all out early."

"We want our money," a beefy man in overalls said at the front of the line.

John couldn't lay hold of the man's name. "Of course. No one is saying you can't have your money, but what are you going to do with it when you get it?"

"We'll have it in our possession," the man said.

"Then what? Hide it under your mattress?" He laughed and held up his hand. "Please, friends, there is no need for panic."

"I got a telegram from my uncle," someone yelled from the back. "His bank in New York closed down, and he lost everything."

People cried out and surged toward the counter. John tried to reason with them, but they shouted him down, demanding their money. He signaled to the tellers, who came forward. Their nervous smiles would only serve to inflame the crowd.

"Please, in an orderly fashion," he called. "Panic will make things worse."

His final statement pricked the bubble of agitation, and he saw the crowd visibly relax. He allowed himself a sliver of hope until the man in overalls thrust his fist into the air.

"This is no different from 1873!" he yelled. "Banks failed all over the world." His fist came down on the counter. "Give me my money!"

Just like that, the run started. Though John tried several times to restore order, no one paid attention. The tellers began to pay out money from deposits, and the line diminished, then ballooned again. He wished he'd asked Addie to pray before he left the house. It would take a miracle to get through the run and still be solvent.

Within an hour, Paul pulled him aside. Perspiration dotted the older man's forehead.

"We're almost out of cash," he whispered, wiping the back of his hand across his damp face.

"Let me look." John strode back to the vault and slipped inside. Only two stacks of money were left.

The bank had failed.

His knees gave out, and he sank onto a nearby chair. Those poor families were about to lose their life's savings. Anger burned in his belly. Henry hadn't even considered the possible effects of his actions on the people of this community. How could John go out there and tell the people that the money was gone?

He considered the ways he might pull this out yet. He might announce the bank was closing for the day rather than tell them the money was gone. But that would only postpone the inevitable. No bank would loan Henry the cash, not considering the current situation. The people waiting out there—shopkeepers, factory workers, home-makers—were going to have to know sooner or later that their worlds had shifted.

He got heavily to his feet. While Henry might prefer to avoid the situation, John wasn't going to do it. He'd speak the truth today, even if it pained him. And it did. He dreaded the disbelief and disil-lusionment on the faces of these anxious people.

Carrying the last two stacks of money, he returned to the counter and distributed the funds into the tellers' cash drawers. "Carry on," he said. "Let me know when the money is gone."

He watched those in line jostle for position, then step to the windows and demand their money. Reddened, fearful faces waited and watched as their turn neared. Three people served, then seven. Five minutes. Ten. It wouldn't be long now.

Paul shot a desperate glance John's way and held up his hand. John stepped into the crowd and held up his hands. "Friends, I'm sorry, but the bank is going to have to close its doors. Our cash is gone. I'm going to do what I can to call in loans to pay you, but for now, I must ask you all to leave."

The din increased to a roar. People pushed the others around them. He heard more cries for money, actual sobbing, and his gut clenched. Someone shoved him, and he struggled to keep his balance before going down into a sea of feet. Someone yanked him up, then planted a fist in his face and another in his stomach.

He welcomed the pain. A kick landed against his thigh, and the agony spread up to his waist and down to his ankle. Then another slammed into his head, and fog rolled across his vision. He fought his way through the blurry vision and reached for support. A hand grabbed his and hauled him to his feet. He reeled, and a hand seized the back of his collar and pulled him free of the kicks and punches still aimed in his direction.

"Lieutenant North, are you all right?" Paul propelled him down the hall while the other teller blocked access.

John nodded, and sharp pain circled his neck at the movement. "Thanks, Paul."

"What are we going to do now?" the older man asked.

John buried his head in his hands. "Only God knows."

Edward's inheritance was gone. Addie's too.

Addie's hands perspired inside her gloves. When the policeman had called today to tell her they were releasing Josephine's body to the mortuary, she'd called Katie to accompany her. This visit wasn't one she wanted to make alone. Addie sat on the buggy seat beside her friend and adjusted her hat.

"Is there anything I can do?" her friend asked.

"Pray for me," Addie said.

"Of course." Katie gathered her skirts and clambered down from the buggy.

Addie did the same. "Stay," she told Gideon. Edward had a cold and was napping, so she'd been allowed to take the dog. The plate glass of the mortuary windows gleamed. When she stepped inside, not a thread or a crumb was on the carpet. A light scent hung on the air. Cinnamon perhaps? A man in a suit came from the back to greet them. His muted smile added to the atmosphere of quiet competence.

"Miss Eaton?" he asked, his gaze flickering from Addie to Katie.

"Yes," Addie said. "I'm here to pay for Mrs. Sullivan's preparation."

"Of course. The body is not quite prepared yet. We only received Mrs. Sullivan from the police this morning. But if you come back tomorrow, she'll be ready."

Addie couldn't restrain a shudder at what faced her. "My friends have offered to have the funeral in their parlor. Would you deliver the casket to the Russell home?" With the preparations for the ball in full swing, having the funeral at Eaton Manor was out of the question.

"Gladly." He handed her an invoice.

She counted out the money for the coffin and embalming. "What about a burial plot?"

"I've arranged for her to be buried at the church at the top of Mercy Hill, as you requested."

"Thank you. The viewing will be Sunday and Monday. I'd like the burial to be Tuesday."

"That's all been arranged," he said in a soothing voice. "Is there anything else I can do for you?"

"I think that's everything," she said. "I appreciate all you've done."

He gave a small bow. "I'm here to serve you, Miss Eaton. Let me know if there is anything else I can do."

She murmured her gratitude and escaped into the fresh air, with Katie on her heels. She stood on the sidewalk with her chest heaving.

Katie touched her arm. "Are you all right?"

Addie nodded. "I couldn't have borne it if you hadn't been with me."

"So many things hitting you all at once," Katie said.

Addie linked arms with her friend. "Papa always said when I'm blue to find something to do for someone else. I'd like to buy some food and take it to the Whittaker family."

"I love the idea! The market is down a block. Do you have enough money?"

"I have plenty." She'd found the bankbook for the money her adoptive parents had been paid for her upkeep. The vast sum in the San Francisco bank had left her speechless. Nearly thirty thousand dollars. Unbelievable.

She and Katie filled bags full of groceries, then packed the buggy and went to the tenement row. Lifting two bags of food, Addie whistled for Gideon, then went to the front door. Climbing five flights of stairs with her burden would be a challenge, but it had to be done. With Katie behind her, she started up the steps. Gideon ran on ahead, turning to look back at her as if to ask why she was so slow.

Huffing, she finally reached the fifth floor. She paused to drag in a lungful of oxygen, then led the way to the door. It hung open, and the smell of cooked cabbage wafted out. A child's plaintive cry tugged on her heartstrings.

"Mrs. Whittaker?" she called. "It's Addie Sullivan. Can I come in?"

When the child only wailed louder, Addie stepped through the doorway. She saw the kitchen, so she carried the bags to the table and set them down. Katie unloaded the parcels while Addie went in search of the distressed child with Gideon at her side. The dog bounded ahead, his tail straight up and his ears alert.

"Mrs. Whittaker?" she called.

The older girls would still be at work, so the child must be one of the younger ones. Addie stepped into a small bedroom. The drapes over one tiny window blocked all light from the room, and she squinted to make out a small girl crouched by the side of the bed. Addie glanced at the bed and saw Mrs. Whittaker's pale face on the pillow.

Gideon rushed to nose the little girl. The child threw her arms around the dog and cried harder. Addie knelt beside her, but the girl flinched when Addie tried to touch her. She rose and touched the woman in the bed. Mrs. Whittaker's breathing was labored, and her eyes were closed. Her color was bad. Pasty.

Addie smoothed the woman's damp hair. "Mrs. Whittaker, can you hear me?"

When there was no response, she opened the drapes and struggled with the sash until she managed to raise the window. The woman needed fresh air. She went to find Katie, who was putting groceries away in the few cupboards and the ice chest.

"Did you find her?" Katie asked.

"She needs a doctor. She's unconscious."

Katie closed the cupboard door. "I'll fetch him."

When her friend was gone, Addie went back to the bedroom. There'd been no change in Mrs. Whittaker's condition. The little girl still had her face buried in Gideon's fur, so Addie sat beside her and began to sing "In the Good Old Summertime" to her. The little one began to sniffle, and the sobs stopped. She finally lifted her head and peeked at Addie.

"Hello," Addie said, smiling. "I'm Miss Eaton. This is Gideon. We came by to help your mama. Can you tell me what happened?"

"Mama won't wake up," the child said.

Addie guessed her to be about three. "How long has she been sleeping?" Probably a useless question. A child this young had no conception of time.

"A long time. She didn't fix me anything to eat. I'm hungry."

There was nothing Addie could do for Mrs. Whittaker until the doctor arrived. "I can fix you something to eat."

"We don't got no food. My sisters went to see if the neighbors could give us some bread and milk."

"I brought some."

Addie held out her hand, and after a brief hesitation, the little girl took it. Addie led her to the kitchen and prepared the child bread and jam, then poured milk from the glass bottle in the ice box. She pulled out the rickety chair and lifted the little girl onto it to eat.

"What's your name, honey?" she asked.

"Goldie." The little girl took a huge bite of her bread and jam. She looked like a squirrel with her cheeks puffed out.

"You eat while I check on your mama." Addie went back to the woman's bedroom, where Gideon stood watch.

No change. Five children. What could be done for them? Mrs. Whittaker was going to have to go to the hospital. She needed a sanatorium, though the nearest one was in San Francisco. Someone would have to care for these children. The oldest was ten. Addie could only imagine the expression on Mrs. Eaton's face if she brought home these dirty children.

Maybe Katie could help.

She turned at the sound of footsteps and saw Katie rushing through the door with the doctor in tow. He sped back to the bedroom without asking directions, and Addie knew he'd been here before. She followed him and stood back while he examined the unconscious woman.

"I've instructed the ambulance to come," Dr. Lambertson said without turning from his patient. "I've been trying for two weeks to get Mrs.

Whittaker to go in for treatment. She's in a very bad way."

"What can you do for her?" she asked, turning to view the woman's white face. If Mrs. Whittaker wasn't struggling so hard to breathe, Addie would think she was dead.

"She needs rest, good food, clean air. She won't get it here. Not with five children to feed."

Addie bit her lip. She wanted to offer to stay with the children, but she had to get home. Her family would be enraged.

The doctor straightened. "The children will have to go to the orphanage overnight at least. Maybe several weeks. And Mrs. Whittaker may not survive."

He turned a kind eye on Addie. "You'd better run along, Miss Eaton. This isn't a healthy place for you to be. Your father would have my head."

"What about the children?"

"I'll take care of delivering them to the orphanage."

It wasn't what Addie wanted. She stood in the doorway, trying to decide if she dared buck the Eaton's expectations. She was trying so hard to fit in. To be part of the family. She couldn't risk it.

Twenty-eight

THE DOCTOR STEPPED back. "I think you'll live, John."

John wasn't so sure. Every muscle ached, and his gut throbbed from the kicks. "Thanks, Doc." He slipped off the examining table.

"I'll give you a packet of pain powder. Take it with food. And rest."

"I'll try."

The doctor's smile vanished. "How bad is it, John? The bank, I mean?"

"Bad." He still hoped to be able to call in some loans and stay afloat. He'd spent two hours going over the books and trying to find a way to avert further catastrophe. The chances were slim to nonexistent.

The doctor's worried frown deepened. "Did my wife show up?"

John buttoned his shirt carefully over the bandage. "Yes, sir. She was one of the first in line. Your money is safe."

The doctor leaned his head back and sighed. "Thank you, God."

"Hundreds more weren't so lucky," John said. He put on his hat and thanked the doctor again before limping out to his buggy.

People on the street glared and stepped around him. News traveled fast, especially bad news. He suspected Henry might have already heard by the time John got back to the manor. In fact, he expected his father-in-law to be waiting for him at the door. It astounded him that Henry hadn't come to the bank.

He left the town limits behind and breathed easier as the cool shadows in the trees fell across his face. Birds chirped overhead, and the babble of the river running beside the road soothed his spirit. He wanted to hold his boy in his arms and forget today had ever happened.

Not likely he'd be allowed that privilege. Henry would want a complete description of the day and a plan of attack for pulling them all from ruin. And though John could throw it back on Henry's shoulders, the reality remained that this disaster affected his son as well.

At the manor, he turned the motorcycle over to the groom, then strode inside. The servants scurried up and down the stairs with armloads of decorations and chairs for the ballroom on the third floor. The ball was tomorrow night.

Clara greeted him at the door. She was paler than usual. "Is it true?" she demanded. "Is our money all gone?"

"The bank failed," he said.

Her lids fluttered, and she sagged. He caught her and half carried her to the sofa in the parlor. "Sally, get some water," he called to a servant he saw passing by the doorway.

He fanned Clara with his hand until Sally returned, then held the glass to Clara's lips. She swallowed, then sputtered. Her eyes opened. Daze changed to panic when her gaze locked with his.

"What are we going to do?" she shrieked. Her hands went to her hair, and she yanked on it until it came free from its pins.

"Hush, Clara." He pulled her arms down. "Henry has more assets. You'll be fine. It's the common people in town who have lost their life's savings." Even if the other businesses were mortgaged, they were bringing in money. Henry's kind always made out.

He pushed her back against the sofa. "Rest. Where's Henry?"

"On his way home." She moaned again. "We must put on a brave front. It's too late to cancel the ball."

Saturday night, Addie stood in a corner of the third-floor ballroom in her borrowed finery. The space glittered with gaslight from the chandeliers and sconces around the gilded room. The gleaming wood floor bounced back the brilliance. The tray ceiling rose to a skylight that allowed moonlight to filter into the room as well.

The luxurious fabric of the dress she wore rustled with every movement. Behind her black velvet mask, she could observe without fear of people watching. She tried to imagine herself as

Alice Roosevelt, confident and in control. But no amount of mind trickery persuaded her to move from her corner. Her hands perspired inside the gloves that came past her elbows.

Laughing couples swung by as the live band played. None of them looked familiar in their fancy attire and masks. She hoped no one would ask her to dance until her nervousness eased. This was her first time at a ball, and she would likely embarrass herself and her family by stepping all over her partner's feet. A sumptuous display of food was spread on white linen-covered tables along the west wall. She scanned the crowd for John but knew she wouldn't recognize him if she saw him.

Just as well. Her thoughts kept going back to the plight of the Whittaker family. She should have done more. And the entire family was in an uproar about the bank failure. John had been grim and distracted when she got back from town, though she'd longed to share her day with him. She'd seen him and her father engaged in serious conversations throughout the day, but she'd been distracted with Clara's demands for final arrangements for the ball.

Every muscle tightened when she saw Lord Carrington approaching—without a mask and dressed in his suit. She glanced away from his determined face to see if she could find help from any quarter. Behind her was a door to the hall, so she turned and slipped through it.

She heard Carrington call, "Miss Eaton." She closed the door, then rushed away.

She should never have agreed to come. Her father was going to try to auction her off to the highest bidder. Her vision blurred, and she lifted her skirts to hurry. When she heard a male voice call out behind her, she put on another burst of speed. Then she recognized it as John's voice. She turned to see him striding toward her in a black tail coat and pants and white bow tie. He wore a black velvet mask, but she would have recognized those broad shoulders anywhere.

"Not leaving so soon, are you?" he asked when he reached her.

"Lord Carrington was in pursuit," she said.

He nodded, a smile tugging at his lips. "And you ran like a rabbit."

"Like a jackrabbit," she agreed, smiling. "How did you know it was me?"

He touched a curl hanging to her shoulder. "No one else has hair like that."

His comment brought her pleasure. "Thank you. I think." She smiled up into his face.

He put her hand on his arm and turned back toward the ballroom. "It's necessary for us to face our fears. I promise to protect you."

"How easy for you to say," she said. "You aren't out of your element like I am mine. I don't even know how to dance."

"We can remedy that." He laid his right hand on

top of hers, where it rested on his left arm. "I'm not the best dancer in the world, but I can waltz without breaking your toes."

"I can't give you the same promise," she said. "You'll be risking your feet if you dance with me."

"I do believe it would be worth it," he said, leading her back into the crowd.

Her father hailed her before they'd taken three steps toward the dance floor. "Julia, come here, please." He stood in his tails with Clara on one side and Lord Carrington on the other. "Lord Carrington has been looking for you."

The Englishman bent over her gloved hand. His blue eyes shone. "Please, call me Thomas," he said. "You look lovely, Miss Eaton."

"Addie," she said without thinking.

"Julia," her father corrected with a warning glint in his eye.

"It will take me some time to get used to that," she said. She caught John's smile, then bit her lip and glanced away.

"Would you care to dance?" Lord Carrington extended his arm.

Before she could admit she didn't know how, John interrupted. "We were on our way to the floor when Henry called us over," he said. "Shall we continue?" he asked her.

She placed her hand on his arm, and he led her to the center of the room. "What do I do?" she whispered.

He slipped his hand on the right side of her waist and took her left hand in his. "Follow me."

The warmth of his hand penetrated the silk layers of her dress. His spicy scent filled her head. If she leaned forward, she could put her ear against his chest. Would his heart be pounding as hard as hers?

He counted off the rhythm in her ear. "One, two, three."

Awkwardly at first, she let him guide her around the floor. Her skirt billowed around her in a most delicious way, and she couldn't stop the smile that sprang to her lips as she figured out how to do it. "I'm waltzing!"

"And quite beautifully," he said, smiling down into her face.

She rested her head against his chest and felt him wince. "Did I hurt your bruises?"

"It was a most delicious pain," he said, smiling down at her.

She stopped in the middle of the dance floor. "I have a poultice to put on them. If I'd known of your injuries last night, I could have prevented much of your pain today."

His smile widened. "Being with you is the best medicine, but I'll allow any ministrations you want to make after this thing is over."

She allowed him to whirl her around the floor again. She was out of breath by the time the dance ended. Lord Carrington came to take his turn, then another gentleman, whose name she didn't remember. She kept an eye out for Lord Carrington's reappearance, but she saw him in conversation with John. John winked at her as she danced by, and she knew he'd occupied the odious man on her behalf.

She'd first thought her attraction to John was simply because she wasn't used to male attention. But she'd had plenty of it over the past two weeks, and she still sought him out. She loved him.

TWENTY-NINE

A LADY NEVER perspired, but Addie felt a definite glow on her face after the last dance. Mr. Eaton waved her to his side again. She was happy to oblige, since he stood alone. Her dream was to find their hearts were in tune, that she was the daughter he'd dreamed of.

"Having a good time?" he asked, smiling when she reached his side.

"It's lovely. And a little disconcerting. So much attention." She flipped open her fan and waved it over her face.

"It's because you're an Eaton, Julia. Always remember that."

She nodded, her smile fading. "I'll keep that in mind."

"Lord Carrington is quite smitten."

"He's nice enough, but a bit above me."

284

"You mustn't allow yourself to think that way. Thomas would be a splendid match for you."

"I'm not looking for a husband, sir."

"Call me Father," he said, his voice gruff. "I've looked for you for a long time."

"Yes . . . Father." The word didn't roll off her tongue as easily as she'd hoped.

"Now, back to the Carringtons. They're an old and established English family. And rich."

"I don't care about money," she said, when it was clear he was waiting for a response from her.

"I want you to marry into a title. That's the one thing the Eatons lack. We're self-made. But with you as an English lady, the Eaton reputation can only grow."

"As I said, I'm not looking for a husband, Father."

"Of course you are. It's what every woman wants. And what could be better than a husband like Carrington? What else could you do with your time but find a good man and bear children?"

"I'd like to become a nurse," she said. Saying it out loud made her realize how ridiculous it was. An Eaton tending to the sick. He'd never allow it.

"What the devil are you talking about?" he sputtered. "The Eaton name is not an asset to be squandered. I suspect Carrington will apply to me for your hand. And I'll be happy to grant it."

She took a step back. "Surely not without my permission!"

"A father knows what is best for his daughter. You need to trust my judgment, Julia."

She met his gaze and lifted her chin. "I want to love the man I marry."

"Love," he scoffed. "Don't be so naïve, child."

"You loved my mother."

His voice softened. "That I did. And you'll come to love your husband."

She wanted to tell him of her love for John, but now wasn't the time. It would take some time for her father to realize she had a mind of her own. "Yes, sir."

"Father," he corrected again.

"Father." She managed to speak without breaking down, but she longed for her room and her dog.

"Good girl," he said, his smile breaking out again. "I'll make sure of a very good match for you, Daughter."

Daughter. It soothed her heart to know he loved and accepted her. To know she finally had an extended family. It was a whole new world.

"Father, that little girl who was hurt at your garment factory—Brigitte Whittaker?"

"I did as you asked. She and her sister are toting fabric now."

"I'm so grateful. I stopped by the tenement yesterday, and Mrs. Whittaker is quite ill with consumption. I'd like to do something."

"Consumption. There's nothing much to be done

for that. I forbid you to go back to that place. Full of noxious vapors and sickness." He patted her shoulder. "Put it out of your head."

She nodded, but her frown remained.

It was after midnight when the last guests filed off to their bedrooms. Most had come in from San Francisco and would be staying for the weekend. She resolved to avoid the majority of them. Lord Carrington had pressed her hand and invited her for a yacht ride on the following Friday, and she'd been forced to accept, with her father's gimlet eye on her. Though the thought of a day on the water appealed to her, she prayed there would be others on the boat as well.

One lone hall light illuminated the back stairway to the second floor. She went down the steep steps to avoid a last-minute encounter with Lord Carrington. She stepped into the second-floor hall and moved toward the sanctuary of her bedroom. John's door was open as she passed, and his light was on, but she saw no sign of him in the room. Averting her eyes for her unseemly curiosity, she scurried toward the end of the hall.

He stepped out of Edward's room as she neared it. "Addie, hold on a moment," he said, grasping her arm. "Edward has had another spell."

"Oh no!" She started to enter the room, but he blocked her passage.

"He's fine now. Sleeping with Gideon at the foot of his bed."

"I miss him," she said. "Gideon."

His eyes softened. "I imagine Henry has forgotten about finding a mate for him. I'll see what I can do. Edward would be quite taken with a puppy, and perhaps Gideon could pass along his intuition."

"I hope so, because you'll be going back to the city soon, won't you?"

"I will. I'd hoped to take you with me."

She dropped her gaze. "I'm not sure my father will allow it."

"What do you want, Addie?"

At least John used the name her soul responded to. She raised her gaze from the carpet. "I want to be with you," she said. "Such a bold thing for me to say."

He reached out and wrapped a curl around his finger. "We must see what we can do about that."

Laughing revelers rounded the hall corner and approached. He dropped his hand back to his side, and Addie fled to her room. A choice between John and her family might be fast approaching. She wanted both, which wasn't likely to come about.

The overpowering scent of flowers made Addie's head ache. "It's so good of you to host Josephine's funeral," she told Katie and Mrs. Russell.

Mrs. Russell patted her hand. "My dear, it was the least I could do for my best friend's daughter." She glanced around the parlor. "A respectable attendance from the Eatons and those who do business with them."

"They were very kind," Addie agreed. She started to say they'd come only out of duty but bit back the words. It was time she learned a little discretion in her speech.

Flowers nearly smothered the room. The casket containing Josephine's body was in one corner, and even more flowers surrounded it. A table of food, finger sandwiches, and desserts had been spread for the visitors. This day would soon be over, and the undertaker would arrive to take Josephine to the grave site.

She saw a familiar top hat approaching through the window. "Oh no, it's Lord Carrington," she said. "He's been pursuing me most relentlessly."

"He's a very nice man," Mrs. Russell said. "A trifle old for you, perhaps, but wealthy and generous. I know your mother thought most highly of him."

Addie's face burned at the rebuke. "I'm sure you're right," she said. "But I'm not interested in him."

"Lord Carrington pursued your mother most persistently. He was livid when she turned him down and married your father. Thrown over for a commoner."

"But he is pursuing me. He must be quite old if he was in love with my mother."

Mrs. Russell tugged at her glove. "I often wondered if he had something to do with your mother's departure."

"What do you mean?" Addie asked.

"He came to see her two days before she left. Laura sent a note to me that night."

"What did it say?"

"That she'd learned something dreadful." Mrs. Russell shook her head. "But when she came to tea the next day, I could not persuade her to reveal what it was she'd discovered."

"She might have learned this thing from Lord Carrington."

"I've often wondered," Mrs. Russell said.

Addie tried to control her excitement. "I'm going yachting with him on Friday. I shall ask him directly."

"You think that's wise?" Katie asked. "He may not want to drag up old conflicts."

"I'll press him."

"You're such an unconventional young woman," Mrs. Russell said. "I quite admire your forthcoming spirit. You should come to the next suffrage meeting."

"One of the maids invited me," Addie said. "I haven't had time, but I'll come soon."

Mrs. Russell smiled. "You've been too busy adjusting to your new position. And spending time with the dashing lieutenant. I don't blame you. He's quite handsome."

"He's a good man," Addie said. "I sense loneliness in him. He's like the missing piece of me."

"Such a poetic thought," Katie said. "I don't know if I'll ever feel like that about a man. Sh, here comes Carrington." She extended her hand. "Lord Carrington, so kind of you to come."

"I wouldn't stay away." He pressed Addie's hand. "Have the police found who did this thing?"

She removed her hand when he would have kept it. "Not yet. They are not optimistic that they'll find the criminal."

Another couple came through the door, and Mrs. Russell hurried off to greet them with Katie in tow. Addie wanted to call at least one of them back to help her deal with Lord Carrington.

He claimed her hand again and tucked it into the crook of his arm. He led her toward the table of food. "I'm famished, my dear. What can I get you to eat?"

"Nothing, sir. I've already eaten."

"Oh, call me Thomas."

"My father taught me to call my elders sir and ma'am," she said. She barely restrained a gasp when she realized how offensive what she'd said must sound to him.

The muscles in his arm tightened under her fingers. "I realize you have your cap set for young North," he said, stopping short of the food table. "You should know there was plenty of talk when Katherine died."

"What kind of talk?"

"She was leaving him, you know."

"I know."

"Such a freak accident to be mowed down by a streetcar. Some said John pushed her in front of that car."

"I don't believe that for a moment," she said, raising her voice. She withdrew her hand and restrained herself from slapping him. "If you'll excuse me, I'd better speak to the other guests."

Shaking, she stalked off to the door in time to see John arriving on his motorcycle. She stepped from the house and went to greet him.

He dismounted and put the kickstand down. "Is something wrong?"

"That vile Carrington practically accused you of murdering Katherine! He said people believe you pushed her under the wheels of the streetcar."

His brows rose, and his eyes flashed. "I've heard that rumor." He smiled then. "Nice of you to defend me, but it's not necessary."

"It was necessary. He spoke loudly enough for others to hear him." She took the arm he offered, and they strolled toward the house.

"Carrington must have noticed our relationship."

Her fingers tightened on his arm. "Do we have a relationship, John?"

"I don't know who else gets away with being so blunt with me," he said. A smile curved his mouth.

The words *I love you* hovered on her lips, but she bit them back. He might find her amusing.

Intriguing, even. But he didn't love her. Not yet. She would do everything in her power to make that happen.

"How are you doing?" he asked, studying her face.

"I miss her even though she never loved me. Now she never will." Her voice broke.

John's other hand covered hers. "I'm sorry, Addie."

"I like to hear you say my name," she whispered.

He embraced her, and she laid her head against his chest. His heart beat fast in her ear. She let herself dream that in other circumstances he might have kissed her.

"We should go in," he said, drawing her away from him.

Thursday was to be a day beyond reach of the Eaton family's expectations. Addie relished the hours that stretched ahead of her as she took a family buggy to Mercy Falls. The last few days had been gloomy as the Eatons conferred about what to do. She'd heard her father say the estate would have to be sold unless she managed to land a wealthy husband. The weight of the responsibility nearly crushed her.

At church on Sunday, Katie had invited her to dessert today at the Burnett's Confectionery Kitchen, with a promise of chocolate. Addie had eaten chocolate only a few times in her life. Her papa would sometimes bring her a Hershey's Bar from the mainland, and she would eat one square a day until it was gone. But more than the promise of chocolate, the thought of sharing the afternoon with Katie lifted her spirits.

She parked the buggy in the lot, then walked down the sidewalk to the candy store. Through the plate-glass window, she saw Katie standing at the ornate glass and oak display. The bell on the door tinkled when Addie stepped inside. Her mouth watered the moment she smelled the delicious scents inside the shop.

Katie smiled when she saw her. "I took the liberty of ordering for you. I wanted you to try my favorite. A hot-fudge sundae with pecans."

"What is that?" Addie couldn't take her gaze from the tempting array of chocolates, pralines, and hard candies.

"Ice cream with chocolate and nuts."

"Ice cream?" She'd heard of it but never had it.

Katie led her to a small wrought-iron table and chairs. "You'll see." She sat and pulled off her gloves.

Addie did the same, though she wanted to buy an intriguing candy called a Tootsie Roll. A passing contraption caught her eye. "There's John on his Harley-Davidson."

Katie twisted in her chair to stare out the window. "It makes a most dreadful noise," she said, raising her voice over the rumble. "And it appears unsafe."

"I think perhaps that's why he loves it. It's the one place he can be a boy again," she said.

She became aware that Katie was staring at her with her mouth gaping in a most unladylike manner. "Is something wrong?"

"You're in love with him?"

"What? With whom?"

"Don't play the ingenue. With John North. It's as plain as the ribbons on your hat."

Heat rose in Addie's cheeks. "He's an intriguing man."

"You're blushing! It's true. You're in love with him."

Addie turned back toward the counter. Now would be a good time for their dessert to arrive. "I don't know what love is."

"Your heart pounds when he's around. You watch for him in a crowded room. You daydream about what it's like to kiss him."

The heat intensified in Addie's face. "That's infatuation. Even I know the difference. How does one know it's love?"

Katie laid her gloves on the table. "I'm no expert, since I've never been in love myself, but I've watched my friends get married. They say that the man they love makes them want to be better than they are. That he brings out the best in them and complements their weaknesses. And they do the same to their husband."

"I don't know if it's love," Addie said. "I care

about him. I want to see him learn to enjoy life. He's always so serious."

"I hope you don't get your heart broken, Addie," Katie said, her smile fading. "Lieutenant North is a dangerous man."

"Dangerous?" He was certainly dangerous to her peace of mind.

Her friend nodded. "He has such a charming way about him."

"That's hardly a negative trait."

"Perhaps not. But that doesn't negate the fact that he may not be as interested in you as he seems."

She put her hands on her cheeks. "I never said he was interested!"

"How else could he have stolen your heart? He's paid you some attention."

Was that all her feelings were? An inexperienced girl's misunderstanding of a man's attention? The proprietor placed a mouthwatering dish in front of her, but she could barely concentrate on the amazing concoction of flavors.

THIRTY

FRIDAY MORNING, ADDIE watched Edward's form on the pinto pony. She was still exhausted from the events of the past week, and the last thing she wanted to do was go for a boat ride with Thomas Carrington.

"Back straight. Heels down," she called. The horse she rode was a quick and responsive mare named Whisper. Ferns as high as trees bordered the clearing where they rode. Addie kept an eye on Gideon to ensure Edward wasn't on the verge of an attack.

"Papa will be so surprised," Edward said, his cheeks flushed. "He never let me ride before."

"He was rightly worried about you. It would be dangerous for you to become ill while on a horse. It was all I could do to persuade him to let you try."

The boy's grin stretched wider. "I can do anything with Gideon."

It was true. Since she'd arrived at Eaton Manor, she'd seen Edward's confidence grow. This latest adventure was to be a surprise for John's birthday. She glanced at her watch, a gift from Mr. Eaton. It had once been her mother's, and Addie couldn't stop admiring the diamonds and the delicate workmanship. It was nearly ten o'clock, and she had to be ready for the dreaded yachting trip at noon. Lord Carrington's staff was preparing a picnic lunch for aboard the boat.

She opened her mouth to tell Edward it was time to head back to the house, when a flock of birds rose from a bush near him. The pony reared with its eyes rolling.

Addie rode forward and snatched at the reins, but the pony evaded her. "Edward, hang on!"

The boy's knuckles were white as he gripped the

reins. Then the horse bolted straight for an opening in the thick ferns. Gideon barked and followed.

"Rein him in!" she shouted. She urged her horse after Edward. The ferns and towering trees blocked out the sun. It was like stepping into twilight. She caught a flash of white and saw the pony racing toward the stream. Edward still clung to his back, with Gideon on the pony's hooves. Once the horse hit the stream, Edward's chances of being seriously injured by rocks would increase.

"Rein him in, Edward!" she screamed, urging her horse faster. "Pull hard on the reins!"

The boy straightened from his hunch over the pony's neck. She saw him yank on the reins. "Don't let up. Pull!" she yelled. Edward continued to pull on the leather. The pony began to slow, then finally stopped, his sides bellowing with exertion. Foam flecked his sides.

Addie dismounted and ran to pull Edward from the pony. "Are you all right?"

His eyes filled, but he nodded. "That pony can run fast. But I did it, Teacher. I made him stop. And I didn't fall off."

She hugged him. "I'm very proud of you. You were quite the little man."

John's voice spoke behind her. "You are quite the little man, Edward."

"Papa!" Edward released Addie and ran to this father. "Did you see me? I didn't fall off even when the birds spooked the pony."

John lifted his son into his arms. "You were very brave." He kissed Edward's cheek. "You were right," he told Addie. "He needed to learn to ride."

She clasped her hands together. "Thank you for trusting me. I want him to enjoy being a child."

"So do I."

Edward wiggled to be let down. "Miss Addie said we could go wading in the stream!"

John raised a brow. "I'd rather you didn't, Edward."

Addie curled her fingers in Gideon's fur. "You could come with us."

"Yes, Papa, you come too!" Edward tugged on John's hand.

Addie nearly giggled at the consternation on John's face. She grabbed her horse's reins and led him through the redwoods and Sitka spruce. They passed rhododendrons, huckleberry, and redwood sorrel. The roar of the waterfall grew louder until its cold spray misted her face.

"Take off your shoes," she said.

"I-I have bank figures to go over."

She only hoped he found some way out of the overwhelming pressure on her to save the Eaton family. "Everyone deserves some time off. We won't be long."

Edward took off his shoes and pulled his knickers higher. "Hold my hand, Papa," he said, pulling on his father's fingers.

With a roll of his eyes, John sat down and pulled

off his shoes and socks, revealing long white feet. No calluses. He'd obviously not been accustomed to walking barefoot on the beach, as she was. Gideon barked and ran ahead of her to the water. He jumped in and snapped at the small fish swimming in the stream. He eyed a frog until Addie commanded him to leave it alone.

She waded out into the stream. "Come on in, Edward." Her skin quickly numbed from the frigid water. Minnows darted between rocks in the clear water, and larger fish swam from her splashes.

"Ooh, it's cold!" Edward waded toward Gideon. He turned to face his father. "Come on, Papa."

"I'm coming," John growled. He rolled his pants legs up a little more, then gingerly stepped into the water. He grimaced. "Boy howdy, is it cold!"

Addie giggled behind her hand. "You'll get used to it in a minute."

He still wore his bowler, vest, and jacket, but with his pants rolled up and the wonder on his face, he reminded her of a little boy dressed in his father's clothes. She leaned down and flicked cold water at him. A dollop splashed on his cheek and rolled down his neck.

His eyes went wide, then he grinned and took off his hat. He scooped up a hatful of water and started toward her. Adrenaline kicked in, and she scurried backward with her hands out. "I give, I give!"

He advanced on her. "You're not getting off that easy."

"Do it, Papa!" Edward splashed water as he practically danced along beside his father.

Gideon barked excitedly as if he approved as well. "Traitor," Addie told him.

Her feet slid on the moss-covered rocks. She threw out her hands to try to regain her balance, and John caught her arm. She clutched at him, and in the next moment, she was in his arms, and they both tumbled into the stream. Cold water filled her mouth and nose and soaked her clothing. Her water-heavy dress dragged her down, but she managed to sit up. Laughter bubbled from her throat when she saw John. His wet hair hung in his face, and his suit was soaked.

"Hungry?" She picked a flopping minnow off his shoulder and tossed it back into the water.

"That was too small to keep anyway," he said.

The current caused by the waterfall kept trying to force her back down, and she only managed to resist its pressure by holding on to John. He had his arm around her back and his hand at her waist. She was close enough to see the flecks of white in his eyes—like starbursts. A rather comfortable position, or it would have been if not for the freezing water.

"I suppose we'd better get up," she said, her head buttressed by his shoulder.

"I'm in no hurry. The damage is done." He kept his left arm around her, but dumped a frog out of his hat with his right. "You're right. The water doesn't seem so cold now." He put his hat on his knee.

"I'm sorry your suit is ruined," she said.

"It's the most fun I've had since I was a boy." His tone was wistful. "No wonder Edward loves you."

Her pulse kicked up a notch when his face came closer, but he stopped, then scrambled to his feet and held out his hand to lift her from the rushing water.

"Are we still on for the concert tomorrow night?" he asked.

"I can't wait," she said.

"You're going with Carrington today, aren't you?"

"Yes. I don't want to, but my father insists."

"Don't let him force you into anything you don't want to do, Addie."

"What would you do if your family's future depended on you?" she whispered.

He sighed and rubbed his head. "Your father has brought this on himself. What if this is discipline from God?"

"I'd never thought of that," she said. "If I intervene to save him, I could be circumventing God's will." She would have to think about this.

THIRTY-ONE

THE SEA SPRAY hit Addie's face, and she adjusted her parasol. What she really wanted to do was toss it into the sea foam. Playing this new role of lady wasn't something she relished yet. The bow of the yacht rode the waves like a champion. The steam-powered vessel had two masts and stretched over two hundred feet along the waves. The lounge chair she reclined upon pointed her toward a stunning view of the cliffs along the coast.

She'd expected others to be on board when she saw the size of the craft, but only crewmen scurried along the deck. She and Lord Carrington were the only passengers, a gaffe she wasn't sure how to rectify. If she'd known beforehand, she would have invited Katie along to chaperone.

"Comfortable?" Lord Carrington asked.

"Quite. She is magnificent."

He beamed. "I had her built two years ago. She rivals anything in the Royal Navy."

Her nose caught a whiff of roast beef. The chef would soon have dinner ready, and she prayed they could eat on deck. She didn't want to be below deck and at Carrington's mercy. She shifted on the chair and stared at the passing coast.

"You seem ill at ease, Miss Sullivan. I assure you I'm completely harmless," he said.

She turned to face him. Distinguished mustache,

salt-and-pepper hair at the temples, erect posture. He appeared honorable, but what did she know of men and their motives? If her journey to find her heritage had taught her one thing, it was that she was an innocent surrounded by people of murky motives.

"Why so serious?" he asked, a dimple appearing in his right cheek.

"I learned something interesting about you."

The amusement in his blue eyes faded. "About me?"

She twirled the parasol but kept her gaze on him. "I heard you wanted to marry my mother."

"You believe in going for the jugular, I see."

"Is it true?"

He nodded. "It is. You have the look of her, you know."

"I've only seen pictures. They do a poor job of capturing her essence. Her vitality, her spirit."

"Her hair was redder than yours, and she was very fair. Your eyes are like hers, green and sparkling with life."

"You must have loved her very much."

He broke eye contact. "Enough to let her go when she made her choice."

"Did you break off all contact with her then?" Addie held her breath while she waited to see if he would lie to her.

"Yes."

Her fingers tightened around the parasol. She

should have expected less than the truth, especially if he had anything to do with her mother's disappearance. "No contact at all?"

He shrugged. "She sent me a note when I was in the city about a week before she left. She asked that I come to see her. I did so."

"What did she want?" she asked, careful to keep any judgment out of her voice.

"My help. She wanted to leave."

She barely bit back a gasp. "*You* helped her leave?"

He nodded. "I've never told any other person. Certainly not your father."

"He would blame you for her death."

His gaze veered to the distant shore. "And I feel somewhat responsible. If I'd urged her to stay, would she still be alive?"

"Did she say why she was leaving?"

He hesitated. "She felt her life was in danger."

Addie's gasp escaped her throat this time. "Did she say from whom?"

He took off his hat and rubbed his forehead. "Look, Julia, this is all such a long time ago. Why go dredging up these memories now? What difference does it make?"

She snapped her parasol shut and leaned forward to grip his forearm. "Thomas, what if she was murdered?"

"She was lost in a storm."

"Her body was never found."

His lips twisted. "That's hardly unusual on the ocean, is it not?"

"No," she admitted. "But I was found on the shore, wet but fine. So where was she? How did I get there?"

"The providence of God, I suspect. What possible proof do you have for such an outrageous thought?"

"I found some letters of hers. And she left a note indicating she was fearful." She bit back the information about the clues. "I think there would have been *some* evidence that she perished on the boat, if she did," Addie said. She couldn't explain her growing belief there was more to the story than a tragic shipwreck. There was no evidence to prove her mother had even died on that boat.

She considered who might have wanted to harm her mother. Her father? But no, he'd been possessed as he'd searched for her and had changed afterward. He was too cool and collected to feign that kind of passion. What about Clara? Her sister was a formidable rival, and Clara got what she wanted after Laura died.

Thomas rose and held out his hand "Let's go enjoy that lunch the chef has prepared for us."

His candor had calmed her fears about him. She accepted his assistance and followed him to the dining room below. It was only later she realized he never answered her question about whom her mother feared.

John unbuttoned his jacket, then buttoned it up again. The new tuxedo was a bit loose and looked better closed. He combed his hair again, then tried it on the other side. No, it was better in the normal manner. He changed it, then rubbed his face. His shave had gotten all the stray whiskers.

He straightened his tie for the third time, then picked up his hat and exited his room. Edward was playing with toy soldiers on the floor with the dog. "Good night, son," he said. "Be good for Yvonne."

"I will, Papa." Edward kissed him. "You smell good."

John tugged at his tie when his neck heated. "It's just hair tonic," he mumbled, knowing it was more than that. The saleswoman at Oscar's Mercantile had assured him the cologne was the one the women asked for most often for their husbands.

"See you in the morning." Leaving his son, he strode down the wide staircase to the entry. Women liked to make a fashionable entry, didn't they? She wouldn't be ready yet. But when he reached the front door, he found Addie waiting on the entry settee with her hands folded in her lap.

When she saw him, she rose with a brilliant smile that stole his voice. "I didn't want to be late. I'm so looking forward to this. I quite adore Scott Joplin's music. I've never been to a nickelodeon."

He wasn't quite sure what he mumbled as he offered his arm and escorted her through the door.

She would be the most beautiful woman there tonight. The emerald gown brought out the color of her eyes. Auburn curls peeked from under the velvet turban she wore. A swatch of something filmy protruded from the top of the hat. The same style on Clara the other night had looked attractive, but on Addie it was elegant and breathtaking.

The carriage was waiting. He helped her inside, then climbed in behind her. The driver set off as soon as John shut the door behind them. Her perfume made him dizzy.

"Did you make your dress?" he asked.

She smoothed the folds of the skirt. "No, there wasn't time. Clara loaned it to me. She's being very solicitous now that their future hinges on me."

"You look lovely," he said.

The dimple in her cheek flashed. "You seem to have survived the dip in the stream yesterday."

"My suit didn't." He watched the light dim in her eyes and cursed his poor choice of words. "It was worth it to see Edward's enjoyment, though."

The sparkle came back to her face. "You should do it more often."

"I should," he agreed. He'd nearly kissed her yesterday. Maybe he should have. He shifted on the seat. "I want no secrets between us, so I want you to know I've done some investigating."

"Of me?"

He nodded. "I made the decision before I knew you as well as I do now. I'm sorry if you find it offensive. I have a son to protect. And I find I want to protect you as well."

A cardinal flitted from a redwood tree, and she watched its path. "And what did you find out?"

"Everyone in Crescent City spoke of you and your parents most highly."

She put her hands to her hot cheeks. "I hardly knew the townspeople. What must they think to be asked such questions? What could they possibly have to say?" Straightening in her seat, she turned to stare at him.

"That you're an angel in skirts. Taking food to the poor, mending clothing for free, ministering to the sick when you weren't working hard on your parents' behalf." He smiled. "They say your father told glowing stories. Exactly my impression of you. I'm relieved. But I'm afraid it brings us no closer to helping you figure out who attacked you or paid for your upkeep."

Addie slipped her hand into his. "Tonight, let's think of happier things."

The happiest thing he could imagine would be to have her at his side for the rest of his life. The errant thought nearly made him gasp. He'd realized his attraction, but it was only now that he understood how deep it went.

The carriage pulled up in front of the nickelodeon. Women in colorful dresses on the arms of men dressed in tuxedos streamed toward the entrance. The driver opened the door, and John stepped down onto the street, then helped Addie out. He straightened when he saw the admiring glances other men threw her way. Her eyes were wide as she took in everything: velvet seats and curtains, gilded ceiling, ornately carved railings. The level of excitement in the audience created a rising hum of conversation.

He stopped to introduce her to the mayor, several society women, and a couple of Henry's employees before they found their box seat in the balcony. Once the drapes behind them were closed, he settled beside her and planned to watch her reaction to the ragtime music.

The audience thundered its approval of Willie Richards. The handsome man of color bowed, then took his place at the piano. He first thundered out "Maple Leaf Rag," and John's foot kept time to the music.

"He's quite extraordinary," he whispered to Addie, who was lost in the music.

She gripped the oaken railing in front of her, and he thought she might leap over the balcony. At least that's the reason he told himself it was all right to take her gloved hand. She only removed it long enough to clap at the end of the number, then slipped her hand back into his in a natural movement that touched him.

Her fingers tightened on his when Richards began to play "The Entertainer." "It's my favorite," she whispered.

John paid more attention to Addie than he did the music. The concert was over much too soon. He had her wait with him in the box until most of the crowd cleared out, then led her down to meet the musician. He stood back, smiling as she gushed her enthusiasm to the pianist. When John finally led her back to the carriage, her hat was askew, and high color lodged in her cheeks.

He helped her inside the carriage, then told the driver to take them for a ride along the seaside before heading home. When he settled beside her on the leather seat, she slipped her hand into his.

Her eyes shone in the moonlight. "Thank you for a night I'll never forget," she said. "It was quite wonderful, John." Her lips parted in a gleaming smile.

He leaned closer until their breaths mingled. "I'm glad you enjoyed it."

Her face was turned up to his. He shouldn't find her so tempting, but he did. He drew his fingers across her cheek. It was soft as the velvet in her hat. He bent his head and brushed her lips with his. She inhaled and went rigid.

"Don't be afraid," he murmured. "I won't hurt you." He kissed her again, pulling her more firmly into his arms.

One gloved hand lodged against his chest. The other arm stole around his neck. The sweetness and purity of her lips was like nothing he'd ever dreamed of or imagined. He deepened the kiss and realized how deeply he'd fallen in love with her. Not because she was an Eaton, but because she was Addie. Delightful, laughing Addie.

He pulled away and smiled into her half-closed eyes. The heady fragrance of her hair, her skin, filled his head. Words of love hovered on his lips, but he held them back. It was too soon. He might frighten her.

Her eyes came open, then her fingers crept to her lips. "You kissed me," she said. "I dreamed you might tonight."

His heart stuttered, then leaped to a steady rhythm again. "I should say I'm sorry, but I'm not."

She touched his cheek. "I wondered what love felt like," she said. "Now I know."

He crushed her to his chest again. There was no pretense with her. He kissed her again, not caring to hold back the depth of his love.

His breathing was ragged when he raised his head. "Oh Addie, Addie, what did I do before you came into my life?"

Tears shone on her lashes. "I don't think I lived before tonight."

"We must be married. Quite soon, darling girl. I can't wait for long."

"I'd marry you tonight," she said. "Right now."

He traced the curve of her cheek with his finger. "I'll ask your father for your hand tonight."

A shadow darkened the joy in her eyes. "What about Lord Carrington?"

"What about him?"

"Father seems quite set on a match with him." She wet her lips. "I've been thinking about what you said. That God might be disciplining him. You might be right."

The shadow didn't leave her eyes, and the fear in her face spread to him. Henry had to consent.

THIRTY-TWO

ADDIE KEPT TOUCHING her fingertips to her lips on the ride back to the manor. John loved her! She couldn't take it in. Her lips felt fuller, softer. Different. She was going to be married. Life could change just that fast. She couldn't wait to tell Katie. Her father had to agree. He just had to. His own daughter would be the new mother of his grandson. What more could he want?

John kissed her quickly when the carriage stopped in front of the manor. "I'll talk to your father now."

"I'd like to be there. Is that allowed?"

"It's not usual," he said. "But I can't deny you anything tonight."

Her heart would not stop its insistent knocking against her ribs. "I'm so happy," she whispered.

He clambered down and held out his hand. "I'll do my best to keep you that way," he said, his eyes smiling.

She looped her arm through his and allowed

him to lead her toward the house. "That's Lord Carrington's brougham," she said.

"Perhaps he'll leave soon so we can talk to your father." He opened the door for her.

The flowers on the entry table perfumed the hall. She and John followed the voices to the drawing room, where she found Lord Carrington and her father smoking cigars. The claret was out on the table, and both were talking more loudly than usual.

Her father turned his head and saw her in the doorway. His face was flushed, but he bellowed out her name. "Julia, my dear, I have wonderful news for you. Come in. You too, John. You might as well hear this now."

She glanced at John, then slipped into the room. "What is it, Father?" She'd never get used to calling him Father.

His smile was expansive, and he preened. "Your future is all settled, my dear. Lord Carrington has graciously asked for your hand, and I've given my permission. The wedding is to be at Christmas." When she opened her mouth, he held up his hand. "I know that's not much time to arrange all the fripperies you ladies like, but Clara will help make the arrangements. You'll be Lady Carrington." He beamed at her.

The bright bubble of her joy burst in her chest. Instead of being upset at the denial of a proper proposal, Lord Carrington smiled.

"But Father, I hardly know Lord Carrington," she said.

Henry waved his hand. "There'll be time enough for that after the wedding."

She glared at the Englishman. "I don't know you well enough to marry you, sir. And you're much too old for me."

"Julia!" her father gasped.

She whirled toward her father. Her face was hot, and her hands shook. "It's true. He also wanted to marry my mother. How can you even think of allowing him to marry me? Did you know he came to see my mother before she died? What if he had something to do with her death?"

"Go to your room!" her father shouted. "You know nothing about this."

"I know more than you think," she said. "I'm not going to marry him."

Lord Carrington rose and stepped to where she stood. He took her hand and raised it to his lips. "I'll leave you to absorb the news, my dear. You're overwrought. I shall call on you tomorrow." His eyes held kindness. "I'll see myself out."

She stood mute as he walked from the drawing room. When the front door closed, she glanced at John. His eyes were steely. She took his hand, and he squeezed it.

Her father poured himself another glass of claret and drank the whole thing. "I realize you were caught off guard, but I'll not have my own daughter speak to me with such disrespect."

"I meant no disrespect, Father, but I'm not going to marry that man. Don't you even care that he might have had something to do with my mother's fate?"

"Oh my dear, you're being much too melodramatic." Her father leaned back. "Carrington is a good man."

Was her father being deliberately obtuse? "You don't know that!"

John dropped her hand and stepped forward. "Henry, I must protest this arrangement. Carrington is much too old for her."

He set down his glass. "What the devil, John? This is no business of yours."

"It is indeed, sir. I want to marry Addie myself. I love her, and she loves me."

Hearing John say the words brought back Addie's joy. She stepped to his side. "He's right, Father." She linked hands with John. "I love John. I want to marry him and be a mother to Edward."

Her father slammed his fist on the arm of the chair. "Ridiculous!" He shook his finger at John. "I gave you one daughter, whom you made miserable. I'll see Julia dead before I see her married to you."

John paled. "Then we'll marry without your blessing."

"You'll do no such thing!" Henry surged to his

feet. "Go to your room, Daughter. We will discuss this between us."

"I won't marry Lord Carrington, Father. I won't!" She ran from the room and nearly tripped over her skirt in her mad rush upstairs. Sobs tore from her throat.

When she reached her room, she hurled her hat across the room, then fell onto her bed and wailed.

The grandfather clock in Henry's office chimed two in the morning. John's movements were jerky as he pulled open the desk drawers and went through them. He barely controlled his anger. Henry had no right to treat Addie like she was some kind of property to be bartered off. He knew what had to be behind this: money. Carrington was probably buying her the way he would a horse.

He heard footsteps in the hall, and he quickly killed the gaslight. The room plunged into darkness. The door opened, and a shadowy form filled the doorway, then moved into the office. There was no place to hide, so he sat motionless until the moonlight allowed him to recognize the figure.

"Addie," he whispered.

She gasped and turned toward him. "John?"

He rose from the chair and embraced her. "What are you doing up?"

She pulled away, then went to the doorway and shut the door. "Turn on the light."

"What's happening?" He lit the light and adjusted the glow.

She joined him at the desk. Her hair spilled onto her lilac dressing gown, and he couldn't take his eyes off the long curls that hung nearly to her waist.

"You've been crying," he said, noticing her reddened eyes. He took her in his arms again. "We'll convince your father."

Her head nestled against his chest and her fingers clung to his shirt. "I can't marry Carrington, but this is what I've longed for." She raised her head and stared at him with tear-filled eyes. "I wanted to be part of a big family. To have roots. If Father doesn't consent to our marriage, everything I've worked to find will be gone."

"Are you saying you won't marry me without his consent?"

She bit her lip. "I would rather have his blessing, but I can't marry Carrington." She glanced over his shoulder at the desk. "What are you searching for?"

He guided her to the desk chair. "I want to find proof of your father's mismanagement. I thought if I could show you that he's reaping what he's sown, you'll be able to let go of feeling responsible for his future."

"I already know he's done this himself."

He pulled out more desk drawers and lifted the contents onto the top. "Sort through these and see what you find."

She picked up the top sheet of paper. "What am I looking for?"

"Contracts. Legal notices. Bank accounts." He settled in a chair with another stack of paper. They read in silence for several minutes until he heard her gasp and saw her pale. The paper in her hand shook.

He rose and stepped to the desk. "What did you find?"

She held out the paper. "I think it's a will. My maternal grandfather's."

Not what they needed, but it had obviously upset her, so he took it and began to read. The first part detailed property and money left to Clara and Walter. Both were substantial. He read on.

To my daughter Laura I bequeath the bulk of my entire estate. In the event of her death, the estate shall pass to her daughter. If she leaves no heirs, the estate shall pass to any offspring Clara or Walter produce.

He rubbed his forehead and puzzled out the meaning. Edward was the beneficiary? He was the only descendant. No, wait, he wasn't thinking right. His gaze went to Addie's face. She was the legal heir. She was Laura's daughter. "He wasn't going to tell you this," he said slowly. "He's never told me that all this belongs to Edward, not him and Clara. All he's ever mentioned is the tract of land I showed you. It's all been a lie."

She blanched even more. "He's acted like this was all his." She straightened. "Not that it matters now. It's all gone."

"No it's not," he said slowly. "This is all in a San Francisco bank. It's still intact."

"Then why is he so desperate for me to marry Carrington?"

"It's the title he's always craved, not so much the money."

She winced. "He cares so little for me. How has he managed this? How can Walter and Clara not know?"

"Walter was abroad when your grandfather died. And Clara would have let Henry handle matters of the estate. He covered it all up."

"We have to find that other clue," Addie said. "Maybe it's all connected to my mother's disappearance."

"There's no time like the present."

He tucked the will into his pocket and led Addie up the stairs and down the hall to the attic steps. They creaked under his weight as the couple climbed to the attic. He lit the gaslight. "I'm not sure where to look first."

Addie scrutinized the attic's shadowed contents. "My mother loved music."

"And you. I know there is a trunk of your old toys around here, because Edward found it once. I think it's in the northwest corner." He stepped past shrouded furniture and stacks of pictures to the alcove. Two chests were under the window. "I think it was this one." The brass latches on the chest were battered. He lifted the lid. "Yes, this is the one." He began to lift out dolls, clothing, and a tiny tea set.

Addie picked up a rag doll and sat down on a rug. "I remember this! The eyes, especially." She traced the outline of the embroidered face.

John joined her on the carpet and put his arm around her. "I bet you were a beautiful little girl. I hope we have a daughter with your eyes and hair."

"I want another son, a brother for Edward too," she said. She leaned over and kissed him.

Her lips tasted of strawberry jam. She wound her arms around him. He deepened the kiss, and passion ignited between them. He couldn't get enough of her soft lips. Her body was soft beneath his, and he realized they were lying on the carpet instead of sitting on it, though he had no memory of how they got there. It took a monumental effort to roll away and sit up. His pulse hammered in his chest. He wanted to hold her again, but he knew he didn't dare. She was much too tempting.

She touched his arm. "John?"

He forced a smile. "We've gotten sidetracked. Let's see if there's anything else here."

The smile she turned on him stole his breath. Such trust and love. He'd nearly broken that trust. He bent over the chest and pulled out small items.

She picked up the tea set and peered inside each

cup, then lifted the lid on the teapot. "John, there's something here!" She thrust her fingers into the pot and withdrew a tiny scrap of paper.

"Get it under the light," he said when he saw her squint at the tiny print.

She scrambled to her feet, and he followed her to the sconce on the wall. Her brow wrinkled as she strained to see the words. "It reads 'Fort Bragg.'" She stared at him. "The first time I talked to Katie was when she called to pass along a message from Father's secretary about having completed the arrangements for his trip to Fort Bragg. She said he went twice a year."

A memory surged to the forefront of his mind. "There's an insane asylum there."

Addie's hand went to the pocket of her dressing gown and emerged with a paper. "This clue. The one about that reads 'insane asylum.'"

He knew what she wanted from her thoughtful expression. "You want to go to Fort Bragg." But his gut twisted at the thought of digging any deeper into this morass.

THIRTY-THREE

PEOPLE NOTICED WHEN she came to town. Monday morning, Addie could barely make it from store to store without being stopped with a smile and friendly hello. Before it became known she was an Eaton, people were friendly, but now that her identity was common knowledge, they gave her deference.

She knew her smile was lopsided as she spoke and went on her way down the street. Dawn had come with her still wide-eyed and sleepless over the revelations of the night before. Her father cared nothing about her and never would. All that mattered to him was more money and power.

She rounded the corner and saw her uncle outside a tavern. He was staring into the window with a faraway expression that cleared when he turned his head and saw her. "Julia, my dear, you look lovely. What are you doing in town today?"

She brushed a kiss across Walter's cheek. "I had some errands to run." Did he know about the will? She didn't see how he could and have a relationship with her father. He needed to know what she'd found though. She owed him so much. "I found some other things my mother hid," she said.

He took her arm and drew her off the main sidewalk. "What kind of things?"

"Notes. Clues. One reads, 'Fort Bragg' and the other one reads, 'Father murdered.'"

He blanched. "Did she mean *our* father was murdered?"

"I'm not sure, but that's what I'd assumed."

"Fort Bragg. Henry goes there on business a few times a year."

"So John said." It was all she could do to hold

back the contents of the will she'd found. She had to find out more before she told him.

"I'll put my investigator on it," he said. "Thank you for keeping me informed. Now I must go, my dear. I have an appointment. I'll see you at dinner."

"Let me know if you find out anything," she called after him. She resumed her brisk stroll down the sidewalk and reached the hospital, a small brick building down the block from the garment factory. Mrs. Whittaker had been taken in more than a week ago, and Addie should have checked on her before today. Her only excuse was how unsettled her life had been.

She climbed the steps to the second floor and found the nurses' desk. After asking the nurse where to find the older woman, she went to the end of the hall. The scent of carbolic and alcohol hung in the air. The coughing of patients told her she'd reached the right ward. She pressed her hand against her diaphragm and took a deep breath. Pinning on a smile, she stepped into the ward.

She walked between the rows of beds. The stench of blood and sickness nearly gagged her. Gaunt, pale faces turned her direction as she traversed the length of the room, searching for Mrs. Whittaker. When a voice called out her name, she turned and saw the woman struggling to sit up in a bed she'd just passed. Mrs. Whittaker had lost weight and was deathly pale.

She lifted a limp hand to Addie. "Miss Sullivan, is that you?"

Addie rushed to the bed and pressed the woman back against the pillow. "Rest, Mrs. Whittaker. I stopped by to see how you are."

The woman fell back, panting. She dabbed at her lips with the handkerchief. "I'm better. Stronger. But my poor children."

"Have they been to see you?"

Mrs. Whittaker shook her head. "The county orphanage won't let them." She reached over and clutched Addie's hand. "Would you go see them? Make sure they're okay. It would mean so much to me to know they aren't being mistreated."

"I'll do what I can," she said. "Can I get you anything? Food, something to drink?"

"I'm fine, dear. Or I will be." Her violent coughing into the handkerchief left flecks of blood.

"I'd better be going, then. I'll pray for you." Addie fled the ward.

She raced past nurses pushing squeaky carts and a doctor walking at a fast clip. Out in the sunshine, she gulped in fresh air that had never smelled so sweet.

"Julia?"

She turned at her father's voice. He stood in his bowler with his suit buttoned and a flower in his buttonhole.

He glanced from her to the hospital. "What were you doing in there?"

"Visiting a friend."

His brows gathered. "Who would that be?"

She held his gaze. "Mrs. Whittaker."

"The mother of the girls who work at the garment factory. Julia, I expressly forbade you to get involved with that family. You could catch her disease. You're an Eaton. Good works are fine, but please limit them to something I approve."

She curled her fingers into fists in the folds of her dress. "I care about this family, Father. I want to help them."

He took a firmer grip on his cane. "Then give them money."

"I want to do more than that. Those children were taken to the orphanage. I can't bear to think of them there. Five children, Father." Her voice broke.

"My dear, there are children all over this country in orphanages. You can't take in all of them."

She put as much appeal in her voice as she could muster. "Maybe not, but we could take in these."

His brows rose, and his expression of horror said it all. "Absolutely not!" He took out his pocket watch. "I must go, my dear. I'll see you at home tonight. Lord Carrington is coming for dinner."

"Father—" But he was gone before she could object.

She walked on toward her buggy, then saw Katie on the other side of the street. Addie darted between two buggies to intercept her friend, who looked fetching in a blue dress framed with lace at the neck. She carried two bags in her left hand.

Katie shifted one of the bags from her left hand to her right. "Addie, I was just thinking about you!"

"Do you have time for ice cream?"

"Oh, I wish I did. I have some clothing to deliver to the orphanage. Why don't you come along with me?"

"For the Whittaker children?"

Katie nodded. "Mama and I canvassed the neighborhood for items. I have a nice assortment. The children would be so glad to see you."

Addie took one of the bags from her. "I could use your advice."

Katie's blue eyes widened. "Is this about John North?"

Addie fell into step beside her, and they walked toward the orphanage. "Not just John," she said.

"What's wrong?"

"I don't even know where to begin. John proposed Saturday night, and I said yes."

"Addie, I'm so happy for you."

"Don't be. When we arrived home, Father informed me that he'd given my hand to Lord Carrington."

Katie stopped on the sidewalk. "No!"

Addie nodded. "He won't listen to reason. He's insisting I marry Carrington."

"But he might have had something to do with your mother's death! And he's *old*, Addie. Old enough to be your father."

"I know."

Katie tipped her head and held Addie's gaze. "You've changed since I met you."

"In what way?"

"When we first met, you were like Gideon. Eager, happy. You said what you thought with never any guile. Now you're so eager to please your father that you're letting him mold you into some idea he has of the proper daughter."

Addie started to speak but wasn't sure if she even had a defense. Was Katie right? She thought about her recent decisions. She'd barely objected when her father forbade her from helping the Whittaker family anymore. "There may be some truth to what you say."

Katie held up the bag of clothes she carried. "Two weeks ago, you would have been the one gathering donations. You would have moved into the apartment and cared for the children yourself instead of letting them go to the orphanage."

Addie's eyes burned. "I wanted my father to love me."

"We all crave approval. But at what cost, Addie? I think this price is too dear."

Addie's knees nearly buckled. When was the last time she'd opened her Bible? She hadn't even asked God what he would have her do in this situation. "You're right," she whispered. "I have to go." She thrust the bag into Katie's hand and ran back the way she'd come.

Addie fell face-first into the soft moss. The roar of the falls filled her ears and drowned out the sound of her sobs. Edward was eating his lunch under the careful watch of his nurse, so she'd been free to take her dog. Gideon whined and licked her cheek.

This perfect dream was crumbling in her hands. And she'd let it, because she'd allowed other people to become more important to her than God.

"I'm sorry," she whispered against the softness of the moss. "I wanted so much to belong."

You belong to me. I am the only Father you need.

The words impressed themselves on her heart. How easily she'd been enticed away from the things that truly mattered. "I thought I was strong, Lord. That nothing could shake my faith."

And nothing had. Only her willful decisions to let what other people thought matter more than what God wanted. Without so much as a backward glance, she'd dropped her desire for God's will and followed her own. Her life would mean nothing if she let the world creep in.

She groaned as she remembered the desperate face of Mrs. Whittaker. Addie had let her father's disapproval keep her from doing what she knew was right. And those children. She'd abandoned them to the orphanage. God had urged her to help, but she'd been afraid.

She sat up and swiped at her face, then opened the Bible she'd brought. Gideon crowded close and put his head on her lap. Her study of the names of God fell out. She picked up the pages. *El Shaddai. All-Sufficient God*. Why had she thought she needed any man's approval? Only God's mattered.

She flipped to Proverbs 3. "Let not mercy and truth forsake thee," she read. "Bind them about thy neck. Write them upon the table of thine heart." She shut her Bible. With God's help, she'd cling to the truth and follow him, not the whims of man.

She rubbed Gideon's head, then pushed him off. She rose and turned toward the path, but stopped when she saw John approaching through the ferns. Had he come here for solace or had he come in search of her? She waited for him to see her.

Brushing the ferns out of the way, he strolled as if he had all the time in the world. His head was bare, and he'd removed his jacket. His sleeves were rolled up to reveal his strong forearms. She thought of the scripture that mentioned God's strong right arm. This was a man she could depend on. A man who would be strong where she was weak.

Gideon bounded forward, then groveled on his back for John to rub his stomach. At the dog's appearance, John's gaze went toward the spring.

Their eyes met, and he stopped. A grave smile tugged at his lips. "Addie. There you are."

"Were you looking for me?"

"Yes. I knew you'd be here." He glanced at the waterfall. "This is your special place with God, isn't it?"

She nodded and stepped closer to him. "I feel him here."

He wound a curl around his index finger. "You've changed me, Addie. Sitting in church yesterday, I realized how far I'd fallen away from God. I want to remember what it was like to want to follow him."

His fingers in her hair caused warmth to spread out from her belly. "I haven't been a very good example lately," she whispered. "I let what everyone else wanted come first."

"I told you it would happen."

"You did. But no more."

His hand became more entwined in her hair. He glanced at her bare feet. "I'm glad. I love the real Addie. The one who plays ragtime on the piano, and the girl who splashes me with water and runs barefoot through the house."

He pulled her closer, then bent his head. She stood on tiptoes and wound her arms around his neck. Addie inhaled his breath, his essence, into her lungs. He was part of her. She was bone of his bone, flesh of his flesh. His lips met hers, and she tried to put how she felt into her kiss. Her surrender, her love. She would go anywhere, forsake anything, for him.

When his lips lifted from hers, he searched her face. "Will you defy your father and Carrington?"

"Yes."

"We might move back to San Francisco."

"I'll have you and Edward, no matter where we live. That's enough."

John glanced at Gideon, who still sprawled on his back, with his belly exposed. "That's one way to get the dog for Edward."

She poked him in the ribs. "So that's all this is? A ploy to get my dog?"

Gideon rolled over and looked on expectantly at the word *dog*. John laughed and prodded the animal with his foot. Gideon's expression turned blissful. "Whatever works."

Her smile died when he held her face in his hands. "I'd take you, dog or no dog. That spring behind us reminds me of you. I saw you described in the Bible this morning. It was in Isaiah 58. 'And the Lord shall guide thee continually, and satisfy thy soul in drought, and make fat thy bones: and thou shalt be like a watered garden, and like a spring of water, whose waters fail not.' "

She inhaled and pondered the words. "Which part is me? The fat part?"

He threw back his head and laughed. "No, darling. The spring of water. I was so jaded before you came into my life. You make everything new and fresh. Thank you for that."

She nestled against his chest again until she

heard the sound of her father's automobile. "He's home. I have to tell him."

"Actually, he's leaving. For Fort Bragg. I came to get you so we could follow him—if it's still important to you."

She ran her fingers across the faint stubble on his cheeks. "Bless you for that. But yes, I want to know about my mother. What about his dinner guest? Carrington was coming."

"Your father canceled when he got home for lunch a few minutes ago."

He took her hand and they ran toward the house with the dog at their heels. Addie prayed this day would finally bring her some answers.

THIRTY-FOUR

THE RENTED COACH awaited John and Addie when they disembarked at the quay in Fort Bragg. Gideon stayed close on her heels. John had made the decision to bring him, because he might be of assistance to them, though they both worried about Edward. Molly had promised to watch him closely.

Addie could hardly think as they walked past the remains of gutted fish and heaps of fishing nets. Addie held her hankie to her nose, but it did little to block the stench of rotting meat. The pier bustled with fishermen, buyers, and travelers awaiting passage on the next boat to the city.

"We'll never find him," she said, once John

handed her into the carriage and climbed in beside her.

"Our driver says he's taken Henry many times over the years. He goes to a home outside of town. So that's where we're heading." He took her hand. "We have to be careful, Addie. We can't go rushing in there demanding to know what he's doing."

"I know. And it's likely a dead end." She pressed her trembling lips together. "It's good of you to humor me."

"I'd do anything for you, Addie," he said, his eyes soft.

She squeezed his hand. "And I do love you for it." She craned her neck to stare out the window as the cab rolled through town. The bustling seaside port seemed to subsist on logging and fishing. They soon left the streets behind and rolled along a country lane that wound through Sitka spruce and wildflowers. The towering edifice at the top of the hill had to be the insane asylum. The stonework and shuttered windows gave it a secretive air.

John leaned forward. "Let us out here. Come back in two hours."

The driver nodded and pulled the horse to the side of the road. John helped Addie out of the cab, then paid the driver while she called Gideon to her. When the clopping of the horse's hooves faded, he took her hand, and they walked along the road to the side of the building.

"Why don't we go to the front door?" Addie asked.

"We can't walk in and ask why Henry comes here twice a year or why he's broken his routine and come here today. If there's anything unsavory going on with the residents, they are hardly going to admit it."

She clung to his hand and stared at the large home. Her silly vapors had brought them on a wild goose chase, and she would be embarrassed when they found out nothing. Hiring the boat and their lodging wouldn't have been cheap either.

The road wound around to the back of the asylum. A garden with a labyrinth and clipped hedges caught her eye. Stone benches and a small waterfall looked serene and inviting. Several people wandered among the flowers on the other side of the fence.

Her fingers tightened on John's forearm. "Isn't that my father?" She pointed toward a man sitting beside a woman on a bench.

John peered. "I think you're right. I can't make out much about the woman."

"Can we get closer without being seen?"

"I think so. There are so many huckleberry shrubs through the back field. We can hide behind them as we get closer. Mind your skirt, and hang on to me. The ground will be uneven."

She nodded and clung to his support. He led her down into the valley from the road. They moved from shrub to shrub until they stood five feet from the stone wall. The barrier was eight feet tall without a gate on the backside.

"We can't see anything now. We had a better view from up on the road," she said.

"We might be able to hear something."

He took her hand and led her to the wall. Holding his finger to his lips, he sidled down the stone structure in the direction of the bench where they'd seen her father sitting. She strained to make out the conversation on the other side of the wall.

"Are you chilled?" Her father's voice spoke. "I can get you a shawl."

He continued to speak of the weather, his day, and the news from the city. There was no response from his companion. John and Addie exchanged puzzled glances.

Addie peered through the gloom but couldn't make out the woman's features.

"I have to leave you now, my dear," her father said. "It's been good to see you."

Addie and John waited. She heard footsteps fade along the cobblestone path to the building.

"How do we get into the garden?" John asked.

"There might be an access near the building."

She followed him along the perimeter. Attached to the stone building was a small gate. Wild roses grew beside it and perfumed the air. He tugged on the padlock, but it didn't budge. He shrugged and dug out a pocketknife. He poked and prodded until he succeeded in popping the lock. Once the lock was removed, he twisted the handle and opened it slowly.

"Coast is clear," he said, stepping through.

She followed him with her pulse hammering in her throat. A six-foot-high clipped hedge blocked the rest of the garden from view. When they stepped past it, she realized they were in the maze. Finding their way out might not be easy. John led her down a few false paths, but they finally came out by a fountain that gurgled its welcome.

Addie's gaze fell on the woman who sat on the bench. Her breath came fast as she noticed the woman's faded red hair, high cheekbones, and green eyes. It had to be her mother.

Addie knelt in front of the woman and took her cold hand. "Mama?" This lady was an older version of the portrait Addie had seen at the Eaton manor. She knew without any doubt that this person was Laura Eaton.

The woman's eyes focused on her, and a tiny frown crouched between her brows. "I had a little girl once." Her trembling hand touched Addie's hair.

"This woman is your mother?" John's voice shook.

Unable to speak, Addie nodded.

The woman's slurred speech and wide stare hinted at the reason for her compliance. "I think she's drugged." John said, glancing around the garden. "Looks like no one is out here." He checked the time. "We've got an hour before the cab comes back."

"We could start walking to town."

"Someone will be looking for her soon. It's nearly sundown."

She realized he was right. The quality of light had changed. "We could hide if someone comes." She grabbed his hand. "Please, John, I can't leave her here."

"I agree." He knelt by her mother. "Mrs. Eaton, it's time to go."

"Go," she agreed, her eyes vacant. She came to her feet when he tugged on her hand.

A bell chimed. "That's probably the dinner bell," Addie said. "We have to hurry. Someone will be coming." She took her mother's hand. "Come along, Mama."

Saying the words hit her. *Mama.* She had a living mother, even if she was damaged. She led her mother to the gate, and they stepped through. John pulled it shut behind him, then fiddled with the lock.

"It's broken," he said. "I'll have to leave it."

They hurried across the field. Addie was thankful for the darkness that now quickly began to fall. They would be harder to track when a search ensued.

"It's a big place," John said. "I expect they'll

search the building first and won't realize for a while that she's missing."

"I hope so."

"Our hotel is on the edge of town. I'll register us while you stay outside with her. I'll come get you when it's safe to go to our rooms. She'll need to stay with you."

Addie tightened her grip on her mother's hand. "Of course."

They reached the road and began the trek toward town. Her new shoes pinched her toes, and she prayed she could endure walking until the cab came. "How much longer before the cab arrives?"

John checked his watch. "Forty-five minutes."

An eternity. "This road doesn't seem to be well traveled."

"A blessing for us," he said.

They trudged toward town. Head down, her mother walked slowly, pausing often to touch a flower or a tree branch. Addie watched her for any sign of coming out of her stupor. How long might something like that take? Hours? Days? She suspected an evening dose came with dinner.

"How could he do it?" she blurted out. "How could he put her in a place like that?"

"You don't know he did, Addie. Don't jump to conclusions."

"He let everyone believe she drowned, though he knew differently."

"Maybe he was trying to spare the family the

339

shame of knowing she was in this state." He nodded to her mother, who was humming tunelessly.

Addie clenched her fists. "There's more to this, John. I feel it."

A light bobbed ahead of them in the road. "There's the cab," he said, relief highlighting his tone. He held up his hand, and the buggy slowed, then stopped.

The door opened, and her father stepped onto the road. His mouth was tight, and his eyes narrowed. His gaze went from Addie to her mother and back again. "Get in," he said.

Addie took a step back. "You locked my mother away. How could you?"

"There's more to the story than you know. Get in and I'll explain."

Addie glanced at John, who shrugged. There was nowhere for them to hide. She took her mother's unresisting arm and helped her into the carriage. Gideon leaped in after her.

"There's room for only three inside. I'll ride up top with the driver," her father said. "Make no judgment yet, my dear. You'll understand when you hear the full story."

Addie didn't reply. Nothing he could say would change what he'd done in her eyes. Even if her mother was quite mad, she deserved better than being hidden away for a quarter century.

The carriage set off with a jerk. It continued on

toward the asylum. "He's not turning around," John said. He leaned forward and spoke through the open window. "Why aren't we turning around?"

Her father didn't acknowledge him. Addie stood and put her head through the window. "Father, why are we not turning around?"

"Your mother needs her medication," he said without turning to look at her. "You see the state she's in, my dear. Why else would she be here?"

The carriage lurched, and Addie fell back onto the worn leather seat. "We have to escape. I can't let her go back to that place." She held her mother's hand. The older woman had stopped humming, and her faded eyes showed a trace of awareness.

John pressed his lips together. "I wish I had my pistol," he said.

"When the carriage slows to turn into the lane, let's jump out," she said. "It will have to nearly stop."

He nodded. "I'll take your mother with me. You jump out the other door."

The vehicle slowed. Addie grabbed the door handle.

"Now!" John thrust open the door and grabbed her mother's hand. They both hurtled through the door.

Addie tried to do the same, but her door was stuck. She slid across the seat and prepared to leap from John's side.

"Oh no, you don't!" Her father grabbed at her from the front window.

She beat at him with her fists but couldn't tear free of his grasp. Gideon growled and leaped forward. He sank his teeth into Mr. Eaton's wrist.

Her father howled. "Get him off me!"

While he was thrown off center, she leaped from the carriage and hit the grass. Pain flared through her shoulder and back, and she bit back a moan. Holding her arm, she rolled until she saw the carriage stop. Gideon jumped from the coach and ran to her.

"Good boy," she gasped. She forced herself to ignore the pain and ran back to where John stood with her mother.

"Run!" he yelled. He grabbed her hand in his left one and her mother's in his right, and they plunged into the pine forest.

THIRTY-FIVE

THE DARKNESS PRESSED in on them. John stopped to let his eyes adjust to the lack of light. "He'll have trouble finding us in the dark," he said, groping. "I can't see my hand in front of my face."

"Let's hide under a tree," Addie suggested. "Maybe we can circle back and get to the road and hike out of here."

"Good idea." He swept his hand across the air and moved forward until his fingers touched the pine needles of the nearest tree. "Here. And hurry. I think I hear him."

He pushed Laura under the tree, and Addie followed. The dog belly-crawled to join her. John squeezed under the sheltering limbs with them. The dead needles were soft under him, and the tree above them released the scent of pine. He squeezed Addie's hand when something crunched nearby.

The sound grew nearer. It sounded like a hand brushing at every tree. He held his breath and lay with his cheek resting on the pine needles. The darkness was complete, but he sensed Henry was near.

"Kids, this has gone on long enough," Henry's voice was right beside him. "I know you're here somewhere. Let's talk about this. You're overreacting."

Addie's fingers squeezed John's. Hard. He couldn't hear her breathe either. The feet by his head shuffled, and the scent of pine intensified. Then the steps went farther into the woods.

"Julia?" Henry called again. "Come on out, Daughter. This is ridiculous. You don't need to fear me. I'm only doing what's best for your mother."

The footsteps moved deeper into the forest. Henry's voice grew distant until John couldn't hear it any longer. He strained to make out whether his father-in-law might be circling back to trick them. There was no sound but the wind in the tree boughs.

"I think it's safe," John whispered.

He rolled out from under the pine. When soft sounds told him Addie and her mother had done the same.

Addie clasped her hands together. "I knew he wouldn't find us. I asked God, and he wouldn't let me down."

Oh, how he loved her simple, childlike faith. His own faith seemed weak by comparison. He rose and held out his hand. He helped her to her feet, then raised her mother from her prone position. The poor woman moaned under her breath, and he wondered if her medicine was wearing off.

"This way," he told them.

He led them back the way they'd come. The moon was out when they stepped out of the forest's shadows. But it was only a sliver and cast very little light. He glanced up and down the road but didn't see the carriage.

"Where is it?" Addie asked.

"Maybe the driver didn't want to be involved in what was happening and went back to town."

She stepped closer and took his hand. "Could we go to the asylum and borrow a buggy?"

"They wouldn't loan us one."

"I was thinking we might borrow it without asking."

He grinned, though he knew she couldn't see him. "Why, Miss Adeline, how shocking."

"We wouldn't hurt it."

"It's a great idea. Let's see what we can find."

They set off toward the asylum. The ground was uneven and hard to gauge in the dark. Several times he caught Addie or her mother when they stumbled. The dog kept jogging ahead, then turning back as if to ask why they were so slow. John kept pausing and glancing behind them but saw no sign of Henry.

They reached the building, then wound around to the west, where a large barn stood. The door was unlocked, so he shoved it open and peered inside. It was dark, so he lit a lantern by the door and held it aloft to check out the resources.

A brougham was by the door, and two horses snorted in alarm at the lantern. "Come in," he told the women.

Addie led her mother inside, and he shut the door. "You hold the light while I harness the horse."

He soothed the nearest horse, a mare, then led her to the carriage and hitched her up.

"I heard something," Addie whispered.

He stopped and listened. Shouts, calls from the house. "They've realized she's gone," he said. "Get in. We're ready to get out of here."

He took the lantern from her and set it on the floor, then helped the women inside. He waited for the dog to leap inside too. With the door shut, he blew out the lantern, then shoved open the doors. There was still no one in the yard. He clambered onto the driver's seat, then grabbed the reins and guided the horse out of the barn. When he slapped the reins on the mare's rump, she took off at a lively clip for the road.

So far so good. The carriage reached the road, and he turned the horse's head toward town. With the straightaway in front of them, he prayed for a smooth journey. The horse broke into a canter, and he spared a glance back at the asylum. Men were running from the building toward the barn. They'd realize the horse and carriage were gone. He let the horse have her head, and her stride lengthened.

When he passed the area of the forest where they'd hidden, he stared but saw nothing. It was only when he saw the lights of the hotel that he began to relax. The question was, what were they going to do next? It probably wasn't safe to stay at the hotel. There weren't many in town. Henry would have no trouble tracking them down.

Addie's mother made anxious noises and tugged at her skirt. Maybe she needed the medication her father had mentioned. It might not be safe to withdraw it all at once. Addie should have thought of that sooner.

"Who are you again?" her mother asked in a thin, reedy voice. She sat with Gideon's head in her lap.

"I'm Julia, Mama. Your daughter."

"I wish it were true," the older woman said.

Addie patted her hand. At least her mother

seemed to be improving. Outside the window the moon gleamed on the water. The quay was just ahead.

"Why are we going back to the quay?" she asked John through the window.

"We've got to get out of town. Your father will track us down if we stay."

Addie leaned against the leather seat back until the carriage stopped and John jumped down to open the door. This felt like a bad idea.

"How are we going to get a boat at this hour?" she asked when he opened the door. "And what if Father comes here to stay on his yacht for the night?"

He lifted her from the carriage. "We have to try. I'm not sure what else to do."

The activity at the quay had changed to men laughing and drinking. She heard the occasional splash as someone threw something into the water.

"John?" A man's voice spoke out of the shadows. Lord Carrington stepped into view.

Addie's muscles clenched. She stepped down from the carriage and blocked his view of her mother. "Lord Carrington."

"Miss Eaton." He raised a brow. "Eloping?"

"Not exactly."

"Thomas. Is that you?" Her mother's voice was thin and weak.

Lord Carrington grew rigid. His eyes widened. "W-Who is that?"

Addie stepped out of the way. "My mother." She watched him come forward and peer into the carriage. She heard his gasp.

"Praise be to God, it is you, Laura." His voice trembled.

If nothing else, Addie knew he would help save her mother. There was no doubt how he felt about her. "We need your help, sir. Most especially, my mother needs it."

With obvious reluctance, he took his gaze from her mother and turned to her. "I am at your disposal, Miss Addie."

"My father had her locked away in an asylum. He's looking for us now. We have to escape. Quickly."

"Of course. My yacht is moored in the bay. My man is right here with the dinghy." He reached into the carriage. "You can come out now, Laura. No one will hurt you." He helped her down with the utmost tenderness.

Her mother stood blinking at the lights. "I'm so cold," she said, her teeth chattering.

Lord Carrington glanced at Addie. "Do you know what's wrong with her?"

"I think she's overdue whatever drugs they were giving her."

"Laudanum?" he asked.

"I'm not sure."

"I have some aboard ship in the medical kit. We'll wean her off it more gently."

"You sound as though you know of these matters."

He smiled gently. "You wouldn't want to know the things I've seen." He nodded toward the pier. "Come. Let's go." Still holding Laura's hand, he led her away.

John stopped a young boy and arranged to have the horse and carriage returned to the asylum. "I don't trust Carrington," he said as they followed the gentleman and her mother.

She pressed her fingers on his arm. "We have no choice, John. Where can we go?"

His nod was grudging. "I wish I had my pistol," he said again.

She followed him to the end of the pier, where a dinghy bobbed. John kept glancing behind them. When he went rigid, she turned to look also.

"It's my father," she said to Lord Carrington. "Hurry."

The deckhand helped them down into the boat. Gideon hesitated, then made the leap to the craft. So far, her father hadn't spotted them. But he'd seen the carriage. He opened the door and peered inside. As Addie sat down, she saw him emerge.

She grabbed the railing. "He's seen us!"

"He's too late," Lord Carrington said, shoving off.

The men took every available oar and rowed toward the yacht. Addie watched her father gesture and shout from the pier, but she couldn't make out his words. She prayed for the Lord to slow him down, to help them escape. Her father managed to commandeer a dinghy, but he nearly fell as he tried to maneuver into it.

Their dinghy reached Lord Carrington's yacht, and moments later they were aboard. The men lashed the dinghy to the side, and Lord Carrington hurried to the cabin to tell the captain to shove off. It seemed an eternity before the large craft began to move away from shore. There was no sign of her father, but his ship was fast. And he wouldn't give up easily.

Her mother was shaking uncontrollably now. Her teeth chattered, but perspiration dotted her forehead. Addie embraced her and led her to a lounge chair, where a throw lay waiting. She draped her mother's form with it.

"Mama, I'll take care of you," she said.

John eased her into the chair and lifted her feet onto the lounge. Her mother's eyes were clearer, even though she suffered from a condition Addie didn't know how to ease. Gideon sat at her feet.

"Who are you again?" her mother asked through her chattering teeth.

"I'm A-Julia. Your daughter, Julia."

Her mother's eyes widened. "That's impossible," she gasped.

Lord Carrington arrived with a small bottle. He administered some drops to her mother, and the shaking began to ease. "Not too much," he muttered. He had her sip coffee, then watched her head drop back and her eyes close.

"How long will it take for her to become lucid?" Addie asked.

"Hard to say. A few hours. A few days."

"I have so many questions to ask her."

"I can answer some of them," Lord Carrington said.

Addie curled her fingers around John's hand. "Why didn't you answer them the other day?"

"I wasn't sure what camp you were in. If you loved your father, it would be difficult for you to hear the truth about him. My priority was to get you out of that house. That's the real reason I offered marriage. I do hope you'll forgive my ungallant confession."

John's bark of laughter held relief. "Then you'll put up no objections to dropping your suit?"

"I'll not stand in the way of true love," Lord Carrington said.

"Why was I not safe in that house?" Addie demanded.

"Because your father is a murderer."

THIRTY-SIX

THE SALON BELOW deck was appointed with plush fabrics and comfortable seating. Lord Carrington had insisted on dinner before he continued with explanations, but Addie could barely eat the delicious food when all she wanted was to know what he'd meant.

"Tell me," she finally demanded as the men leaned back with their claret. She glanced at her mother, whose eyes were closed. Her color was better, though, and her chest fell up and down with reassuring regularity.

Lord Carrington put his wine on the table. "You asked me why your mother summoned me before she left."

Addie nodded. "But you didn't tell me."

"You weren't ready to hear it."

"We are now," John said, his voice grim.

"I'll tell you," her mother's reedy voice said. She sat up with her eyes open and clear.

Addie moved to her side. "Mama?" She took her mother's thin hand. It was cold as the waves. Gideon whined and nudged their linked hands.

Her mother held on with a tight grip. "Are you really my Julia?" she asked.

Addie barely managed to choke out the words. "I am."

Her mother's wondering eyes traveled Addie's form. "Praise God," she said. "I believed you'd drowned." She passed her hand over her forehead. "So many jumbled memories."

"Take your time," Lord Carrington said, moving to her other side.

"Thomas. You too. I prayed for rescue so many years. How many?" she asked. "How long was I locked away?"

"Twenty-three years," Addie said gently.

Tears flooded her mother's eyes. "A lifetime," she murmured. She swallowed hard. "It was all Henry," she said. "He orchestrated everything. I thought he loved me."

"I'm sure he did," Addie said, seeing her mother's distress.

"He did at first. I believe that. But he grew to love my money more. He killed my father to get his hands on all of it."

Addie gasped. So did John. Only Lord Carrington remained unmoved, and he'd surely heard this story before. Addie clung to John's hand. This was going to be worse than she'd dreamed.

"I can tell them about it," Lord Carrington said. "You don't have to do this, Laura."

"I want to." Perspiration beaded her forehead. "Could I have some tea?"

"Of course, darling." He sprang to his feet and went to the galley.

Addie swallowed down the massive lump forming in her throat. She wanted to bury her face in Gideon's fur and cry. Even when her father was after them, she'd held on to a shred of hope that there was an explanation for what he'd done. To discover he had a soul as black as Satan himself left her fighting tears.

"I'm here," John murmured against her hair. "We'll get through this. Just rejoice that your mother is alive."

353

Addie forced back her tears. "You're right."

"When did you find this out? That he'd killed your father?" John asked her mother. "Just before you left?"

She nodded. "He knew I'd discovered the truth."

"How did he do it?" John asked.

"Poison. It looked like a heart attack, but I found the poison in Henry's dresser before he disposed of it. When I accused him, he admitted it. He said he was tired of waiting for Father to die. He had a bad case of gout, and Henry claimed death would be a release. A release—from gout!"

"I'm so sorry," Addie said. She didn't remember her grandfather, but she could see her mother's pain.

"There was some reason Henry needed money quickly. He'd asked Father and was refused. So Henry killed him."

"And you fled," John said. "With Julia."

Her mother nodded. "He told me no one would believe me. That he'd put me in an insane asylum and I'd never see my daughter again. So I ran."

"After you hid the clues. We found them," Addie said.

"And you tracked me here?"

"We followed . . . Henry." Addie didn't want to call him Father. Not after what he'd done.

Lord Carrington returned with a cup of tea and toast. He offered it to her mother, who nibbled on the toast and took a sip of tea.

"Did you finish the story?" Lord Carrington asked, settling beside her.

She shook her head. "Not yet." She set her tea on the table. "Henry boarded the same ship as Thomas and I, but we didn't know it. He drugged me, and the next thing I knew, I was at the asylum. It was one he practically owned. I heard him warn them to keep me drugged at all times, because I'd killed my father and was extremely dangerous. That they shouldn't trust what they thought was lucidity. They were happy to do whatever he said because of the money he'd given them over the years."

"What about me?" Addie asked.

Her mother's eyes held grief. "I told him I'd left you at my grandfather's. I never dreamed he would sink the ship to cover my disappearance. I don't know how you were saved."

"I do," Lord Carrington said. "I'd taken you to my room so your mother could get some sleep. The next morning she was gone. I couldn't find your mother and feared Henry had thrown her overboard. A storm rolled in. I heard an explosion, then the captain yelled to get to the lifeboats. I overheard a crew member say it was a bomb."

"An explosion?" Addie asked. She rubbed her head. "I remember a man carrying me on a burning ship, then throwing me into the sea. That was you?"

He nodded. "I actually threw you into a lifeboat. It sank, though, and you ended up in the sea."

"Henry sank the steamer on purpose?" John asked.

Lord Carrington shrugged. "That's what I've always believed."

"But how did I end up at the lighthouse?" Addie asked.

"I'm coming to that." He picked up the tea and put it back in her mother's hand. "Drink, Laura. You must get something down. It will help fight the drug's effects."

She nodded and sipped at her tea, then took another bite of her toast.

"As I said, I ran to a lifeboat with you, but it was too full for both of us. I handed you over to a woman in the boat, then dived overboard. I thought I had a better chance of swimming on my own than going down with the ship."

"And you made it," she said.

"I did, but the lifeboat didn't. The storm upended it. The waves tossed me onto the beach farther up the shore, and when I came to, I thought you'd been drowned with all the others. A couple of days later, I came back to this area to search and saw you on the lawn with the lightkeeper. You were giggling and fine."

"So you said nothing?" she asked.

"I knew I couldn't raise you myself. For one thing, I had no visa, so I'd be unable to adopt you. I'd hoped to catch up with your father as well, and a child would slow me down. I arranged

356

for one of my lawyers to offer Roy Sullivan money to care for you."

Addie's head whirled. "It was you! So you knew all along where I was?"

He nodded. "I was quite dismayed to find you at Eaton Hall a few weeks ago. I knew it was only a matter of time before your father eliminated you. He would never let you live to take his money."

Her chest constricted. "So you were trying to protect me for all these years. Why?"

He shrugged. "You should have been mine."

"I wish you were my father," she whispered. She turned and buried her face against John's shoulder.

"What's next?" John asked Carrington.

The three of them stood on the stern of the ship watching the dark sea. Addie's mother had fallen asleep below.

John gestured to the water. "You realize Henry's yacht is one of the fastest. I'm sure he's chasing us."

"We're running with no lights, and it's a big ocean," Carrington said. "I hope to make Eureka and summon the police. We have Laura as a witness."

"Will he say she's insane and can't testify?" Addie asked.

Carrington's lips tightened. "He might, but the three of us know better."

John expected a battle. Henry wouldn't go down without a fight.

Addie gasped and put her hand to her mouth. "Josephine. The woman who raised me. Someone killed her. W-Was it Henry?"

He put his hand on her shoulder. "I don't know, Addie, but it makes sense that he might have. Or, more likely, ordered it done. I doubt Henry would sully his own hands."

"But what about the attack on Mr. Driscoll? And me? And the man who tried to take Edward? Are those incidents tied to Henry as well?"

She was trembling. John embraced her, his arm circling her waist. "I can see how he would think you and Driscoll were a threat, but Edward is his own grandson!"

"But he's also the heir to everything."

"Not while your mother lives. She is. And you after her."

"And he knew she was alive. So Edward would be the one he would want to eliminate perhaps?"

He shook his head. "For what reason? Henry won't live forever. Who would inherit if Edward were out of the picture?"

"Wait a minute," she said slowly. "I found a blackmail note in Henry's office right after I first came."

"Blackmail? Any idea what someone might have against him?" Carrington asked.

"The note demanded ten thousand dollars or the blackmailer would tell the world about Henry's child. At least I assumed it was Henry's child. There was no one named in the note."

"His child. Could that be you, Addie?" Carrington asked. "Who knew of your existence besides me?"

"No one that I know of," she said. "We lived quietly in the lighthouse." She paused, her brows gathering in a frown. "Oh wait. There was the solicitor you hired, Lord Carrington. But Uncle Walter was unable to find out anything from him."

"I suppose it's possible he told someone. An employee, perhaps, who deposited the money into Mr. Sullivan's account."

Addie stepped away from John's side. She paced the deck. "So my father knew of my existence before I came to the manor?"

"I suspect that's possible," John said. "If so, when you arrived, he would understand he had to work fast. There could be only one reason you were there—you'd found out the truth."

"And of course he would know of Driscoll's involvement, as he was the one who brought you," Carrington said.

Addie returned to John's side. Gideon accompanied her. "But if I'm the child mentioned in the blackmail note, why would Edward be threatened? That piece still doesn't make any sense."

A splashing sound wafted over the water. John held up his hand. "Listen. I hear a boat. If that's Eaton, we may have a chance to capture him and get him to the authorities. Then he can explain it all."

An explosion battered his ears, and in reaction,

he swung Addie behind him. Seconds later, something splashed in the waves off their starboard. "He's firing on us!"

Addie peered past him. "How could he do such a thing?"

Carrington ran to the helm. "If he sinks us, he's rid of everyone standing in his way." He yelled down into the hold. "Start the engine!"

A few moments later a rumble started under John's feet. The yacht picked up speed. It had been running silently on sails, but now that they'd been discovered, speed was all that mattered.

"Get below!" John yelled to Addie. "Your mother will need you." When she ran for the salon with Gideon, he turned to Carrington. "Do you have guns?"

Carrington shook his head. "I've never had any need of something so barbaric."

The yacht in pursuit fired on them again, and John realized it was getting closer. Why hadn't he brought his pistol at least? He paced the deck.

"More speed!" Carrington shouted.

The rumble in the bowels of the ship grew, and a bit more distance opened between the two yachts. "Is that Mercy Falls?" John asked.

"Yes," Carrington said. "If we can make it to town, he won't dare do anything to us there."

"You don't know Henry," John said. "He'll twist this around and accuse us of something atrocious." He strained to see through the gloom.

"I think we're leaving him behind. When we reach shore, I'll go to the constable, while you get the women to safety. We'll meet back up when I've finished pressing charges."

John shook his head. "Henry owns the town, and it was his influence that got the constable the position. I fear we'll be hard-pressed to convince the constable to arrest him."

"You might be right. We could press on to Eureka."

"It might be best."

Addie's head rose from the opening to the hold. "What about a decoy?" She stepped onto the deck. "My mother is terrified. Mr. Eaton can't be allowed near her. I want to take her to safety."

John folded her in his arms. He could feel the shudders that seized her body. "What do you have in mind?"

She glanced at Lord Carrington. "We have the dinghy. Mercy Falls lighthouse is just ahead. Mama and I could hide out in the lighthouse. I can padlock the door from inside, and we can go up into the light tower until you come for us."

"He'll follow Carrington's yacht."

"Yes. You can lead him away and find help so Mama never has to see him again. Once the authorities have him in custody, I'll unlock it."

"I don't like it," John said. He held her close. "I don't want anything to happen to you."

"We'll be fine."

"You could go with the women," Carrington said.

"I'd rather do that," John said.

Addie shook her head. "Lord Carrington, you need the strength of John's word with yours. Henry is too influential a man for a foreigner such as yourself to challenge alone."

John held her close. "I don't trust your father," he said.

She pulled back and gazed up at him. Her eyes were brilliant in the moonlight. "What could possibly go wrong? My father won't have any idea we're not on this boat."

He couldn't argue. The other yacht was distant enough that he could no longer hear the flap of its sails or the water on its hull. Eaton would never know a dinghy had left with the women.

"All right," he said. "But I still don't like it."

Carrington ordered the dinghy prepared, and the men helped the women into it. Gideon leaped into the boat with them. The hollow spot in John's chest grew as he watched it lowered into the sea.

THIRTY-SEVEN

ADDIE'S MOTHER WAS increasingly lucid, but chills still racked her body. Addie rowed for shore with all her might. The oars in her hands were like long-lost friends. She put her back into the effort and steered the craft toward the light winking on and off on the spit of land to her northeast.

"Are you okay, Mama?" she asked.

"I'm so c-cold," her mother whispered.

"You probably need more medicine," Addie said.

She should have brought the laudanum. What had she been thinking to leave it behind? She rowed harder until the dinghy bumped against the sand in shallow water. She leaped from the boat and dragged the craft onto the rocky shore, then helped her mother.

"Let's get you inside," she said.

Wading through calf-high flowers, she half carried her mother up the steep incline to the house. Gideon ran on ahead. The lighthouse beacon drew her attention. Who had wound the light? She hadn't stopped to wonder who was tending the light since Josephine's death. No lights shone from the home, so maybe neighbors had stopped by to help out.

Her mother trembled, and her teeth chattered. Addie steered her toward the back door that led to the kitchen. "I'll find chamomile tea. It might help you."

Inside, she settled her mother into a chair at the table, then lit the gaslight. The tea was in the pantry off the back porch. No fire warmed the wood cookstove, so she poked at it. No embers glowed in the cold ashes. She would have to start it from scratch. She found kindling and wood, then arranged it in the fire box. The match sputtered when she struck it, then the fire flared to life. She set the kettle on to heat, then turned around to check on her mother.

She wasn't at the table. "Mama?" Addie called.

She walked into the parlor and found her mother holding a picture of Addie up to the moonlight streaming through the window. Addie was about five. Tears rolled down her mother's cheeks. Addie embraced her, and the older woman clung to her.

"You're really Julia," her mother said, her voice hushed. Her hand caressed Addie's cheek, then she glanced back at the picture. "I recognize you. All these years . . ."

"I know. But I've found you now." Addie didn't like the way her mother trembled. It was more than emotion. "Come sit down, Mama. I'll get you some tea."

She snatched a throw from the chair as she passed and draped it around her mother's gaunt shoulders. The kettle shrieked as they stepped into the kitchen. She hurried to grab it from the range while her mother sank onto a chair. Steam rose from the cup of tea as Addie carried it to her mother. While her mother sipped the chamomile tea, Addie ticked through in her mind what she would need for a night in the tower.

Blankets, pillows, food, and water. It might be hours before the men returned.

"I'd like to go to bed now," her mother said.

"I wish we could stay here in the house," Addie

told her. "But we're going to have to go to the light tower and lock ourselves in."

Her mother's eyes went wide, and the tea sloshed over the lip of her teacup. "He's not out there, is he?"

"I don't think so, Mama. But we can't know what's happening. We're safest in the lighthouse. I can padlock us in until the men come back."

"Thank the Lord." Her mother's voice was stronger. She sipped at the tea until it was gone.

Addie heard something. A voice, a scrape. She wasn't sure what. She rose and flipped off the gaslight, then peered out the window. A light bobbed on the water.

"I think a boat is out there," she whispered. "We need to go up now."

She helped her mother to her feet. "Come with me."

She raced up the steps with Gideon and scooped pillows and blankets off the bed in the room at the top of the stairs. By the time her mother finished the climb, Addie had their supplies ready. She led her mom down the hall to the stairs that led into the tower. The light on the boat appeared to be onshore now. The men could be halfway up the slope by now.

"Very quiet," she whispered to her mother.

The stairway door hung open. Addie stepped inside and pulled her mother in with her. She shut the door and fumbled in the dark for the padlock. It wasn't on the door. Where was it?

She dropped the bundle of blankets and pillows and felt along the floor for the missing lock. Her hand grazed the gritty floor, then something metal skittered away. She followed its trail and cornered the padlock. The key was in it. She took it out, then looped the padlock through the door handle and clicked it shut.

When she tugged on it, it stayed snug. "Let's get upstairs," she whispered. "As quietly as you can."

She led the way up the winding metal stairs. Wincing every time their footfalls clanged, she kept checking to make sure her mother stayed on her heels. They reached the top. Another door separated the stairs from the light room. It hung open as well. Looking past the Fresnel lens, Addie stared out past the glass enclosing the lamp. Lanterns bobbed on the hillside. One, two of them.

Her fingers tightened on the blankets. "They're coming," she said. Gideon snarled, and she quieted him with a glance.

Her mother grabbed her hand. "Who?"

"I don't know. It's too soon for John and Thomas to be back with the constable." She dropped the blankets into the corner and arranged a makeshift bed. "I'm sure it's nothing to worry about, Mama. Maybe neighbors arriving to wind the light. If it is, I'll ask one of them to call the police. Why don't you lie down and rest a bit?"

Her mother moved to her side. "I feel much better. The tea helped, but I'm so tired."

Her voice was stronger. Addie helped her lie down, then covered her with another blanket. Gideon lay down beside her. "I'll be here if you need me."

With her mother settled, she went back to her post at the window. She crouched beyond reach of the flashing light. The lanterns stopped at the house and winked out. Whoever they were, they were searching the house now.

Carrington's yacht sped through the night seas. John kept an ear out for Henry's boat but heard nothing, saw no lights.

"How long until we reach Eureka?" he asked.

Carrington stood at the helm with the wheel in his hands. "A few more minutes."

"I haven't heard anything to make us think he's behind us," John said.

He paced the deck back to the stern. Water churned behind the yacht. Stars glittered overhead, and the moonlight gilded the railing with a glimmer of light. Still, he saw nothing behind them, heard nothing but the lapping of waves and the chug of their own engine.

He walked back to Carrington. "Could we shut off the engine and listen for anything out there?"

"Certainly. I'll see to it." Carrington yelled instructions to power down temporarily.

Carrington turned the helm over to his first mate, then walked with John back to the stern. Both men stood and listened.

John strained his eyes through the darkness but saw nothing. "I don't think he's following us."

"You believe he noticed the ruse and followed the women?"

John leaned over the railing. Nothing. "He's wily. He could have been closer than we realized but wasn't firing."

"If so, he would have seen the dinghy shove off."

It made horrible sense to John. "We have to double back."

"You're sure that's wise? We're nearly to Eureka and help."

"How long?"

"Fifteen minutes."

"And another forty-five minutes back. Explaining to the authorities will take at least another hour. We can't risk it. In two hours both Addie and Laura could be missing."

"I have an idea," Carrington said. "One of us could go to the constable, and the other could go back to check on the ladies."

"Addie pointed out they might not believe you."

"True enough, but Henry won't be there to fill them with his lies. I have some standing with my money and title."

"That's our best chance, then," John said.

Carrington gave instructions to his crew. When the yacht reached the dock at Eureka. Carrington leaped over the side into another dinghy and waved the boat on. John watched him row to shore as the yacht made a wide turn and headed back the way she'd come.

As the boat plowed the waves back to the lighthouse, he stood at the bow and prayed for the safety of the woman he loved and her mother. From here, he couldn't see the lighthouse winking its warning.

"Should we be able to see the lighthouse from here?" he asked the first mate.

"Not yet, sir. Another half an hour."

John gripped the railing. If he could swim there faster, he'd plunge into the dark water. He'd never had a premonition before, but his skin prickled and his breath came hard and fast. Something was very wrong.

THIRTY-EIGHT

ADDIE CLASPED HER knees to her chest and sat with her back propped against the wall. She glanced at her sleeping mother, then back out across the dark terrain. It was only a matter of time before the intruders tried the door to the tower. When they found it locked, they would suspect she and her mother were hiding up here.

The padlock might not hold determined men for long. Or maybe they'd think the lighthouse tower was locked because the lightkeeper hadn't been replaced. She prayed for God to blind their eyes, to distract them from their search.

She crawled to the metal stairs and peered into the darkness. It was too impenetrable for her to make out the door. Silence pressed against her ears. But they were down there. She sensed them. Easing back to the window, she gazed out again. Moonlight gleamed on the whitecaps and touched the rocks along the coast. Nothing moved, though.

If only they'd go back to their boat and shove off.

Her mother sat up. A scream tore from her throat. "No, Henry! Please, no!"

Addie leaped to her mother's side. Her heart hammered at her ribs. "Sh, Mama," she crooned. "It's okay. It's Julia." Gideon followed her.

Please don't let them have heard her.

Shouts echoed from below. "Up here," she heard a man yell. She hunkered beside her mother, who covered her face and moaned.

"I'm sorry, so sorry," her mother whispered. "I had a nightmare."

Addie hugged her. Perspiration soaked her mother's hair and the fabric of the back of her dress. She trembled violently.

"I think I'm going to throw up," she choked out.

Addie helped her bend over, then rubbed her mother's back as she retched. The stink of vomit made her gag, but she managed to control herself. "Let's move you over here."

Her mother nodded and dabbed her mouth with the hem of her gown. "Did they hear me?"

The answer was the thunderous pounding on the door from below. Mr. Eaton's voice came from the other side of the door. "Julia, I know you're in there. Open the door this instant."

Addie clutched her mother to her. "Don't answer. Stay very quiet."

It was hopeless to think he'd just go away. They'd all heard her mother. He knew they were there, but it would take time for him to break down the metal door and padlock. God would come through for them. She knew it, depended on it. He would be sufficient to this challenge.

"Get an ax," she heard her father say to his unknown partner.

Could an ax break down a metal door? She prayed not.

"Julia, this is your father. You must open this door now. I'm not going to hurt you. I just want to talk to you."

Hot words hovered on the tip of her tongue. Not hurt her? He'd tried to sink their yacht. If she said nothing, though, he'd have no positive proof she was on the other side of the door.

Her mother clapped her hands to her ears. "Go away, Henry!" she screamed. "Haven't you tortured me enough?"

Addie shrank back against the wall. If only she had a weapon. There was nothing up here but a wrench. It might come in handy, though. She groped for it, and her fingers closed around it.

A fierce banging commenced against the door downstairs. Gideon sprang to his feet and began to bark. The man must have found the ax in the well house. She and her mother covered their ears as the relentless battering continued. Addie wanted to scream at the horrific din. She imagined the metal denting and caving beneath the blows. When the noise ceased, the pressure on her chest eased, and she drew in a breath.

When no more demands came from her father for a few minutes, she eased onto her knees and peered out the glass. A movement below caught her eye, and she realized he was on the rickety cat-walk. She'd forgotten about it. He sidled along the metal support. The moonlight caught a glint at his side. He had a pistol, and he'd be here in minutes.

"Get up, Mama," she said. "Let's go."

She led her mother through the door and to the top of the stairs, but before they could begin to descend, she heard the battering resume on the door below. There was no other exit. If Addie were alone, she could climb out onto the other side of the catwalk and outmaneuver her father, but her mother was much too weak to accompany her.

Addie gripped the pipe wrench. If she leaned out the window, she might be able to use it on the catwalk and loosen it enough that Mr. Eaton couldn't approach.

"Sit tight, Mama," she whispered.

She took the wrench and swung it against the

glass. Her mother screamed as the window shattered outward. Gideon ran in circles and barked. A few shards rained onto the floor and crunched under Addie's feet as she knocked the last few pieces out of her way. Holding on to the window frame, she leaned out and began hammering with the heavy wrench against the metal catwalk. The metalwork trembled under the blows but held fast to the lighthouse.

"Julia, stop at once!" her father yelled.

Pain rippled up Addie's arm from the blows, but she continued to batter at the metal. She saw him draw his gun and ducked back inside as a bullet ricocheted off the frame where she'd been a moment before. He couldn't fire his gun while sidling around the building.

She waited a moment, then peered outside to see him on the move again. She leaned out and swung the wrench once more. This time she detected a weakening of the bolt holding the catwalk in place. With renewed vigor, she pounded at it again. Her father was moving faster now. He was within reach of the nearest window. He'd be inside in moments.

Glass shattered to Addie's left. Her mother had found a wooden box and swung it against the window. Henry's face was inches away.

"You killed my father, Henry!" she shrieked. "I hate you!" She threw the box at him. "I won't let you hurt my daughter too."

He batted it out of the way. One foot slipped

from the catwalk, but he recovered his balance and inched closer. "Laura, darling, you know I did it all for us. For our future. Help me in. We can talk about it."

Addie saw it coming. Saw her mother's dress flutter in the breeze as the older woman hoisted herself into the window. Saw her poised with both feet on the bottom stile. It seemed everything moved in slow motion.

"Mama, no!" Addie scrambled back from the opening where she perched.

Her outstretched hand grasped at her mother's arm. And missed. Her mother launched herself at Mr. Eaton. Gideon lunged and caught the hem of her dress in his teeth. She was far enough out the window that her body struck her husband's. The force of weight knocked him from his perch. They grappled with each other, then Mr. Eaton hurtled toward the ground.

Her mother's dress began to rip in Gideon's teeth.

"No!" Addie shrieked.

She leaned out the window and grabbed her mother around the waist. It was all she could do to get both of them back inside the light tower. The battering at the door began again, and she covered her ears.

The minutes ticked by too slowly. John paced the deck and stared into the darkness. "Why aren't we seeing it yet?"

"We should be," the first mate said.

John squinted in the darkness. "There it is!" He ran along the deck. "Do we have another dinghy? There's no pier."

"Sorry, no."

"I'll swim." He shucked his jacket, shoes, and socks.

"Wait, sir. Let me get the yacht as close as possible and upstream a bit so the current will help propel you to shore."

John nodded but clambered to the top of the railing to be ready. When the first mate gave him the nod, he dived overboard. The cold water shocked him and gave him renewed purpose. He surfaced and gasped in air, then struck out for land. The tide carried him just past the lighthouse, but he struggled to shore, cutting his knees and hands on the sharp rocks.

He staggered from the ocean, with cold water dripping from his body. His legs trembled from the long swim, but he forced himself up the slope that led to the back of the lighthouse. He heard the sound of metal against metal. What on earth?

As he neared the lighthouse, he caught sight of something on the ground at the base of the tower. As he approached, he realized a body lay there. "Oh please, God, no." He started forward.

He ran to the heap of arms and legs and stared down into Henry's face, twisted into a grimace.

John's eyes burned with uncustomary emotion. Where was his Addie?

The pounding of metal on metal had stopped, but he turned toward the back door. Addie had to be here somewhere. He strained his ears to hear her voice, but there was nothing. Not even a bark from Gideon.

"Just the man I need."

John turned at the sound of the man's voice. He squinted in the darkness. "Walter? Is that you?"

The man emerged from the shadows. "Hello, John."

The moonlight glinted on the gun in Driscoll's hand. John looked at it, then back at Driscoll's face. "What's going on?"

The gun came up. "Your fiancée is holed up in the lighthouse. You're going to get her down for me."

"I don't think so."

Driscoll gestured with the gun. "Through that door."

"Nope. I'm not going anywhere with you."

"I'll shoot you where you stand."

John clenched his fists. "Then do it."

The gun wavered in Driscoll's hand. "Addie!" he shouted. "I've got John down here. I'm going to shoot him if you don't come down."

John started to yell out to tell her not to listen, but he hoped if he kept quiet, she'd assume Driscoll was lying. He heard something overhead. He glanced up and saw moonlight illuminating

Addie's face in the lighthouse tower. Their gazes locked.

"Stay there!" he shouted.

Driscoll fired, and a bullet zinged off a rock by John's feet. "I'll aim for his head next, Addie!" Driscoll screamed.

Addie's head disappeared. "Addie, no!" he yelled. He started toward the door to the house so he could gain entry to the tower, but a bullet plowed into the earth by his feet. Driscoll raised the gun to John's chest. All he could do was pray Addie wouldn't come down.

A few moments later she and Laura emerged from the house with Gideon. Her mother leaned heavily against her as they moved slowly.

Laura flinched when she saw her brother. "Walter?"

"Hello, Laura," he said.

"What are you doing?"

"Get over there by John," Driscoll ordered.

The women joined John, and he embraced Addie. Gideon whined and nosed at John's wet pants. Laura continued to stare at her brother.

"Let's take a moonlight stroll," Driscoll said. "That way." He motioned to the path that led to the cliff.

John put Addie behind him. "Why, Walter?"

"Why take a stroll? Because I said so."

"Why are you doing this?" Addie whispered, peeking around John.

"I have no choice," Driscoll said. "My creditors want their money now."

"The man in Henry's office demanding money," John said. "I overheard him tell the fellow it wasn't his debt or his problem. He was trying to get money from Henry for something you owed. Gambling?" He recalled seeing Walter two weeks ago, exiting the alley. "We saw him coming out of the alley where games are going on all the time."

"I remember," Addie said slowly. "I thought he was delivering medicine." She rubbed her forehead. "I found a note in my father's office, asking for ten thousand dollars to keep quiet about a child. I assumed it might be his indiscretion, but it was yours, wasn't it, Uncle Walter?"

Driscoll motioned with the gun for them to move along. "Henry had always bailed me out in the past, but he decided I had to face the music this time. I would have been ruined if the truth came out. I tried to get the money by gambling, but I only succeeded in digging myself into a deeper hole."

"Was that you pounding on the door?" Addie asked. "Why would you work with Henry when he wouldn't help you?"

"When you told me about the clues you'd found, I knew Henry had killed my father. I told him to pay what I needed, or I'd go to the constable. He agreed before he left for his trip to Fort Bragg. One of his men called me from Fort Bragg and told me to meet him here. He said that if I'd help him with a problem, he'd give me double what I needed."

"But why kill us now?" Addie asked, stepping out from behind John.

"It's because of your grandfather's will," John said, keeping his gaze on Driscoll for an opening to attack. "You saw it, too, didn't you, Walter?"

His lips thinned. "I never dreamed Henry would cheat me out of my inheritance that way. I should have had my share all along."

Laura held out her hand toward him. "Did you know Henry had me penned up?"

His eyes held regret. "Not until recently. But you've been dead to me for years. I can't let sentiment keep me from my needs. Now that Henry is dead, the Eaton estate is all mine, so long as I take care of this problem here. Very tidy, don't you think?"

John's muscles coiled. "So with us out of the way, you inherit what's left. Once you dispose of Edward too." He had to save them. His son's life depended on it.

Driscoll waved the gun. "Enough of this chatter. Move or I'll shoot the dog."

Addie cried out and reached for Gideon. "Come with me, boy," she said.

John clenched and unclenched his fists.

"Follow the little lady," Driscoll said. "I'd hate to shoot her dog."

John didn't have a choice. He caught up with Addie and kept his body between her and the madman. Driscoll marched them out to the edge of the cliff.

"Right there is fine," Driscoll said from behind him.

John turned quickly. For all he knew, Driscoll was going to shoot him in the back.

"Was this your plan all along?" Addie asked. "When you brought me to the manor?"

"Quite honestly, I wasn't sure how I might use you to get the money I needed. I had thought Henry might be so grateful to get you back that he'd give me the money to pay my debts. When my creditor attacked me before I had proof, I knew I had to move faster."

"You killed Josephine, didn't you? Looking for more proof," Addie said. "That's how you came up with the pictures of me as a child."

"I watched her leave, but she came back to the house before I was finished. She tried to black-mail me."

"Did you arrange to have Edward kidnapped?" John demanded, curling his hands into fists.

Driscoll raised a brow. "It was the syndicate. They'd thought to exert pressure on me and Henry to pay what I owed."

John saw Driscoll turn the gun toward him, then his finger tightened on the trigger. It was now or never. But before he could make a move, Gideon leaped silently out of the dark. His teeth fastened on the arm that held the gun.

Driscoll wrestled with the dog. "Let go, you mangy mutt!"

John jumped and tackled Walter. The man was wiry and stronger than he expected. John tried to get the gun, but the older man kept it just out of reach. Gideon continued to worry Driscoll's arm, but he hung on to the weapon in spite of all efforts to dislodge it.

"Let go of me," Driscoll panted.

John kneed him in the groin, and Driscoll groaned but fought back. He kicked out at the dog. Gideon yelped, then leaped into the fray again as Driscoll pinned John to the ground and began to bring the gun around. The dog bit into his wrist again, and Driscoll grabbed Gideon by the neck with his left hand and began to choke him.

John struggled to get his leg free so he could kick out. He reached for a loose rock by his head, but before he could bring it up, Driscoll slumped onto him. John lowered him to the ground, then glanced up into Addie's face. She still held the rock she'd used to strike Driscoll.

"Wicked arm you've got there," he said. He shoved Driscoll off, grabbed the gun, and struggled to his feet.

Addie collapsed into his arms, and Gideon came to nose at his hand. "I'm glad you two are on my side." He saw lights on the water. "Here comes the cavalry."

"A little late," Addie said.

"I don't think you need the cavalry. You're strong, my love. And you have a fearless sidekick in Gideon."

"And I have you," she whispered.

Addie warmed her hands with a cup of hot cocoa in front of the fire at the Russell home. Gideon lay at her feet with a self-satisfied smile on his doggy face. She'd fed him until he could eat no more as a reward for being such a hero.

Mrs. Russell bustled in with oatmeal cookies, fresh from the oven. "Are you warm enough, my dear? You were shaking so."

"I'm fine now. It was shock, I think. Is John back yet?"

"I thought I heard his buggy stop outside. Katie went to let him in." Mrs. Russell put the cookies on a side table. "Katie and I will leave you two to sort things out."

Katie led John into the room. Addie drank in the sight of him. They'd nearly lost what they had. Her heart swelled at how good God was. He'd seen them through this valley. She waved back at Katie as she disappeared up the steps.

"Addie." John was at her side in two steps. He knelt and took her cold hands in his warm ones. "I couldn't wait to get back to you."

She took comfort from his grip. "What's happened with Mr. Driscoll?"

"The doctor says he'll live."

"He's in jail?"

John joined her on the sofa, but he kept control of one of her hands. "Yes, but don't feel sorry for him, love. He nearly killed you. And his own sister." He released her hand and slipped his arm around her.

She burrowed into the comfort of his embrace. The clean scent of him reassured her. "I'm so glad it's over. You saved my mother, John."

He kissed the top of her head. "We did it together."

"I'm too tired to think," she said. "I can't impose on my friends for too long. I'm not sure what to do."

He tipped her face up and brushed a kiss across her lips. "You'll marry me, of course. As soon as it can be arranged."

Her pulse skipped, and she pulled back. "Right away?"

His eyes were smiling and full of love. "I'd marry you tomorrow if we could arrange it that quickly."

The thought of being a family with him and Edward brought heat rushing to her cheeks. "I'd like that more than anything in the world," she said.

"Tell me what to do and I'll arrange it."

"There are so many things to do, I don't know where to start," she said, laughing.

The smile left his face. "When, my love?"

The possessiveness in his voice heated her cheeks even more. "I need at least two weeks. I have to make a dress."

"I'll buy you one."

"I want to make it. I'll only have one wedding day."

He released her hair from its combs and plunged his fingers into the mass of curls. As his lips claimed hers, she realized how God had given her every desire of her heart.

EPILOGUE

THE ROAR OF the ocean was music in Addie's ears. Her white lingerie dress, while simple, was the only wedding dress she needed. John insisted she appear barefoot to take their nuptials. Silly man, but how wonderful to be loved for who she was.

"Kneel there by Gideon. Our hero," Katie said. She had her Brownie camera on a tripod and was documenting the day. Her dark hair gleamed against the lilac bridesmaid dress Addie had made for her.

Smiling, Addie knelt on the grass with the lighthouse in the background. Gideon crowded close, and she put her arm around him.

"Just a moment. Don't move," Katie called.

Addie froze her smile until she heard a click. "Are we done?"

"Done!"

At her friend's announcement, Addie rose and stretched. Guests in buggies were beginning to arrive. Though Clara's offer to use the manor house had been generous, Addie belonged here, not in fancy drawing rooms or on manicured lawns. Her true home was by the sea, with the lighthouse winking overhead. The wedding would be at sundown, when the light could be wound.

"I see you watching for John," Katie said, linking arms. "You're not supposed to see him before the wedding."

Addie tucked a strand of hair behind her ears. "Do you think I should have put my hair up? John wanted it down, but it seems almost disrespectful on such a momentous occasion."

Katie held her at arm's length and studied her. "I've never seen a lovelier bride."

"You'd say that if I wore a flour sack."

"It would be true. You are just glowing. I hope a man looks at me someday like John looks at you."

Addie turned her friend toward the lighthouse. "It will happen."

"Uh-oh, John is here," Katie said. She grabbed at Addie when she would have turned toward the road. "Oh no, you don't. Inside with you, before he sees you."

"Katie!" Addie protested.

"No bad luck allowed." Katie steered her to the back door.

"I don't need luck. God has this all under control."

"I'd have to agree, after seeing all you've gone through."

The girls stepped into the kitchen. The yeasty scents mixed with cinnamon made Addie's tummy grumble. She'd been too excited to eat today. The neighbors had pitched in and brought the food. Clara had paid for cake and ice cream to be delivered. Everything was in order.

"Where's Gideon?" Katie asked as she affixed Addie's veil to her head, then added flowers.

"With Edward." Addie clasped her hands together and glanced at the clock. "It's time." The butterflies in her stomach took flight.

She peeked out the window. Guests had begun to mill around the yard. The tulle on the bower by the cliff rippled in the breeze. Piano music came to her ears from the instrument John had arranged to be moved to the yard. "The Entertainer" rang out, and she smiled. Who else was lucky enough to have ragtime played at her wedding?

Thomas Carrington poked his head into the kitchen. "Ready?" His eyebrows rose. "You look quite lovely, Addie."

She pulled her veil over her face and joined him on the back stoop. "Thank you so much for agreeing to give me away."

His eyes were moist. "I'm honored to be asked."

"How's Mama?"

"Excited. Still weak though. I have her on a lawn chair in the front row."

The music changed to another ragtime tune. Addie tucked her hand into the crook of his arm and stepped into the grass. As the piano music tinkled, she strolled between smiling friends and neighbors toward the bower. The Whittakers smiled and waved as she passed. Clara had taken the children into her house, and Mrs. Whittaker planned to join the children and take over as housekeeper as soon as she was well enough. Mrs. Russell dabbed at her eyes as Addie approached. She waved at Addie from her spot near the front, and John's father gave a grave nod.

Addie's eyes met her mother's for a moment. All the love and pride she'd longed for were in those serene green eyes. Her mother blew her a kiss, and Addie returned the gesture.

Then her gaze locked on the bower, where John awaited her. Dressed in a double-breasted frock coat and tan trousers, his dark eyes under the top hat caught and held hers. Edward stood beside his father, with his hand on Gideon's head. He tugged at the round collar on his shirt. The knickers he wore already had grass stains on the knees.

All three watched her approach, but she had eyes only for John. A slight smile played at his lips, and the love in his eyes brought moisture rushing to hers.

He stepped out to take her hands.

Lord Carrington stepped between them. "Not yet, son. She's still mine at the moment."

John's hand fell back to his side, and he smiled. "I've waited for her all my life, Carrington. No one's standing between us now."

Lord Carrington grinned and passed her hand to John's. His eyes stayed on her through the ceremony, which she barely heard as she repeated her vows. When he slid the ring on her finger, she caught her breath. She had a family. A husband who loved her. A son. God was so good. He'd provided every desire of her heart.

After the ceremony, John led her away from the crush of well-wishers. "I want to talk to you a moment."

They stood at the base of the lighthouse, which blinked out its warning every three seconds. He embraced her, and she nestled against his chest. His hand crept to her hair, and his fingers entwined in her curls.

"You're distracting me," he murmured.

She lifted her head. "Oh? You had something to say beyond telling me how much you adore me?"

"You have no idea how much." He bent his head to kiss her. His lips nuzzled her jawline and her neck. "Do you still think I'm your Robert Browning?"

Heat seared her cheeks. "You promised never to bring up that book. I shall take great pleasure in watching you jump over the falls."

He grinned. "I'm taking you with me."

"That wasn't part of the arrangement," she said, somehow managing to keep a straight face.

One eyebrow lifted. "Didn't you just promise whither so I goest? Or something like that?"

"You might have to remind me of that when we're at the top of the falls."

He chuckled, then sobered. "Now, back to what I have to tell you."

Her skin still tingled from his touch. She pulled away. "I'm listening."

"I've managed to keep Mercy Steamboat out of bankruptcy. The creamery too. Your mother and Clara should be all right financially."

"Mama has Lord Carrington too."

He nodded. "But I wanted to do what I could to help Clara and you." His gaze was troubled. "I need to talk to you about where we will live."

"We'll be in San Francisco, won't we?"

He shook his head. "I resigned my commission, darling. I can't take you from your mother. You searched for her so valiantly, and she fought for you so hard."

She swallowed over the constriction in her throat. "You did that for me?"

"I'd do anything for you."

She kissed him. "You're a good man, Lieutenant."

He smiled. "I'm not a lieutenant anymore. I'm a private citizen."

"Where shall we live, then?"

"There's a house I want to show you. It's down the lane and faces the water. I'll purchase that if you like it."

"I'll be by the sea! I know I shall love it."

He smiled. "I see the wheels turning behind those beautiful eyes. You're wondering what I'm going to do."

"You're going to run the Eaton holdings," she said.

He inhaled. "How do you do that?"

"Women's intuition," she said, brushing a kiss across his lips. "You're so good at organization. It makes sense."

"I'll never be able to keep anything from you."

"I hope you don't try."

He kissed the tip of her nose and exhaled. "I'll do the best I can with the other businesses. They're all struggling under Henry's mismanagement. Things will be tight for a while."

"We'll be fine. I'm not a spendthrift. And we have my money."

"I plan to support my family myself." His smile was tender. "I'm worried about the people who lost so much in the bank failure."

Her smile faded. "Me too."

"I have an idea that might help some. Clara has moved to a smaller place in town that her grandmother left her. The income from the creamery and the steamboat will sustain her. With your permission, I'd like to sell Eaton Hall to a group that wants to turn it into a sanatorium."

He was such a good man. She clung to him. "Oh, John, I'd like nothing better! But will that be enough to repay the people who lost their savings?"

He shook his head. "I wish it were. But I can repay some of the money at least."

"I've thought of another solution. I wasn't sure you'd agree, but I'd intended to talk to you about it tonight."

"What is it?"

"The land. We could sell it to the investors you mentioned. Surely that would be enough to give the bank customers their money."

His brows rose, and a smile lifted his lips. "Addie, you'd want to do that?"

"Of course. Would it be enough?"

"I believe it would," he said, pulling her close. "You are a remarkable woman. But I've also gotten an offer from a group who wants to turn it into a park area. It's nearly as much money."

"John, how wonderful! Let's do that."

"We'll have no resources to fall back on though."

"We have God. He'll see to anything we need. He always has."

Day-to-day dependence on God was all she needed to flourish. She laid her head against her husband's chest and listened to his heartbeat. Together, they formed a strong cord of three strands. There was nothing brighter in her future than that reality.

"Let's go home," she whispered.

DEAR READER

I HOPE YOU'VE enjoyed this book as much as I've enjoyed writing it. Though writing a historical novel was a bit of a departure for me, I think you'll agree it's also my trademark mystery and romance, blended together and flavored with a strong sense of place. That place just happens to be Northern California in 1907. We stayed at a wonderful hotel/bed-and-breakfast in Ferndale, the inspiration for Mercy Falls. The Victorian Inn made me feel like I'd stepped back in time. If you get into that area, check it out at http://www.victorianvillageinn.com/.

I sharpened my writing pencil on historical romance, and it's been a fun experience for me to go back to my roots—with the addition of the mystery thread I so love to write. I'm a nut about lighthouses and the Gilded Age (I live in a house built in 1895), so all those elements found their way into *The Lightkeeper's Daughter*. I studied the Painted Ladies, houses of this era that were embellished with gingerbread trim and painted many colors to bring out their beauty. Dave and I turned our own home into the middle-class version, and it was featured in the October 2008 edition of *Victorian Homes*.

If you enjoyed this book, drop me an e-mail. I love to hear from readers! Contact me at colleen@colleencoble.com, and check out my Web site at www.colleencoble.com. You can also follow me on Twitter at http://twitter.com/colleen-coble, and I'm on Facebook as well. Thank you all for giving up your most precious commodity —*time*—to spend it with me and my stories.

Much affection,
Colleen Coble

ACKNOWLEDGMENTS

IT IS SUCH a privilege to do another project with my wonderful Thomas Nelson family. Publisher Allen Arnold (I call him Superman) is so passionate about fiction, and he lights up a room when he enters it. Senior acquisitions editor Ami McConnell (my friend and cheerleader) has an eye for character and theme like no one I know. I crave her analytical eye! It was her influence that encouraged me to write a historical romantic mystery, and I'm glad she pushed me a bit! Marketing manager Jennifer Deshler brings both friendship and fabulous marketing ideas to the table. Publicist Katie Bond is always willing to listen to my harebrained ideas. Fabulous cover guru Kristen Vasgaard (you *so* rock!) works hard to create the perfect cover—and does it. And of course I can't forget my other friends who are all part of my amazing fiction family: Natalie Hanemann, Amanda Bostic, Becky Monds, Ashley Schneider, Heather McCulloch, Chris Long, and Kathy Carabajal. I wish I could name all the great folks who work on selling my books through different venues at Thomas Nelson. You are my dream team! Hearing "Well done" from you all is my motivation every day.

My agent, Karen Solem, has helped shape my career in many ways, and that includes kicking an idea to the curb when necessary. Thanks, Karen, you're the best!

Erin Healy is the best freelance editor in the business, bar none. She sees details the rest of us miss, and it doesn't hurt that she's an amazing suspense writer. Thanks, Erin! I couldn't do it without you.

Writing can be a lonely business, but God has blessed me with great writing friends and critique partners. Kristin Billerbeck, Diann Hunt, and Denise Hunter make up the Girls Write Out squad (www.GirlsWriteOut.blogspot.com). I couldn't make it through a day without my peeps! And another one of those is Robin Miller, conference director of ACFW (www.acfw.com), who spots inconsistencies in a suspense plot with an eagle eye. Thanks to all of you for the work you do on my behalf, and for your friendship.

I'm so grateful for my husband, Dave, who carts me around from city to city, washes towels, and chases down dinner without complaint. Thanks, honey! I couldn't do anything without you. My kids—Dave, Kara (and now Donna and Mark)—and my grandsons, James and Jorden Packer, love and support me in every way possible. Love you guys! Donna and Dave brought me the delight of my life—our little granddaughter, Alexa! It's hard to write when all I want to do is kiss those darling, pudgy feet. She is the most beautiful baby ever!

Most importantly I give my thanks to God, who has opened such amazing doors for me and makes the journey a golden one.

Reading Group Guide

1. Addie desperately wanted to belong to a family. How easy is it to change who you are to gain approval?

2. How do you gauge your self worth? How *should* it be gauged?

3. John wanted to protect his son from the world. What are the pros of this? The cons?

4. Addie is a romantic at heart and an optimist. What are consequences of looking at the world through rose-colored glasses?

5. It's said that opposites attract. Why do you think this is true?

6. The Bible says we are to respect our parents. Where do you think the lines are between respect and obedience?

7. God warns us that the love of money is the root of evil. What is it about wanting more and more that corrupts?

8. When I researched this book, I noticed a strong correlation between today's world and the turn of the 20th century. In what ways are they similar? Different? What can serve as a warning for us today?

9. Is it better to be a conformist or to be an individual? Are you always just one of these, or sometimes do you conform while other times you stand alone?

10. People treated Addie differently when her true identity became known. Why do people elevate those with money and power? Do you treat someone differently if they are wealthy?

Center Point Publishing
600 Brooks Road • PO Box 1
Thorndike ME 04986-0001 USA

(207) 568-3717

US & Canada:
1 800 929-9108
www.centerpointlargeprint.com